Nikki Mottram writes crime fiction and has a background in child protection. She has a psychology degree from The University of Queensland and has worked in London and Australia in positions protecting and promoting the welfare of children at risk of harm. She has been published in the Boroondara Literary Awards anthology and shortlisted for the Fish Short Story Prize and the Hal Porter Short Story Competition. In 2018, she was the recipient of a Katharine Susannah Pritchard Writers' Centre Fellowship. She grew up and resides in Toowoomba, and brings to her work an understanding of rural communities.

CROWS NEST

First published 2023 by University of Queensland Press
PO Box 6042, St Lucia, Queensland 4067 Australia
Reprinted 2023

University of Queensland Press (UQP) acknowledges the Traditional Owners and their custodianship of the lands on which UQP operates. We pay our respects to their Ancestors and their descendants, who continue cultural and spiritual connections to Country. We recognise their valuable contributions to Australian and global society.

uqp.com.au
reception@uqp.com.au

Cover design by Christabella Designs
Cover photograph by Terry Cooke, AusStockPhoto // Shutterstock
Author photograph by Syd Owen
Typeset in 12/17 pt Bembo Std by Post Pre-press Group, Brisbane
Printed in Australia by McPherson's Printing Group

University of Queensland Press is supported by the Queensland Government through Arts Queensland.

University of Queensland Press is assisted by the Australian Government through the Australia Council, its arts funding and advisory body.

A catalogue record for this book is available from the National Library of Australia.

ISBN 978 0 7022 6577 8 (pbk)
ISBN 978 0 7022 6726 0 (epdf)
ISBN 978 0 7022 6727 7 (epub)

University of Queensland Press uses papers that are natural, renewable and recyclable products made from wood grown in well-managed forests and other controlled sources. The logging and manufacturing processes conform to the environmental regulations of the country of origin.

CROWS NEST

NIKKI MOTTRAM

For Alex, Emily and Jack

A woman, silhouetted in the light, was slumped over the steering wheel. The high beams of the panel van cut through the misty eucalypts, the car doors were outspread like wings – an angel of death.

She was miles from nowhere and the air was still. Trees like bones stood straight and pale in the moonlight. The temperature began to dip in the unnerving silence.

A mopoke called out, the first sound since the gunshots.

She suddenly realised she'd lost track of time.

The wind whispered through the trees and the sky turned white. The distant pain in her body ebbed as her breath turned to ice. She was floating. Through the tops of the trees, through infinite space, far beyond them all. The caw of crows welcomed the dawn.

She closed her eyes.

1

Dana headed north along the highway, her half-packed suitcase on the seat beside her. She passed prickly pear and creek beds, barbed-wire fences and desiccated trees. A flock of crows flew overhead in the late afternoon sky and as soon as she spotted them, a lone dropping hit the bonnet of her Mercedes. The car had been a gift from her husband, as was the ring on her finger, but as she gazed at the leather interior, the Art Deco diamond, she wondered if she'd ever care about any of it again.

She was still jittery from the fight they'd had before she left Castlecrag. He'd acted outrageously at his fiftieth. Let himself be dragged into their bedroom by that woman, the door slamming shut behind them. Hugh had sworn nothing happened, but Dana knew he liked her. Melinda, with the hard jaw and hooded eyes.

The kangaroo leapt from the side of the road and the windscreen shattered. She hit the brakes, a moan escaping her lips as the car fishtailed and skidded along the shoulder of the road before slamming to a stop against a tree. The radiator hissed and her heart hammered. She unbuckled her seatbelt and staggered from the car, observing the damage to the bonnet.

The kangaroo was lying about five metres behind her, its head flung back and a pool of blood at its mouth. Its neck looked broken, but she edged along the road to see if it was alive. A familiar feeling of dread filled her chest as she took in the kangaroo's delicate forelimbs and velvety ears. Its helpless eyes were like Oscar's – that cold morning when she found him in his cot, chilled and blue, the vomit on his jumpsuit like an oil slick.

She knew she should check for a joey but the idea was repulsive. A nightmare of images flashed through her brain – a deformed foetus, an injured youngster, having to snap its neck in a mercy killing. She paused, trying to build the courage to look. What would she do if it lived? Bundle it in her suit jacket and take it to Toowoomba? She pushed up her sleeves and shook her head. *Get on with it, girl.*

The fur around the pouch was surprisingly soft. She opened the flap and was relieved to find the moist pink cavity empty. She sank to her knees, tears stinging her eyes, the sky above her a heartbreaking display of fading pinks and blues. Beyond the endless telephone lines and a solitary windmill, the horizon shimmered. She pulled herself up and returned to the car. With shaking hands, she leant forward and flicked on the hazard lights then reached into her handbag for her Nokia. No reception.

Her chest tightened as panic set in. She stumbled up a nearby service road in her platform sandals and checked her phone. Nothing. She made a turn into a dusty paddock, hoping for a better signal. Yanking the wedges from her feet, she staggered forward another fifty metres and almost wept when two bars appeared. She started calling her insurance company then stopped, realising she hadn't renewed her policy. She swore under her breath, grit her teeth and called them anyway.

A woman named Barbara answered and asked for her name.

She took a shaky breath. 'It's Dana Gibson. I've hit a kangaroo. I'm on the Gore Highway, between Goondiwindi and Toowoomba, just past Captains Mountain service station. The reception's bad.'

Barbara's voice was calm and motherly. 'That's fine, we'll get someone to help you as soon as possible. Are you okay? Do you have any injuries?'

'I'm fine.'

'Right, I need you to park your car as far to the left side of the highway as possible, turn on your hazard lights and fasten your seatbelt.'

'I turned on the lights,' said Dana. 'But I'm worried—' The line dropped out. 'Fuck,' she cried, only just preventing herself from hurling the phone into the dirt. She picked her way to a straggly tree on the other side of the field and stabbed the buttons to redial. The thrum of cicadas drilled into her brain. There was an agonising wait and finally, on the tenth ring, she got through.

'Dana?' Barbara asked.

'Yes, thank god,' she said. 'My licence plate is SMV 158 … I have an awful feeling I haven't renewed my policy.'

'That's okay,' said Barbara, her fingers tapping against the keyboard. 'I'll check it now.' There was a brief pause. 'By the looks of this, the policy was renewed a month ago.'

Hugh had paid her car insurance, and she'd never been more surprised in her life. Since when had he done any of the chores – taken the clothes to the dry cleaner, lodged the tax returns?

'I've logged the job with roadside assistance,' said Barbara. 'They should be no more than an hour away.'

Dana longed to keep Barbara talking, to hear her calm, soothing voice, but she detested weakness and instead thanked her and hung up. As she returned to the car, she could see crows fighting over the carcass of the kangaroo. She rushed towards them; her face contorted with rage. 'Leave it alone!' She clapped her hands until the birds scattered into the sky.

She fought a wild impulse to call Hugh, but what would she say? *I accused you of having an affair, but could you drive a thousand kilometres and pick me up?* Speaking to him now would only confirm that he was right, she'd been foolish to take an agency job. And in a place she hadn't been to for twenty years. Still, she yearned to take refuge on his chest and have him console her. He'd warned her not to drive at dusk, to stop overnight and break up the long drive, but as usual she hadn't listened.

As she opened the car door and sat down to wait, she recalled how badly she'd behaved during their last argument. She'd slapped him. Actually slapped him. 'I can't believe you'd choose her, when you could have chosen anyone else.' And after she'd paused for breath, 'She's not even attractive.'

Hugh hadn't yelled back, was red-faced when he said, 'You could hardly blame me if I had. When was the last time we were in the same bed together?'

Dana ran a hand through her hair as she tried to remember. She'd been sleeping in the spare bedroom for a while now. What started with finishing late at work and not wanting to disturb him had stretched into weeks, then months. She'd been so busy managing a high-risk investigation and assessment team she'd barely noticed their time apart. Instead, she'd filled her head with cases of child abuse and neglect, the sad and sometimes hopeful stories of the families who came onto the radar of Community Services.

She'd watched as Hugh paced around their kitchen, stress etched on his face. Truth be told, she enjoyed sleeping alone, having the freedom to stretch out, to toss and turn after a harrowing day at work. But she knew it bothered him, knew it violated one of his deeply held beliefs about coupledom. Had she been a decent partner she would have done everything in her power to remedy the situation. Instead, she'd followed him into the lounge room and continued their argument.

Glancing in the rear-view mirror she could see the indents in the leather seat where the baby capsule had been. Hugh must have removed it at some point and she realised that what they'd hardly spoken about since the funeral was the loss of Oscar. Everything in the house reminded her of him. The nursery, lovingly decorated in Winnie the Pooh prints, the white sleigh cot and velvet comforter that had only been in use for a few months.

Just before she'd left for Queensland, as she'd hoisted her bag and opened the front door, Hugh touched her arm. He gazed at her with bottomless sadness and said, 'We're alright, aren't we?' She didn't know. All she knew was that she needed some time and space to think things through without the constant reminders of what her life could have looked like.

As the last of the sun faded she flicked on the interior lights, the diamond on her hand sparkling up at her as she took her new Alanis Morissette CD from the wallet. She placed it in the Discman and put on her headphones. By the time 'You Learn' started, the bright yellow beams of a tow truck were cutting through the darkness. It pulled up ahead of her and made a U-turn on the highway.

A thin-hipped man in fisherman pants sprang from the vehicle holding a torch. In the dim glow of the tail-lights, she could make out a Sanskrit tattoo on his bicep and a hoop in his ear.

'Dana Gibson?' he asked. 'That's an unusual name. How do I say it?'

'Day-na,' she replied, answering the question she'd been fielding her entire life.

'Jimmy,' he said, pumping her hand and holding eye contact for longer than necessary. 'Let's see what we've got.' He swung his torch around, surveying the scene. 'Man …' He exhaled. 'Those roos are vicious little buggers. I'd say this one's done a pretty good number on your car.'

He scratched the skin on his chest where it met a blue singlet. *Wife-beater.* The word echoed in her mind. There was something about the way he kept eyeing her that sent shivers up her spine.

'I don't get it.' He shook his head. 'They get dazed by the headlights, but instead of jumping away from the car they jump into it.' He returned to his vehicle and came back with a towing hook. 'You can wait in the truck. I'll be here a while.'

'Sure,' she said, grabbing her handbag and phone. 'Thanks,' she added, remembering herself and handing him the keys. She walked over to the passenger side of the truck, hiked up her skirt and hauled herself into the cabin. Her wedges came to rest on a bed of Coke cans and food wrappers. The air inside had the dead-oil smell of McDonalds. She switched on the overhead light and leant over to study her reflection in the rear-view mirror. Her mascara was smudged, her blue eyes and pale skin red from crying. If Jimmy found her attractive, he was clearly desperate. *Move along*, she addressed him silently. *Nothing to see here.*

She slid her hand into the side door compartment and pulled out a ragged *Hustler* magazine. She started flicking through the pages, but when she landed on a picture of two women with a feather boa, she shoved it back where she'd found it. Dana peered through the grimy back window. Haloed in the truck's spotlight, Jimmy was still bent over her car.

She yanked open the glove box. She knew she was intruding, but if being a social worker had taught her anything it was that a person's vehicle could tell you more about their life than a made-up story. A sea of wrappers fell to the floor and she reached inside and pulled out a leather holster. Inside was a serrated knife coated in a sticky substance. She turned it over in her hands and read the inscription: *guaranteed sharp*. She snapped the compartment shut.

A road train roared past and the cabin shook. The beams of the tail-lights glowed menacingly before receding into the darkness. She sat back in her seat and tried to relax. She'd been on the road for almost ten hours and she was almost there – she couldn't give up now.

The driver's door opened and Jimmy dragged himself into the cabin next to her, clicking the buckle of his seatbelt. 'That towing hook on that flash car of yours was a bastard to find. But, on the upside, at least I got to rescue a hot redhead.' He chuckled as the engine roared to life and he eased the truck onto the highway.

She ignored him and changed the subject. 'I wasn't too worried about breaking down. Barbara from the hotline said someone would be out within the hour.' Dana had a good mind to call her and abuse her for sending this lunatic.

'Where you coming from?' he asked.

'Sydney.'

'Sydney?' He laughed. 'That's where they have the Mardi Gras!'

'That's right,' she said, repulsed, but not wanting to get on the wrong side of him.

'But you're not gay, darl.' He wagged his eyebrows. 'Are you?'

She rolled her eyes as though it was a big joke, but her chest was tight as she wiped her sweaty palms along her skirt.

He reached for the CB radio from the rack and spoke into it. He had a twitchy, nervous quality as he tapped the steering wheel, making her wonder about amphetamines. Her mind raced ahead to the coronial reports she'd read about women being murdered after accepting lifts from strangers. And while she was no hitchhiker, she wondered whether she'd inadvertently put herself in the same position.

'What brings you to Toowoomba? No wait—' he said before she'd had a chance to answer. 'It's work, isn't it? You've driven here in your fancy car with your nice clothes because you're going to show these country people how it's done.'

'You're right,' she said evenly. 'I signed up with a social work agency and I've been sent to Toowoomba.'

He grinned, pleased with himself. 'Where are you working?'

'Department of Families.'

'Families, hey,' Jimmy said, sharply interested. 'Your lot do child support?'

'No,' Dana said truthfully.

'My ex-wife lets me see the kids every second weekend and gets half of what I earn. Major bitch. You have any kids?'

'A boy,' Dana lied, thinking he might be less likely to harm her if he knew she had a child. 'He's at home with his dad at the moment – his dad's in the police force.' Another lie.

He was undeterred. 'And you've been in a relationship longer than six months?'

'Yes,' said Dana, wondering what on earth he was getting at.

'Congratulations,' he said bitterly. 'As soon as you have a kid and you've lived together for longer than six months, you get sixty per cent of everything.'

'That seems unfair,' she said, trying to pacify him.

'Yeah.' He smiled. 'But I guess she's a better parent than me in some ways, at least she doesn't get frustrated. Storm used to cry for hours at night, this piercing cry. Sent me mental every time.'

The tension in her shoulders eased. Perhaps he wasn't that bad if he could concede the reasons he hadn't been awarded custody. 'Are your kids in Toowoomba?' she asked.

'No, Crows Nest – a small town forty kays north. Joel's nine and Storm's fifteen. I'd like to have more of them, actually. Move to Bali and have a whole tribe running around.' He rolled his shoulders, stretched his neck from side to side, then leant over and whispered in her ear. 'You know, darl, I've been cooped up in this truck all day and I think it's time we had a bit of fun.' He reached past her and rifled around in the glove box.

Dana's breath came in short, shallow bursts. She couldn't believe she'd been lulled into a false sense of security. Wasn't it the modus operandi of sociopaths to be charming?

She gripped the seatbelt buckle and thought about escape routes, about throwing herself from the fast-moving vehicle. The roar in her ears became so loud it was impossible to think.

2

Jimmy produced a joint, lit it and took a deep drag. He gazed out the window with a faraway look. 'You don't mind, do you?'

Relief swept over her. 'I'd prefer you didn't.'

'Do you know what they say about Toowoomba?' he asked as they rounded the bend at the top of a hill.

She shook her head.

'World's smallest lake. World's flattest mountain.'

She smiled despite herself, remembering the man-made Lake Annand in the centre of town and the treeless summit of Table Top Mountain. 'What else do they say?' She was surprised he'd made her laugh.

Jimmy considered the question. 'Well, the thing I reckon is interesting, but no-one ever talks about, is that in Toowoomba the wrong side of the tracks is like, literally, the wrong side of the tracks. There's this train line that runs right through the middle of town separating east from west, and the east side is posh and the west side is where all the deros live.'

'Really? I'd never thought of it that way, but now you mention it ...'

'The other thing no-one talks about is,' he said, warming to the subject, 'once a year there's a really brutal murder. Like three years ago there was the torso murder, the year after there was a triple murder, and then last year there was that guy who killed his brother and his freaking teacher helped bury him out the back of Mount Lofty somewhere.' He flicked the joint out of the window. 'Mind if I turn the radio on?' he asked, reaching for the open packet of chips sitting between them and cramming a handful into his mouth.

The dramatic music of the ABC news bulletin came on:

Here is the 7:30 pm news for this day, Sunday, twenty-eighth of April 1996. In breaking news, a gunman armed with two high-calibre semiautomatic weapons has killed in excess of thirty people and wounded countless others in Port Arthur, Tasmania, the former prison colony and popular tourist spot.

Dana and Jimmy sat in shocked silence as the broadcast moved on to interviews with family members of the victims. The headlights of the truck shone on the eucalyptus trees lining the sides of the road, their branches like fingers splayed in an ethereal tunnel.

'What do you make of that?' Jimmy asked.

Dana shrugged, too overwrought by the news headline and the events of the day to comment.

He spoke quietly into the silence. 'I reckon that gunman must have been mad. Schizophrenia's a fucking horrible disease.' He didn't seem to mind if she was listening or not. 'My cousin Matty has it, he's been living on the streets for most of his life.' Jimmy's face tightened, ageing him beyond his years. 'It was a real shame when they closed down those institutions. He was at that Baillie Henderson Hospital for years, on the outskirts of Toowoomba.'

'It is a pity,' she said, a tide of exhaustion sweeping over her. Perhaps she had been too quick to judge. Jimmy was far more complex than she'd imagined.

She closed her eyes and thought of Hugh, his look of endless concern as he stood in the doorway and said goodbye. Jimmy was still speaking, but she was drifting in the realm between sleep and consciousness.

'My cuz and I were real close when we were young,' he said.

But whatever came next, she didn't hear.

In the murky recesses of semiconsciousness, she dreamt of her baby, his dimpled smile, the rosebud lips. Always, the inevitable moment when she found him, not breathing, not moving. She came to with a scream, staring uncomprehendingly at the inside of the truck, at Jimmy's startled expression.

'Jesus,' he said. 'Are you trying to kill us?'

She stammered an apology and stared out the window at the dead streets of Toowoomba, a ghost town under unearthly orange streetlights. Mist rose from a creek bed as they drove into town.

'Where you headed?' he asked.

'Just drop me at the mechanics,' she said. 'I'll catch a cab.'

'It's no problem. The mechanic we use is near the airport, so I may as well drop you on my way through town.'

'Thank you,' she said, grateful her ordeal wasn't to be extended. 'I'm in Godsall Street, opposite the park.'

Minutes later, they pulled up in front of a stately old Queenslander overlooking Queens Park. Jimmy lifted her suitcase from the passenger seat of her mangled car and placed it on the footpath.

'You don't have to do that,' she said.

He shrugged. 'It's what country folk do.'

She thanked him and tiptoed up the stairs of the neighbouring house. She pushed the doorbell of the darkened home, wishing she'd called ahead. A light went on and a figure appeared behind the stained-glass window. The front door opened, revealing a woman in her fifties with kind eyes and a short, sensible haircut.

'Susan?' asked Dana.

Her new landlord nodded and pulled her dressing-gown around her. The mantelpiece behind her was lined with hand-painted china plates and framed photos that Dana presumed were of her grandchildren. Dana explained what had happened and why she was late to arrive.

'Good grief,' said Susan. 'How are you feeling? Is there anything I can do?'

'I'm absolutely fine.'

A young boy, about eleven, with white-blond hair and freckles poked his head around the corner.

'Angus, get to bed,' Susan said sternly.

The boy approached, staring up at Dana.

'Come on,' Susan said, putting her hands on the boy's shoulders and gently pushing him back down the hallway. 'I'm looking after him while my daughter sorts herself out,' she explained.

Dana often worked with clients who had guardianship of their grandchildren and had marvelled at their patience. 'He's lucky to have you.'

Susan gave Dana a tight smile as she handed her the keys to the house next door. 'You must be exhausted, love. I'll let you get some sleep and I can pop over tomorrow and fill you in on anything else you need to know. I've left some basics in the fridge to get you started.'

Breathing a sigh of relief, Dana returned to the footpath to collect her suitcase and paused under the streetlight, looking out across the park. She watched as the fog swirled through the tree canopy and swept across the wide expanse of green lawn, the flowerbeds shrouded in darkness. She looked over to the neighbouring Queenslander, which was to be her home for the next few months, and carefully made her way through a gate flanked by green hedges and up a small set of stairs. Wisteria hung from the gutters of the gabled roof over the verandah.

Inside were polished hardwood floors, Persian rugs and a brass bed in each bedroom. She chose the room closest to the front verandah and swallowed two sleeping tablets. The room was airless, the vase of fake flowers on the side table dusty. It took all her strength just to open the window and turn back the heavy, patterned duvet. In a foreign bed, in this strange house, she felt Hugh's absence as though someone had lopped off an arm. Tears welled as she stared at the peeling pressed-metal ceiling. For the life of her she couldn't remember why, all those nights ago, she'd turned him away.

Cold air streamed through the open window the next morning and she roused herself from a nightmare about Oscar and dead kangaroos. Her head was throbbing and she shivered in her nightie as she stumbled out of bed and replayed the voicemail on her phone.

Hi Dana, it's Mum. Give me a call when you're there and let me know you arrived safely. And please let Doctor Harper know that he'll have to send your scripts to Queensland now. That's all, I think. Promise me you'll look after yourself. I'll talk to you soon.

The usual mix of edginess and guilt rose up inside her when she heard her mother's voice. If she'd been a decent daughter, she'd have been indulging her mother in the things she loved – shopping and going to the movies. Instead, Dana deleted the message, promising herself she'd call back later, and stood in front of the full-length mirror in the corner of the room. She lifted her nightie and looked at the red bruise that had formed from the crash last night, beginning at her right shoulder and ending below her left breast.

She walked down the hallway, noting the mishmash of décor on the painted vj walls – a print of an Arabian horse above the fireplace, a cuckoo clock in the lounge room. A pang of homesickness ran through her, a longing for the quiet stone of her home in Castlecrag. If she'd been there now, she'd be strolling along the peninsula beside the boats on Middle Harbour.

She took two aspirin and phoned her new manager. After five minutes of listening to music that did nothing for her headache she was finally put through. She told Helen about the car accident.

'Goodness, you weren't hurt, were you?'

'I'm alright,' said Dana. 'But I might be running late. I just have to call the hire car company and the insurance people to see if they'll replace my car.'

'That's fine, take all the time you need. And don't worry about hiring a car. I'll arrange for you to have one of the work vehicles.'

'That's very kind,' Dana said, unable to believe how generous her new boss was being. In Sydney she'd have been reprimanded for showing up late on the first day.

'Actually,' Helen added, 'Keely has an assessment to do in Crows Nest and I was going to get her to show you the ropes. I'll get her to drop by and pick you up.'

Dana called the insurance company. When she finally got through, a male voice on the end of the line said, 'I'm sorry to inform you, but your car has suffered major damage. We'll have to declare it a write-off. The good news is that it's still under a three-year warranty so we'll refund the cost of the vehicle in full.'

She was silent. Hugh had surprised her with the car after she'd arrived home from hospital with Oscar. Their *family* car. Her eyes pricked with tears as she realised she would no longer have need for a Mercedes wagon.

'Everything alright?'

'Thank you,' she said, feeling ridiculous. 'The payout's fine.'

After she hung up, she got dressed and waited by the front gate for her lift. She'd chosen to wear a skirt and was thankful she'd also worn a jacket, as the breeze had a bite to it. There was an unwritten law in child protection that one wore pants while doing fieldwork, boots even better if a quick getaway was needed. But she'd always felt the need to push back against expectations. It was the same when she'd chosen a double degree in psychology and social work, when her father's plans were for her to do medicine or law. He'd been appalled when he found out she was wasting her HSC marks on a degree that could guarantee neither wealth nor prestige. He'd been even more bewildered when she'd specialised in child protection.

As a beat-up Commodore with unmistakable Queensland Government number plates pulled up across the street, Dana wondered about those choices now. But before she could give it further thought, a young woman in her twenties, with blue hair and a lanyard ID around her neck, wound down the window.

'Hi, I'm Keely,' she said with a snaggle-tooth smile.

Dana introduced herself and walked around to the passenger side. She strapped herself in and detected a smell she'd long associated with work vehicles – baby formula spilt recklessly, the sweat of harried caseworkers, chips ground into the seats. She closed her eyes and rubbed her temples, wondering if six months after Oscar's death was too soon to be back in the field, if frontline work was going to be impossible after the trauma she'd been through.

There was an awkward lull in the conversation filled by the sound of the indicator as they headed north out of town.

'What's this assessment we're going out on?' asked Dana.

'A nine-year-old girl got hurt during a domestic violence incident. Actually, the mum, Sandra, was the perpetrator. Smashed all the plates in the kitchen during a fight with her husband. Her daughter, Billy-Violet, got hit and needed stitches to her forehead. There's also a teenager who lives there, Chrystal – she's the mother's half-sister.' Keely cleared her throat. 'I should probably mention that a police officer, Connor Morgan, is also coming. He's letting the mother know that they're not pressing charges.'

She said the policeman's name carefully, as though she was uneasy about him.

'Do you want me to lead?' Dana asked casually, knowing what it was like to be young and inexperienced, to lose a night's sleep worrying about work.

'It's fine,' Keely said. 'Helen says I need to practise so I can build my confidence.'

Dana glanced over at Keely. Her nose ring and short hair made her look tough, but her eyes were pools of innocence. Keely was supposed to show Dana the ropes, but she wondered whether it would be the other way around. 'Can I read the notification?'

'Yes, it's in my handbag.'

Dana read the first few pages until her eyes blurred and bright floaters blotted her vision. She forced herself to look up as they passed through the small town of Highfields and sped along the highway.

'Helen said you used to be a manager,' said Keely.

Dana nodded, taking in a collection of heritage buildings with a sign, *The Chocolate Cottage*. 'I managed an investigation and assessment team for the Department of Community Services in Sydney.'

'Why'd you give it up?'

'I missed the fieldwork.' Dana squinted into the sun slanting through the trees, wishing she'd brought sunglasses. She didn't mention that she'd wanted to be as far away from home as possible.

'But Sydney's such a cool place. Have you been to Toowoomba before?'

'I have actually.' She had a history with Toowoomba that began on her fifteenth birthday – the first time she'd attended McGregor Summer School for violin lessons. It was strange to think now, the fantasy that had led her to believe she could be a musician, but it had seemed the most natural thing in the world to her teenage self. She'd travelled from her strict home in

Castlecrag, away from newly divorced parents who were making life hell, to a world where anything seemed possible.

'I haven't been here since the 1980s, when my aunt sold up and moved to Noosa,' added Dana.

As she said it, she realised that Toowoomba had retained its romantic air. There was something magical about the way the fog moved in across Queens Park at a moment's notice, the pine trees rising like sentinels from the stately grounds of Toowoomba Grammar School on Margaret Street. It was Toowoomba where she'd learnt to love the camphor laurel trees and country people who laughed without self-consciousness.

She knew she should be drawing Keely out, asking her more questions, but her headache was rapidly becoming a migraine and her stomach had started to churn. She stared despairingly out the window, hoping Keely would pick up on the social cues and leave Dana to her misery.

The road soon curved downhill and the trees began to thin. By the time they drove past the start of town, marked with a sign – *Welcome to Crows Nest, Population 1600* – Keely's chatter had dwindled to silence. Dana peered closely at the sign and took in the five bullet holes that punctured it.

They continued past paddocks of cows and a deserted tourist spot with replica bullocks, before turning into a gravelled car park under the blue and white logo of the Queensland Police Service. The station, Dana was surprised to note, was little more than a single wooden building with a corrugated-iron roof and a lean-to holding cell.

Dana wondered if she was up to going inside, whether she could admit to Keely she was feeling ill and forget about the home visit and everything it entailed. But when Keely gestured for Dana to join her from the ramp at the entrance of the station she told herself it was just a headache. How bad could it be speaking to a mother who'd thrown some plates in a fit of anger?

Inside the police station they announced their arrival to the receptionist at the front desk. A man with a rough-hewn face and silvery beard appeared in the corridor. He wore a suit and tie as though he'd been at court.

'Keely, how are you?' he asked, before turning to Dana. 'Senior Sergeant Ian Steinmann,' he said, enveloping Dana's delicate hand in his meaty one. 'I look after both Toowoomba and Crows Nest stations. I take it you're the new worker Helen's been telling me about.'

'That's me,' said Dana.

Ian gave her a shrewd yet kindly look. 'I'm hoping you'll be able to teach my men a thing or two about child protection with your experience.'

'I'll do my best.'

He glanced at his TAG Heuer watch. 'Right, I've got to go. Connor will be out in a minute.'

Ian disappeared through the swinging reception-room door and a second later another policeman stood in front of them. He was six foot three with pale blue eyes and a crisp white shirt. He dazzled them with a smile.

'So, you want me to meet you out at the Creek Street house?' he said, speaking directly to Keely.

'That would be good.' Keely blushed, making Dana wonder whether the girl had a crush on him.

'What name should I tell them you're going by this week?' he asked. 'Is it Families, Communities or Child Safety?'

'Families,' said Keely. 'The new name's supposed to renew public confidence.'

'It's going to take more than that.' He smirked.

Dana was awed by his arrogance. More than that, she was awed by how attractive he was. He had dark, feathery hair and wide-spaced eyes that were almost feminine.

'I'm Dana.' She put out her hand, tired of waiting to be introduced.

'Constable Connor Morgan.' He feigned surprise, as if he'd only just noticed her. His handshake was firm and lingered a moment too long.

'So, I'll see you both soon?' he said. 'If I haven't arrived by the time you get there, go in without me. I've got a warrant to serve, so I might be late.' He grinned and slid a hand into the pocket of his perfectly pressed pants.

As he sauntered away, two thoughts passed through her mind: the danger she'd seen in his eyes; and the impulse she had to run towards it.

3

The moment they arrived at the old wooden house Dana knew that turning up to work had been a mistake. The property had the desolate air she'd sensed as they drove through town – unmown lawns, shower curtains used to hide an unfinished extension on the verandah and a leopard tree with all its limbs hacked off.

As they started up the concrete path a Ford Falcon reversed down the drive and a man's head appeared out the window. He gazed at Keely's ID tag.

'You from the welfare?' he said with a Scottish accent.

'That's right,' said Keely.

'I've got to rush out and talk to the builder. He's stuffed up our new house and if I don't pin him down, who knows when I'll catch him.' He paused, his eyes lighting up when he saw Dana. 'Sorry to be rude.' The scent of Old Spice drifted from the car as he stuck out his hand for her to shake. 'Paul Kirby.'

'Nice to meet you.' Dana took in his thick red beard and denim work shirt opened to the chest.

'Thanks for coming.' He gave them a hangdog grin. 'Sandy and I really appreciate all the help you guys give us. Drive safe on your way back.'

Plumes of dust flew from the back of his car as he drove away.

Dana went up the stairs first and knocked. She hoped to god her headache would ease enough to allow her to get through the interview.

She could hear footsteps in the hallway and, beyond that, the barking of dogs. She took a deep breath as the door swung open to reveal a woman with gold hoop earrings wearing an oversized Broncos jersey.

'Mrs Kirby?' Dana asked.

'Call me Sandra.'

'I'm Dana and this is Keely, from the Department of Families.'

'What's this about?'

'We've received concerns,' Dana said crisply. 'Your daughter, Billy-Violet—'

'What fucking concerns? What are they saying about me?'

'That's what we'd like to talk to you about,' Dana said calmly, trying to ignore the pulsating pain in her head. 'Can we speak with you inside?'

'Who did you say you were?' Sandra's eyes rolled back. 'Who?' she shouted again, before Dana had a chance to answer.

Dana was suddenly on high alert. Sandra was a cauldron of emotion and Dana would need all of her faculties to calm her. Yet beneath Sandra's brash exterior, Dana sensed vulnerability. The barking dogs became more hysterical.

'Are those dogs restrained?' asked Dana.

Sandra gave them a half-smile. 'They're real vicious, but lucky for you they're out the back.'

Dana and Keely exchanged glances as they followed Sandra down the dark hall into a house that held the chill of the night. Sandra kicked a mountain of clothes out of the way as she passed by one of the bedrooms.

In the lounge room, a large woman with a fresh bandage around her leg was sitting on the couch. She looked up at them from behind dark glasses. Keely and Dana sat down in the armchairs opposite. The smell of cigarette smoke wafted up from the ancient carpet.

'This is my friend, Debbie,' said Sandra. 'Whatever you've got to say, you can say in front of her 'cause she's my bestie.' Debbie removed her glasses and blinked rapidly when they made eye contact, then started polishing the glasses with her t-shirt. Sandra went into the kitchen that backed on to the lounge room and bent down to check the oven. 'I'm baking a Sara Lee apple crumble – Paul's favourite. He's been working so hard lately.'

Dana pulled her notebook out of her bag and glanced up at a portrait on the sideboard. Paul looked honest and calm, staring evenly at the camera, a baby in his arms as he stood between his wife and Debbie.

When Sandra came back into the room she collapsed beside Debbie on the lounge. 'We're building a massive house up on Chestnut Drive,' she said. 'It's going to have a bedroom for each of the kids, an ensuite and a vanity.'

A red-haired girl of about nine – clearly Billy-Violet – darted into the kitchen then out the back door.

'So, what's this about then?' asked Sandra. 'I'll bet you a hundred bucks it's that twat next door. We're too loud, the dog barks too much.' She shot Keely a glittery smile. 'They want the kids to be really, like, zen.' She gestured to Debbie. 'Well, they're not, are they? They're loud little buggers – especially during school holidays.'

Keely cleared her throat. 'Well, the thing is, we've got to come out and do an assessment.'

Sandra's eyebrows shot to the roof. 'We have, have we?'

'That's right,' said Keely. 'We've received allegations that on Friday night Billy got hit by a plate and needed stitches and that there were also screams coming from the house. As late as eleven o'clock at night.'

Dana bit her lip. It would have been better to lead with a comment on the child, something playful and friendly. She was tempted to intervene, but remembered that Keely was trying to build her confidence.

'Look, I can get rowdy, especially on a Friday night … You know what I'm like, Deb. But smashing plates, that's bullshit. And anyway, it's my house, so what if I did?'

'Well, any kind of domestic violence … it puts the kids at risk,' said Keely.

'Oh, I see, everything's my fault now, is it?'

'We'll need to do some checks, with the school, the police. That sort of thing.'

Sandra's face turned hard. 'Do what you want. But there's no problems with my kids. Nothing at all. And to be honest, I'm sick of your lot turning up here. Asking questions. When's it going to be my turn to ask the questions? When do you use the loo? How often do you shag your husband?' She glanced at Dana scornfully.

'Do you get much support?' Dana asked. 'Any friends or family to help you out?'

'Debbie's great,' she said, as Debbie smiled over at them with shy pride. 'But as for my family … I guess there's Chrystal. She's still a teenager, but she's been helping with the baby since we brought her home.'

'The baby?' Dana asked, her body tensing.

'Rubi.' Sandra pulled a face as though she wished she hadn't mentioned it. 'I'd bring her out, but she's sleeping.'

'Can we see her?' Keely asked, raising her eyebrows in Dana's direction to indicate she had no idea about Sandra's new baby.

Dana stared at her feet, trying not to appear rattled. She couldn't have made it any clearer to Helen that she wouldn't work with infants until she'd settled into the job. What kind of person would give a case involving a newborn to someone who'd just lost a baby of their own?

'Sure,' Sandra said reluctantly. 'But make sure you're quiet. If you wake her up, there'll be hell to pay.'

In a room off the hallway a baby was asleep in a lace-covered crib. Dana, Keely and Sandra stood in a semicircle, no-one daring to speak.

Dana drank in Rubi's heavy eyelids, the rosy hue of her cheeks, and felt a rising panic. An elephant mobile hung from the roof, a change table sat against the wall. She thought of Oscar, staring up at her as she'd changed his nappy. It was her routine to use the hand lotion when she was done and she'd been surprised when, at barely eight months of age, he'd pushed the dispenser and rubbed his palms together, bright-eyed, not missing a beat. Dana gasped as though someone had opened up a wound in her chest.

In the next room were two sets of bunk beds. Clothes and Barbie dolls were strewn across the floor.

'Kids, hey,' said Sandra. 'Who'd have 'em?'

I would, thought Dana with a bitterness that surprised her. *Any day of the year.*

Her headache flared with sudden intensity and the room, with its assortment of kitsch banners, *Love* and *You Are My Happy*, made her head spin. She willed back the tears as she thought of Oscar's smiling face.

As they resumed their places in the lounge room, Keely screwed up her nose. Dana looked up as smoke began to fill the kitchen.

'Oh god.' Sandra sprinted to the oven. 'Help, Debbie. Help!' Debbie darted to the kitchen as Sandra yanked the steaming mess from the oven. Her friend held the bin aloft as Sandra scraped the remnants of apple crumble into it.

Down the hall, the outraged cries of the baby started.

'Just leave me alone.' Sandra threw her hands into the air. 'I'm not in the mood anymore.'

Dana took the rubbish bag from Debbie's hands. 'We'll take this on our way out,' she offered.

Sandra flashed her a reluctant smile. 'Thanks, love. Sorry if I've been … well, you know. Me and my big mouth, hey.'

'It's fine,' Dana reassured her.

They hurried down the hall and into the front yard. Dana dumped the rubbish bag in the bin around the side of the house. The air was cool against her face when she caught up with Keely, and after a few seconds her thoughts turned to her new boss and the memory of their first phone call. Helen's sincere promise that no infant would be allocated to Dana's caseload. Dana stood on the path taking deep breaths to calm herself down.

'Bloody hell, that went badly.' Keely's cheeks glowed red.

'Don't beat yourself up.' Dana blinked at the pain behind her eyes. 'We'll come back next week and speak to the girl and the teenager – alone.'

The sky above the surrounding hills had turned grey as dark clouds gathered in the west. A police car skidded up to the kerb and Connor jumped out.

'I haven't missed the visit, have I? I hope not – I'd be devastated,' he said, and laughed.

'We've finished.' Dana pushed past the policeman and strode down the front path, him and Keely falling into step behind her. He was late and now he had the gall to make jokes. 'So whatever you've come to tell her, you'll have to make do without us.'

'Sure thing,' he said, struggling to keep up. 'God, you should see Debbie and Sandra when they're out on the turps. The number of fights I've had to break up because Sandra's been mouthing off, turning one bloke against another. The guy who owns the pub said that before she met Paul, she'd been the town bike so often he could barely keep track.'

Dana stopped abruptly. 'She's a twenty-nine-year-old mother. She's doing her best.' She opened the gate and let it go before he had the chance to come through. It slammed into his shins.

'Aghh!' he cried out, jumping on one foot and rubbing his leg. 'Christ, woman, I was only joking.'

Keely touched Dana's shoulder. 'We should go.'

Dana's face was burning as she opened the car door. She took a final backward glance at the young constable, their eyes meeting across the straggly lawn.

'Holy shit,' said Keely, turning the key in the ignition. 'That was hardcore.'

'It was an accident,' she said, putting her head in her hands, regretting how childish she must have seemed. *What was happening? To have slapped her husband and now this?* She wondered whether she should just admit she was losing it and check back in with Doctor Harper, like her mother had begged her to.

She fumbled in her bag for her valium, frustrated that she didn't have a bottle of water with her. She slipped a couple of tablets in her mouth and wound down the window.

Heading south along the highway they passed a row of houses with rusted roofs, streaked with dirt. As they drove into the city, a sign at the Weiss factory proclaimed delicious mango and cream iceblocks. Minutes later they turned into the underground car park of a cold and austere office tower, the grey concrete of the Condamine Centre incongruent with the surrounding heritage buildings. A group of men with shaved heads and tattoos had gathered in the foyer and a teenage girl tapped Keely on the arm as they entered the lift.

'You the welfare?' the girl asked.

'Sure am.'

Dana was shocked by the lack of security, that Family Services officers were sharing a lift with clients whose children they'd been known to remove. At the Sydney office there'd been security guards at the front desk and visitors were required to sign a register.

The lift chimed when they reached the third floor and they stepped into the waiting room. A mother and daughter looked up dully from their magazines. On the walls was a child-friendly mural with an inscription: *What you have done for the least of these children you have done for us all.* Dana tried to remember where the quote was from. The Bible?

Keely swiped through the security door and Dana followed her along the corridor under a line of fluorescent lights that made her eyes smart. A *Welcome Dana* sign had been pinned to the wall of one of the pods. A KitKat had been left on her new desk beside her computer. She thought about the disastrous home visit and felt guilty about the kindness being shown to her.

She dropped her handbag on her desk and an admin worker gave her a tour of the office. The intake team, interview rooms and kitchen were on one side of the building, while the other was for the admin pod, the children under orders and initial assessment teams.

When Dana returned to the pod a large woman with black court shoes and a discreetly chequered camel coat came over. Dana swivelled in her chair.

'Hi Dana, I'm Helen. Nice to meet you.'

Dana took a deep breath, reminding herself that while her personal life may be in tatters, at least she could be proud of the work she did in her job.

'Can I see you in my office?'

Helen's tone made Dana's stomach lurch and she began to wonder whether someone had mentioned the incident with Constable Morgan.

She followed Helen's determined strides down the hall where they turned right into a corner office. Inside was a tall man with shoulder-length salt-and-pepper hair. He was sitting cross-legged on a chair in front of Helen's desk and stood as they entered.

'Lachlan,' he said, and put out his hand. He had creases around his eyes from smiling and his skin was tanned from the sun.

Helen sat down behind her desk as Dana took a seat next to Lachlan. Outside Helen's window, stately old buildings and modern ones stood side by side. She gazed at a photo of twin West Highland terriers on Helen's desk, trying to reconcile the woman in front of her with being a dog lover.

'I thought I'd get you to come in so we could have a chat about case allocation.' Helen ran a hand through her pageboy haircut.

'Okay,' said Dana, as her breathing returned to normal.

Lachlan was nervously bouncing a foot up and down on his knee. He flashed her an apologetic smile.

What was he doing here anyway?

Helen reached across to her in-tray for a file and opened it on her desk. 'So, I'd like to allocate you the Kirby family, the one you saw with Keely this morning. Ideally, I would have given it to Lachlan as he worked with them at the beginning of the year, but unfortunately his caseload's far too high.' She sighed. 'This family's been on the books for as long as I can remember – I've worked with them, my mother worked with them. There's been intergenerational abuse in that family for forty years. I need someone to work this case and make things better. Can you do that?'

Dana nodded. She was annoyed that, with Lachlan there, she couldn't object to being allocated a case with a newborn.

'And I'm sending Lachlan with you next time, to mentor you – much like I should have done in the first place.'

'Is that necessary?' Dana bristled at the thought of being babysat.

'Yes, to begin with.' Helen thrust the family's case file across the desk towards Dana. 'Crows Nest is a small town and people have long memories. They're not likely to accept you unless you're with someone who has their trust.'

'Like me.' Lachlan gave Dana a self-deprecating grin as she accepted the folder. 'We can figure out a time so I can give you the lowdown on the family.'

After they were excused, Dana stalked back towards her desk.

'What did you think of Helen?' Lachlan asked as he followed along the corridor behind her, striding to catch up.

'Seems nice enough,' said Dana.

'I'm terrified of her,' he said. 'Terrified that if I met her in a dark alley I'd come off second best. She might seem reasonable, but underneath she's tough as nails.'

Dana frowned, not wanting to show her allegiances too early. She sat at her desk and opened the file she'd been given. A newspaper clipping of Sandra and Paul's wedding was stapled to the inside. The photo was of the happy couple along with Debbie, who'd been the bridesmaid. It was a memorable picture and clearly taken in the 1980s. Sandra's dress was adorned with Chantilly lace, romantic era-style shoulders and a high neckline – a knock-off of the dress worn by Kylie Minogue in the *Neighbours* wedding a year or so earlier. Debbie wore a light-coloured taffeta and Paul stood next to her in a matching cummerbund.

Dana was immediately transported to the memories of her own wedding and the understated slip dress she'd worn. When Hugh had seen her outside the registry office his face had been awestruck, but since their family had fallen apart, she'd started to wonder whether he cared about Oscar's death or if what he truly missed was his stylish wife.

A phone rang in the neighbouring cubicle snapping her out of her daydream. She refocused on the image of Sandra. Her first impressions – a mother who'd gather her children close in times of stress rather than push them away. If Dana could get some childcare and house maintenance services in place, then perhaps it would be a straightforward case. She could link the family with support agencies and close the file quickly. Once and for all.

4

Dana sat opposite Lachlan in the stone-floored pub, leaning on a barrel that doubled as a table. She'd just placed the Kirby file in front of them and was forced to slide it down onto her lap as a waiter came from behind the mirrored bar to take their order. He asked Lachlan if he wanted the usual, then took Dana's order, a gin and tonic.

Lachlan nodded at the file in her lap. 'I see you're getting into bad habits already?'

She gave him a thin smile, hoping he'd get the message that she was here for work and not for a casual chat. Nor did she want to bring up the meeting she'd been dragged back into late yesterday afternoon, when Helen had told her about the complaint that had been lodged against her.

Helen had berated her for assaulting Constable Morgan. 'How is it,' she had chided, 'that in one morning you've managed to annoy the local police force and give the community the impression that we're completely unprofessional?'

After her initial shock, Dana had longed to give Helen a piece of her mind, tell her the whole thing had been blown out of proportion, but instead she remained silent. She'd long ago confronted the authority problem brought on by her father and had learnt that the best way to manage such situations was to say nothing.

'So, what can you tell me about the Kirby family?' Dana asked, getting back to the subject at hand.

'Well,' Lachlan raised an eyebrow, appearing surprised there would be no small talk, 'the mother, Sandra, has the two young children as well as caring for her half-sisters. She was raised in the school of hard knocks, if you know what I mean, and got hitched to Paul when she was twenty-one, at the RSL apparently. What did you think of Crows Nest, by the way?'

'It's a nice little town.' Dana ripped a corner from a red beer coaster. She wished Lachlan would get to the point.

He scratched his beard meditatively. 'It's always reminded me of the film *Deliverance*. I didn't want to say it while Helen was around, but whenever I'm there I half expect a little squint-eyed boy to come out on the patio and start playing the banjo.'

'Okay. What more can you tell me?'

He shrugged. 'Sandy's had a tough life. Her two brothers were in and out of jail in their teens and early twenties and her mother was useless. There's a history of domestic violence between her and Paul, the husband, some pushing and shoving, emotional abuse that went both ways. What else?' he wondered aloud and waved at a man who ambled through the doors. 'Paul has an air conditioning business which seems to do well. His childhood was erratic. He was born in Scotland and his father was in the oil industry. They moved around a lot – Saudi and

Venezuela. He's not much of a disciplinarian, but then again, he's always at work so he's not around a lot.'

'Does Sandy work?'

'No, she's a hairdresser by trade, but she's got enough on her plate caring for the children. She's a good mother, I'll give her that. Apart from the outburst when Billy got stitches, I'd say she's a caring mum.'

The waiter placed their drinks in front of them and Dana took a large sip, hoping the alcohol would relax her. Her second day had been filled with meeting new people and grappling with unfamiliar computer systems.

'What's your opinion on the domestic violence between the parents?'

'Honestly,' Lachlan said, sipping from his beer, 'I think a lot of it has to do with when they took the teenage sisters in. Alisha, the eldest one, gave them a lot of grief – stealing, skipping school, running away to be with her boyfriend. It put a lot of strain on the family and I think that's why things got so bad between Paul and Sandra. Alisha moved out a while back, so that's one less issue they've had to deal with.'

'So, you're saying' – Dana's eyes narrowed – 'it's your belief that the violence between them was fuelled by being stressed out by a teenager's difficult behaviour?'

Surely, there were other factors at play? She wondered what on earth Lachlan was doing in social work. Privately, she believed that improving the lives of children was women's business. In her years in the field, she'd yet to meet a male worker her equal.

'I know it seems strange.' He turned his palms upwards with sincerity. 'But things got better once Alisha left. Sandra also has a best friend, Debbie, who's at the house day and night, so I don't think that's helped. Sandra and Debbie see so much of each other the locals think they're lovers.'

'And are they?'

'Not sure. Could just be small-town gossip.'

A blonde woman in a tight black dress and towering stilettos stopped at their table. She embraced Lachlan and they kissed each other's cheeks. Another round of drinks came out. After a brief chat the woman left, promising they'd catch up soon.

Lachlan caught Dana staring at him and grinned.

'How do you know her?' Dana asked. The alcohol had hit its mark. For the first time that day, she felt relaxed and expansive.

'She's the wife of an old school friend,' Lachlan said. 'Are you married?'

'Yes.' Dana thought fondly of Hugh now the alcohol was in her veins. 'Three years next week.'

'And what does he do?'

'He's a landscape architect. Designs gardens for the rich and famous.'

'I imagine there'd be a lot of call for it down there. How'd he feel about you packing up and leaving him to fend for himself?' He nodded a hello at a man walking past.

'There wasn't much he could say. Is there anyone you don't know at this pub?'

'I don't know everyone. See that man by the door? I don't think I've met him.' He smiled, examining Dana's face as if seeing her for the first time. 'Why did you get into child protection? No offence, but you're not really the type.'

Dana took a long breath. 'At the start, it was everything I'd ever wanted. It was meaty and instructive; I was going out with the police, removing children from neglectful homes, placing them with loving foster families. But when I was put into the management role things changed. It got to the point where instead of feeling sympathy for the kids and families, the only sympathy I could muster up was for myself, for having to deal with such crap, day after day.'

She stopped, horrified by how much of herself she'd revealed. In the dim light of the pub, there was an absence of judgement in Lachlan's expression. She realised that they'd only spent a small amount of time together and already she'd disclosed what she'd barely admitted to herself. She glanced at her watch. It was half past five. 'I should be going.' She hastily gathered up the file.

Lachlan swigged the last of his beer and checked his phone. 'Me too,' he said. 'The missus is asking where I am.'

On the way out of the bar Dana wondered whether all country pubs smelt the same. Stale vomit. Control lost.

They stood under a camphor laurel tree in the car park and Lachlan lit a cigarette. 'Let me give you a lift home,' he offered.

'I don't think so,' Dana said flatly.

'What?' He paused, then blinked with comprehension. 'I've only had two beers.'

She shook her head. 'Don't worry about it. I'm only on the other side of the park.'

'Look,' said Lachlan, a shadow passing over his face. 'I don't know who you've pissed off, but in the office they're already calling you Princess Diana.'

'What?'

He grinned. 'It's funny, isn't it?'

'For you, maybe.'

'So who was it? Who've you managed to get on the wrong side of during your first two days?'

'I've no idea.'

He looked at her with disappointment. 'Keep your head down and try to get along with everyone. You'll find it's a nice office once they get to know you.'

'Thanks,' she said, grateful he was trying to help.

He drove away in a beat-up green Range Rover, with The Eagles' 'Witchy Woman' blaring from the stereo. He waved as he skidded out of the gravelled car park and drove down the street.

Dana headed to the Bell Street Mall and collected dinner from a small deli. She crossed at the traffic lights near a church with a sign proclaiming: *Jesus Saves!* As she strode up the incline on Godsall Street, struggling for breath, she vowed to get fit now that she was in Queensland. The sun was lowering behind her. A brilliant apricot setting the sky on fire.

After she let herself in, she went straight to the kitchen and checked the answering machine. There were no messages from Hugh, just three from her mother, begging Dana to call. She flicked on ABC Classic FM, made a simple meal of cheese and olives, and poured a glass of wine.

She sat on the couch, the Kirby file on her lap, and gazed around at the shabbiness of the room with its faded rug and dusty curtains. After her second glass an uneasy calm settled over her. She was almost in a dream when Jacqueline du Pré came on the radio playing 'Elgar's Cello Concerto in E minor'. Her last troubled thoughts before she fell asleep were of Jacqueline's husband, Daniel Barenboim, cheating on her with his mistress in France, their two children born before Jacqueline was dead in the ground.

~

When her eyes snapped open it was night-time. A boy was watching television. *Susan's grandson?* He was sprawled across the rug with his head on a cushion, as though he'd been there for hours. Her mind ground into action trying to figure out how long she'd been asleep. *How had he gotten in?* Then she realised she must have left the front door unlocked when she'd come back from the deli. She tried to recall his name. *Angus?* Though she couldn't be sure. *Dear god*, she prayed silently, *make him go away.*

'It's Angus, isn't it?' she asked.

He nodded, his eyes glued to the TV.

'You can stay for a while and watch the news, but it's late so when it's over you'll have to go home. Would you like some orange juice?'

'No, thanks.' He darted to the dining-room table where her PowerBook 5300 laptop sat. He touched it gently and looked across at her with an expression of rapture.

'Is this the C?' he asked.

'Yes.' She remembered the extra fifteen hundred dollars she'd paid at Hugh's urging to upgrade the screen to an active-matrix display.

She was in the kitchen, pouring a glass of water for herself when Angus yelled, 'Quick! Come look! There's been a murder!'

Dana hurried into the lounge room where the Channel Nine news was on and a woman with shoulder pads was announcing in a serious tone:

In breaking news tonight, police are scouring bushland just outside Crows Nest where the bodies of two women have been discovered. Debbie Vickers and Sandra Kirby were found in a green Holden Kingswood panel van by bushwalkers at five o'clock this evening.

Senior Sergeant Ian Steinmann said the deaths are being treated as suspicious.

Angus rose from the floor and huddled close to Dana on the couch. She felt dizzy as the screen cut to live footage of Ian Steinmann. His face was tomato red as he stood in the foyer of the police station speaking into a couple of microphones. Cameras clicked and bright flashes of white illuminated the room. Ian blinked furiously:

We have a number of officers there and have cordoned off the area and declared it a crime scene. We are talking to witnesses, but we don't know what has occurred, as yet.

A home movie of Sandra playing with a wide-eyed baby Rubi and a faded photo of Debbie with a group of kindergarten children was shown. Next, a close-up of a green Holden Kingswood panel van, shrouded in mist in thick bushland with its doors flung open. The reporter resumed speaking:

Police stated that a post-mortem examination is expected to be completed in coming days and police have asked that anyone who has information on this matter please contact Crime Stoppers on 1800 333 000.

Dana opened the Kirby file on the coffee table as bile rose in her throat. She flicked through the pages with trembling hands until she found the photo of the two women on Sandra's wedding day. They were holding bouquets of ivory roses and their faces shone with the vitality of youth, their whole lives ahead of them. Outside, the screams of possums fighting filled the evening air.

5

On her way to work the next morning, Dana crunched through the red, green and gold leaves blanketing the park. At the Bell Street Mall, a crowd of journalists were jostling for position outside her office building. She chided herself for not anticipating their presence and made a hasty retreat to the back entrance. She'd just turned the corner when she ran headlong into a woman holding a microphone with an officious-looking lanyard around her neck.

'Isabell!' She gasped, taking in the cropped hair and cascade of lines around the woman's eyes. Dana almost didn't recognise her former high school nemesis.

'Dana!' Isabell raked over Dana with the same scrutiny. 'What are you doing here?'

'I'm working at the Department of Families.' She gestured to the adjacent building. 'Having a break from Sydney and doing some agency work. And you?'

Isabell smiled, revealing a mouth crowded with teeth. 'I'm

working for *Sixty Minutes* on the Kirby case. You've probably heard of it. The double murder of that mother and her best friend.'

'Heard of it?' said Dana. 'The whole town's talking about it.'

'Oh, that's right. Someone mentioned that Paul's kids are in foster care.' Isabell's eyes narrowed. 'You're probably working with the family?'

Dana stiffened. 'A lot of cases come through the Department. Just because a family is involved with the Toowoomba office doesn't mean that I'd come into contact with it.' She aimed for her social worker face, the non-judgemental expression she used when people told her intimate details about their lives.

'You don't expect me to believe that.'

Isabell's aggression was what Dana had always so disliked about her. 'Even if I was working with the family,' she said. 'There's no way I could talk about it.'

Isabell shrugged and ran a set of pink acrylic nails through her hair. 'So what's been happening with the great Dana Gibson since high school?' she said, changing the subject. 'No offence, but I almost didn't recognise you.'

Dana knew that Oscar's death had taken its toll, but she'd always believed that the change had taken place on the inside. The comment stung as it became clear that her external appearance had changed, too.

'I'm married,' she said, reaching for her wedding ring. 'What about you? I didn't see you at the ten-year reunion.'

'Oh, Mark and I were in London. We were married a few years back and have three kids.' She rolled her eyes. 'We call them our crazy critters.'

There it was again. The competitiveness.

'Are you going to the school reunion in June?' asked Isabell.

'Not sure yet.' She'd been asked to give the school captain's speech and was planning on going, but the thought of spending the evening with Isabell made her reconsider.

'Anyway.' Isabell barrelled on, unfazed. 'I've been researching the case and it looks like the police really stuffed up on this one. My source told me the police were understaffed and neither of the cops sent out to the scene were detectives or had even investigated a murder before. If they'd been experienced, they would have known that the area needed to be guarded overnight until forensic experts could be called in, but instead the car and the bodies were removed straight away.' She paused. 'If you want, we can do a bit of "I'll show you mine, if you show me yours", if you know what I mean.'

Dana had no intention of playing games. 'Not only is what you're suggesting unprofessional, it's also highly unethical.'

'I'll leave the ethics to you, but if you change your mind, here's my business card.'

Dana stared at the *Sixty Minutes* logo and Isabell's glossy head shot as the journalist turned and hurried across the mall in the direction of the police station.

The reception area was deserted when Dana got out of the lift. The admin worker, in a knitted jumper with a love heart, had a copy of the Toowoomba *Chronicle* spread out in front of her. She looked up, wide-eyed. 'It's horrible what happened to those women,' she said. 'Just horrible.'

In their pod, Lachlan, Keely and a woman Dana hadn't been introduced to were gathered around Lachlan's desk, which was covered in overflowing manila folders. They were deathly quiet as they read the article. Dana stashed her handbag in her desk drawer and joined her colleagues.

'I can't believe it. Just two days ago they were at Sandra's house, burning apple crumble,' Keely said.

Lachlan slid the paper over to Dana. She read the gruesome headline:

SLAYING AT ROCKY CREEK

The bodies of two women have been found brutally murdered in a car at Rocky Creek in Crows Nest. The victims have been identified as Sandra Kirby, a homemaker, and Debbie Vickers, a local kindergarten teacher at the Crows Nest Children's Centre. The women were last seen alive at Sandra's home at Creek Street, Crows Nest, around 10:30 pm on Monday. It is believed that the women left home around midnight and died sometime between 12 am and 6 am. Their bodies were found in the Kirby family's vehicle at the end of a dead-end track in the scrub near Postman's Bluff by bushwalkers at 5 pm Tuesday afternoon. Police state that autopsies of the bodies have yet to occur.

Lachlan's phone rang and interrupted her concentration. 'We'll be there in a minute.' He turned to Dana, his expression unreadable. 'Boss wants to see us.'

When they arrived at Helen's office she was stooped over her desk setting out faxes, the portrait of her terriers on faithful watch.

'Come in.' She waved them through.

Dana took in Helen's un-ironed blouse and lack of make-up and felt a pang of sympathy for her. It was barely eight o'clock and already the air of cool and calm she usually exuded had vanished.

'You've read the paper?' Helen asked, not looking up.

They nodded.

'I just spoke to the sergeant. He confirmed what the article had to say and provided some additional information. Sandra had been shot twice, once in the neck and once in the chest. Debbie was shot in the head.'

Dana realised her pulse was racing. To distract herself, she focused on what had worked in the past – what would best help the children.

'I've had a chat with Ian and he's agreed for you to sit in on the interviews with the family today, as it's likely those kids will need to go into foster care until we've completed an assessment.'

'What about Chrystal's mother?' asked Lachlan. 'We'll have to let her know we're putting her daughter in care, won't we?'

'There's a passing reference to the mother, Rosalyn Lawrence, in the archived history,' said Helen. 'But apparently she was deemed unfit, which is why the girls went to live with Sandra in the first place. I'll do my best to track her down and give her the court documents.'

'Who's going to care for Rubi while the family members are interviewed?' asked Dana, anxious that something terrible might happen to the baby.

'Ian's receptionist has offered to do it.' Helen was silent for a moment, then continued. 'So, the plan is, by the end of the day if there are no suitable family members to look after the children, we'll get a Temporary Assessment Order to grant us guardianship while they're in foster care. I'll have my mobile on me all day, so call if there's anything you need to discuss.'

~

Dana and Lachlan sat behind a small one-way mirror to observe the police interviews. The adjoining room was stark, with chipped white walls, grey carpet tiles and a metal table and chairs.

Dana took her notebook and Parker pen from her bag then looked at her phone as she waited for the interview to begin. Nothing. The blank screen mocked her as she checked for messages from Hugh. *Stupid.* He was no doubt enjoying his time alone. Relaxing into a squalor of half-finished coffee cups, which had always driven her mad. During their final argument, he'd said she was fastidious, unsuited to living with others, but if she was too ambitious, so be it. It was better than getting drunk with his mates, using any excuse to avoid discussing their son's death. If she was honest, she had no idea whether she wanted to resume the relationship, but what was most irritating was that he didn't seem to care either way.

Lachlan stood up and stretched his arms above his head. He started pacing the room, pausing near a desk in the far corner and flicking through a manila folder that had been left there. He took a sharp breath. 'Check this out.'

They stood side by side, staring at a series of crime-scene photos in the folder. The first was of the car, a front-on shot of the Kingswood, which looked like it was bogged, a large sapling was jammed in the undercarriage. The open front door revealed a baby capsule installed in the back seat. It was night-time, and the scene was flooded with pale fluorescence, giving the foliage an unearthly, ghostlike quality.

Lachlan nudged her elbow as he pointed at the photograph. 'The old sin bin.'

She looked at him blankly.

'You never heard that one? Shaggin' wagon?'

She frowned. 'Don't you think it's a bit inappropriate to talk about their car like that?'

She felt light-headed as she anticipated the next photo, bodies in situ. She almost told him to stop, but she couldn't look away.

She was right, of course, the next photo was of the women. Sandra slumped in the driver's seat and Debbie hunched over, head near the gearbox, bare feet touching the ground. They were both wearing thin parachute jackets. Sandra was in a denim skirt, and Debbie in short shorts. Dana was grateful that their faces were obscured, although what she conjured up in her imagination was far worse. Acid burnt the back of her throat.

'Enough.' She jammed her hand over Lachlan's to prevent him turning over any more photographs.

They'd just returned to their seats, on the other side of the one-way glass, when the interview room door opened and Constable Morgan and Sergeant Steinmann filed in behind Paul Kirby. The sergeant instructed Paul to take the seat facing the mirrored glass and positioned himself opposite. Connor sat at the head of the table.

Ian nodded at Connor to switch on the recorder and began the formalities. 'This interview is being recorded,' he said. 'My name is Senior Sergeant Ian Steinmann of the Crows Nest police station. The time is 11:10 am and it's the first of May 1996.'

After taking Paul through his rights and entitlement to receive legal advice, the sergeant informed him that anything he said during the interview could be used as evidence in court.

Paul nodded, staring at the glass intently as if he knew someone was watching. His hair was thin at the front and his ruddy cheeks gave him a youthfulness that surprised Dana.

His eyes, blue under hooked eyebrows, were dulled by the fluorescent lights. He was stocky and had been well fed on Sandra's meals.

Ian cleared his throat. 'To start with … if you could run us through what you were doing the day your wife disappeared – Monday the twenty-ninth of April.'

Paul crossed his arms. 'Like I told you before, I went to work. When I finished I came home, then Sandra and I went shopping to get a Troll Doll for Billy-Violet's birthday tomorrow.'

Lachlan raised his eyebrows in Dana's direction. A lump formed in her throat as she thought of Billy-Violet and the tenth birthday she'd spend in foster care. She forced herself to concentrate, writing furiously in her notebook to record everything Paul was saying.

'We got home at about half past eight and Sandra made the kids dinner and I relaxed and watched TV.'

'What did you watch?' Ian asked.

'*The X-Files*.' His face lit up. 'I remember, because it was about a mutant guy who can crawl through ventilation shafts.' His expression darkened as he must have remembered why Ian was interrogating him.

'What happened next?' asked Ian, tapping his pen against the table in a sharp staccato.

'We ate dinner, baked beans on toast. Then Debbie came over and I watched some more TV while they played Scrabble. I think I dozed off in my work clothes because when I woke up it was about ten o'clock and they were talking about the movie that was playing and about Tom Cruise and how sexy he was.' Paul winced, as if regretting what had happened next. 'Then they decided to see if the foal had been born.'

'Where was this?'

'Debbie's aunt's place – one of those horse studs along Perseverance Dam Road.'

'In the middle of the night?' Connor asked, sounding dubious. 'Why the hell were they out there so late?'

'They'd seen some of the foals born at the farm once or twice before, and it was always late at night.' Paul gazed at Ian steadily. 'Debbie was really into the horses.'

He was holding up rather well, Dana thought, though she suspected he was more nervous than he was letting on.

'And whose idea was it to go?'

'Debbie's.' Paul massaged the stubble on his chin, deep in thought. 'Yep, Debbie's.'

'What happened after they left?'

'I fell asleep again, but I woke up when the baby started crying and I went in and settled her. Then Chrystal came out of her room because the baby had woken her too. We talked for a while, then I went back to bed.'

Dana longed for Ian to ask what they'd been talking about and for how long, but she knew there'd be no way of finding out until the end of the police interview. Lachlan looked across at Dana and shook his head.

'Then in the morning,' Paul continued, 'Chrystal came and woke me up, about seven, because she was worried that Sandy and Debbie hadn't come home yet. I drove to the farm. They weren't there. I called Debbie's work. No-one had heard from her. I went to the servo and told Sarji they'd been heading out to Nancy's farm and asked whether he'd seen them. When he said he hadn't I came home, dropped the kids to school and drove straight here to report them missing.'

'Okay,' said Ian, sighing. 'What about guns? Do you have one? Have you ever owned a firearm?'

'Only when I was a teenager and I lived on my grandparents' farm. I used to go pigging sometimes with the neighbours.'

'And were you a good shot?' asked Connor.

A faint smirk passed over Paul's face. 'I used to go alright when I played paintball with Sandy and the kids.'

Connor stopped the recording. He reached across the table and yanked Paul forward by his shirt so that their faces were millimetres apart. 'You think this is a joke? Your wife and her best friend are brutally murdered and you're making fucking jokes?'

'No. No way. I'm devastated. Sandy was everything to me.'

'Listen, mate,' Connor said, his hands still on Paul's shirt. 'I don't give a shit about this *X-Files* crap and Debbie liking horses. I want to find out who killed them and why.'

Connor let Paul go and wiped the sweat from his brow with the sleeve of his shirt. He stabbed the record button, ready to restart the interview.

'Okay. Do you have any recollection whether Debbie was wearing her glasses that night?' asked Ian.

Paul rubbed his temples. 'She usually did, but as for that night, I couldn't be certain. I didn't take any notice.'

'Right,' said Ian. 'And have you ever been on the track to Postman's Bluff where the car was found – out past the pistol club?'

'I … there may have been, I don't know. I may have been because of the times I went pig shooting.'

'Is there anything else you can tell us about your wife's death? Anything you think might be important?'

'No.' Paul shook his head, frowning. 'That's it. Like I said before – I told you everything.'

'Okay. We'll stop the tape there. It's 11:30 am and I'm ending the interview.'

Connor put his hand to the tape recorder and paused momentarily. His neck turning a deep shade of red. 'Can I see you outside, boss?'

The two officers exited the interview room and Dana could hear their voices in the corridor outside.

'What do you mean you only got half of it on record?' Steinmann hissed. 'Bloody hell, Connor, you're absolutely useless.'

'What do you think?' Lachlan whispered to Dana.

'Not only was it the most unprofessional interview I've ever seen. It was also the most inept,' she said quietly.

The door opened abruptly and Ian came into the viewing room, his face shiny as he pushed a hand to his temple. He looked across at Lachlan. 'I'm going to make some phone calls. Can you let Paul know about the arrangements the Department's making for those kids given he's our only suspect right now? We've got a neighbour who's just called up and said she remembers seeing Paul through the window late that night, but I need to make sure she's reliable and check Chrystal's version of events.' He picked up the manila folder they had been looking at and stormed off down the corridor.

Lachlan stood up and Dana followed him into the interview room. They seated themselves at the table across from Paul.

'At this stage we need to complete what is known as an initial assessment,' Lachlan said. 'And while we're doing that we need to make sure the children are safe. As you're a suspect in a murder case, and we can't rule out that another member of your family was involved, the children will need to stay with a foster carer until the police get to the bottom of this.'

Dana braced herself for Paul to fly off the handle, but instead he hung his head and scratched the hair on his chest. 'You've got to do what you've got to do, right?' He looked up dully at Dana. 'But as soon as you find out I had nothing to do with it, I can have them come back, right?'

She tried to reassure him. 'If that's true they'll be returned to you immediately. And in the meantime they'll be well cared for.'

As he was led away down the corridor, Paul was silent, his head dipped low.

Minutes after Lachlan and Dana returned to the observation room, Chrystal was brought into the interview room by Ian and Connor. She sat quietly, one leg tucked under her. The bracelets on her wrist jangled as she pushed a lock of blonde hair behind her ear. She wore a tie-dyed Billabong t-shirt paired with short denim overalls and her blue eyes had a wide, dreamy quality about them. She was beautiful, in a way that brought to mind a young Meg Ryan, with a dewy complexion Dana would have killed for in her adolescence.

Dana tried to remember what she'd read in Chrystal's file – sixteen years old, chaotic childhood with a drug-addicted mother and raised by a grandfather who'd become sick before she and her sister were taken in by Sandra and Paul.

The click of the recorder brought Dana back to the present.

'All good now?' Ian asked, after he'd taken Chrystal through the formalities of the interview. 'So if you could talk me through what you did the day Sandra and Debbie disappeared, starting from what you did that morning?'

'I went to school and, when I was finished, I went to work,' Chrystal said, head down, staring at the desk.

'And for the tape – can you tell us where you work?'

'At the newsagency.'

'And what hours did you work?'

'Four to six.'

'So you stayed at work all that time?'

'Mm-hmm – yeah.'

She was extremely guarded, thought Dana, though it was impossible to tell if she had something to hide or it was simply the result of a difficult childhood. She wished fervently that she had spoken to her when they visited the Creek Street house, instead of losing her temper with Connor.

'And what happened when you got home?'

'The kids were alone. Paul and Sandy had gone shopping, so I looked after the baby and let Billy watch one of her shows so she'd be quiet.'

'Then what happened?'

'I don't know. They got home about half past eight, I guess. Sandy cooked us dinner because we were starving.' She paused, staring off into the distance. '*The X-Files* came on and Sandy was like, it's getting late, you should go to bed … so I went to bed.' Her voice was thin as she struggled through her longest speech yet. 'Then I was woken up by Rubi crying … I went to her room to sort her out, but Paul was already in there.'

'Did you talk to him?'

'Yeah, he went into the kitchen to smoke, like he normally does, and I followed him because I was, like, really, really awake and didn't think I'd be able to go back to sleep.'

'Do you have any recollection of what time it was?'

'Um, not really.' She shook her head. 'I can't remember.'

'What did you speak about?' Ian asked. Finally, the question Dana had been longing to hear.

'Houses and stuff.'

'Can you be any more specific than that?'

Chrystal wrapped a strand of hair around her index finger, setting off another round of jangling from her bracelets. 'I asked him, if I kept working at the newsagency and saving money, if he thought I could afford to buy my own house by the time I was twenty-three.'

'What did Paul say?'

'That if I worked hard enough I could … and that he might be able to help.'

Dana was touched by her admission. After experiencing so much disruption, all Chrystal really wanted was a place of her own.

'Is there anything else you can tell us about that night?'

'No.'

'Is there anything that happened in the days leading up to Sandra's death that you think might be important?' Ian leant forward. 'It doesn't matter how small or insignificant it might seem.'

Chrystal bit her lip and folded her arms across her chest, staring past them. 'There is one thing.'

'Yes?'

'On the day Sandy disappeared she asked me if I could stay home from work.' Chrystal blinked, fighting back tears.

'And what did you say?'

'That I couldn't.' Chrystal put her head in her hands and began to cry. Ian passed her a tissue. 'I had to do the stocktake,' she whispered.

Ian frowned as Chrystal wiped her nose. 'What reason do you think Sandy could have had for wanting you home?'

'I don't know … I think …' She broke into fresh sobs. 'I think she wanted to tell me something.'

'And do you know what that was?'

Chrystal shook her head and stared despondently at the floor.

'For the tape, I need you to say the answer.'

'No,' she said flatly.

'Okay, I think we'll leave it there.' Connor hit the stop button on the recorder.

After a few moments, Ian came back into the observation room where Dana and Lachlan were sitting.

'I've got to follow up on a few urgent enquiries now,' he said. Then to Dana he added, 'But I'll also have to take your statement, as you spoke with the women the day before they disappeared. We'll leave Billy-Violet's interview until tomorrow. If one of you could let Chrystal know what'll be happening from here that would be good.' He headed out the door.

Lachlan and Dana made their way into the interview room and Dana introduced herself.

'Chrystal,' she said, knowing the girl wasn't going to like what she was about to say. 'Until the police have a clearer picture of what's happened to Sandra and Debbie, we're going to need you to stay with a foster carer to make sure you're safe, and so we can assess the situation.'

'No way,' Chrystal said. 'I want to stay with Charmaine and her mum – like last night.'

'That was okay for a short-term emergency option,' said Dana. 'And it might be okay again in the future if we do an assessment and make sure she's an appropriate person to care for you, but until then I need you and your nieces to stay with one of our foster carers.'

'Why can't we stay with Paul?'

Dana paused, wondering how much she should say, but knew that sugar-coating the facts would simply insult a girl who'd no doubt heard a lifetime of lies and half-truths.

'Paul's a suspect. And until the police can rule him out of their investigation, we can't allow you to live with him. So, we're going to take you home to pack some clothes and the police are going to drop Rubi and Billy-Violet with the foster carer and we'll see them shortly.'

Chrystal gave Dana an angry glare but said nothing. She stood up and waited as they gathered their things.

Outside, Dana settled herself into the passenger seat of the airless work car and buckled her seatbelt. She took a moment to adjust the air vents as Lachlan opened the back door for Chrystal. He had just started the engine when Connor burst from the station doors and sprinted down the wheelchair ramp to catch them.

Dana wound down the passenger window.

'I need to speak to you,' he said.

6

Connor's cheekbones were like razors in the sunlight and he had a certain look, one that said he wanted something. Dana got out of the car and walked beyond Lachlan's earshot towards the shade of a eucalyptus tree.

'You left this.' Connor held out her silver Parker pen as she turned to look up at him.

She cursed herself for being so scatterbrained and wondered whether this was her new normal. 'That's very kind of you.'

'It is, considering that the last time we spoke, you basically assaulted me.'

'I didn't assault you. It was an accident.' Part of her wanted to apologise, but his arrogance held her back. Besides, she was still annoyed that he'd complained to Helen about her behaviour.

He stubbed at the dirt with his boot. 'I was thinking that it might be good to catch up for a coffee at some point. I could give you a bit of a rundown on what's what.' He swiped a fly away from his mouth. 'There's a place in the main street of Toowoomba?'

She hesitated. 'I'll think about it,' she said finally. If nothing else she'd be able to smooth things over with him and reassure Helen there was no need to worry.

She returned to the car and slipped back into her seat. Lachlan was grinning widely.

She held up a hand in warning. 'I don't want to hear it.'

'I'm not saying anything.' He winked at Chrystal in the rear-view mirror, who smirked as he reversed out of the car park.

'Nice car,' said Dana, pointing at the shiny black Holden Statesman parked beside them.

'Yeah, it's a beauty, isn't it,' Lachlan said. 'Ian's pride and joy. Bought it for himself as a Christmas present and apparently he's so keen on it, he won't even let the wife drive it.'

Dana frowned. 'How does a country cop on a country cop's wage afford a brand-new Statesman?'

Lachlan chuckled. 'You may well ask.'

'I am asking.'

'Saving up his pennies, I guess.'

They stopped at the bakery with dust-smeared windows and a cartoon pie on a sign out the front. Dana stood in front of a counter filled with apple slices and cream buns, and wondered what to have. In the end she ordered sausage rolls for Chrystal and Lachlan and a chicken and salad sandwich for herself.

She took the food across the road to the green lawn in the town centre, where she joined the others at a picnic table. When she looked over at Lachlan he was staring at her.

'What?' she asked, shooing flies away from the food.

'You're at a classic country bakery and you order a sandwich. Why not get something they do well? Like the steak pie or Cornish pastie?'

She ignored him and bit into the sandwich with its limp tomato and soggy lettuce, staring at a life-sized statue of an Aboriginal man next to a hollowed-out bottle tree. 'What's the story with the statue?' she asked Lachlan.

'That's Jimmy Crow,' he said. 'He used to give the locals directions and spent his nights sleeping in the middle of that tree. They used to call it Jimmy's crow's nest – hence, the name of the town.' A shadow passed over his face. 'It's been vandalised a lot over the years.' His gaze swept across the park before meeting hers. 'Some idiot even painted it white a few months back.'

They finished up and headed to Creek Street to collect Chrystal's belongings. When they arrived, Lachlan stayed in the car to call Helen, while Dana and Chrystal headed up the concrete path to the house.

Dana blinked with shock as she opened the door. It was like a tornado had whipped through the lounge room, leaving a debris of nappies, lottery tickets and food wrappers in its wake. She tried to decide if the police had crashed through in their search for evidence or if Paul's parenting had collapsed over the past twenty-four hours. She could hardly have blamed him.

Chrystal looked embarrassed. 'It's not usually like this.'

Dana rested a hand on Chrystal's thin, upper arm. 'I know. We were here on Monday. Why don't you go and pack a suitcase of clothes for yourself and Billy-Violet, and I'll decide what to bring for the baby.'

In Rubi's room she found a large striped canvas bag and began filling it with nappies and warm jumpsuits. She'd just started sifting through the bottom cupboard for a set of cot sheets and blankets when she stumbled on a breast pump, which Sandra had no doubt used after Rubi was born.

Dana leant back on her knees and stared out the window. She thought about feeding Oscar his bottle and the way he used to gaze into her eyes. She was thirty-nine when she and Hugh started trying for a child and, after twelve months and not a whiff of conception, they'd gone to a gynaecologist who'd depressed them with the statistical likelihood of a woman falling pregnant at her age. She remembered staring despondently at the polo-horse logo on his shirt as he recommended a laparoscopy to remove any endometriosis. To her surprise, it had worked. Six months later she'd done a pregnancy test and two pink lines appeared. At the time, she felt as though she'd dived through the doors of the baby train carriage before they'd snapped shut without her.

Now they were forever closed, she realised, gazing at a framed photograph of Sandra and Rubi on the windowsill. She'd never see her beautiful boy again, and neither would Rubi grow up with her mother's love.

As she sat beside the cot the full extent of what had happened to the Kirby family suddenly dawned on her. She imagined how terrified the two women must have been, alone in the bush that night, and wondered who had died first, which one of them had to bear witness to their best friend being killed. She shivered as she zipped up the bag and hurried down the hallway to help Chrystal.

Once the court documents and carer paperwork were safely in hand, Dana and Lachlan took the short drive to the home of a foster carer named Carol. They arrived at a simple white weatherboard house with a baby-blue trim and a well-manicured garden. A sign next to the mailbox said, *God Loves You.*

Lachlan got the bags from the boot of the car and they padded over the freshly mown lawn, up the stairs and onto the verandah where the sobs of a child rang out from inside. A woman in her fifties, with glasses on a chain and a cheap nylon shirt, met them at the door as though she'd been waiting.

Inside, baby Rubi was in a bouncer on the floor, while Billy-Violet sat at the kitchen table, head in her hands, wailing. Carol brushed past her to pack the dishwasher as Chrystal raced over to comfort her young niece. Dana felt her blood boil and it was all she could do not to reprimand the woman on the spot. Lachlan cut in before she got the chance.

'Carol, this is Dana Gibson. Dana, this is Carol Smith.'

The women nodded at each other and Carol gestured for them to have a seat next to Billy-Violet.

'How's everything going?' Lachlan asked.

'Good. I've got the beds made up for Chrystal and Billy-Violet in Janine's old room and I'm putting the baby in the spare room. I borrowed a crib from one of Janine's friends so she'll have something to sleep in.'

'It sounds like you've got everything in order then,' said Lachlan.

'Are there clothes for the baby?' Carol asked, barely pausing for breath. 'I had to buy five new jumpsuits when the O'Connor girl was here and the parents took them when she went home. The Department still hasn't reimbursed me.'

'I'll see what I can do.'

'Also,' she said, her questions to Lachlan like rapid fire, 'any behavioural problems I should know about? Stealing, destroying property?' She stared at Chrystal. 'I can't abide teenagers who do that. I was very clear with Helen about that on the phone.'

'No,' Lachlan said. 'I can assure you there's none of that.'

Chrystal's eyes lowered to the linoleum floor and Dana couldn't hold back any longer. 'Look, you need to understand that these girls have been through a very traumatic event. It's really important that you provide them with a lot of emotional support over the next few days.'

'I know,' Carol said, glaring at Dana as though she was dense. 'The whole town has been talking about those poor women and the evil, no-good people that killed them. At Bible study last night it was all anyone could talk about.'

Well that's something, Dana thought, as she rummaged through her handbag for her purse.

Lachlan stood up from his chair. 'You'll have to excuse us. We should hit the road before it gets dark.'

As they were leaving, Dana knelt in front of Billy-Violet and handed her one the Department's business cards, then did the same for Chrystal. 'Feel free to call us if you need anything. Or if there's anything that's bothering you.' She got up and looked directly at Carol. 'It's Billy's birthday tomorrow so we'd really appreciate it if you could do something nice for her.'

Her heart wrenched as the two girls stood solemnly on the verandah watching them leave. Chrystal gave a half-hearted wave. Dana couldn't help but think how innocent and vulnerable she seemed, how ill-prepared she was going to be to face a life without Sandra as her mother figure.

They got into the car and Lachlan started the engine.

'Christ, that was depressing,' she said, scribbling notes in her notebook. 'Isn't there anyone else they could have stayed with?'

'Not really. There's only two foster carers in town and the other one's full up caring for a family of four, plus two more.

What are you writing?' Lachlan stared at Dana's notebook.

'Observations,' she said hurriedly. 'They've had the week from hell and now they have to stay with a woman who asks questions about remuneration in front of them and doesn't comprehend the fact that it's necessary to comfort a child when they're crying. Hasn't she had training?'

'You'd know, it's one thing to teach someone how to physically care for a child, but it's not always so easy to teach the emotional intelligence you need to look after these kids.'

Dana slumped in her seat, trying to erase the image of Billy-Violet on the verandah, a lost soul waiting for a mother who was never coming home.

They drove down the street past a man yanking a bull-mastiff and a graffitied Lions Club sign on the bus shelter.

'So, what's your theory on who killed them?' Lachlan asked, interrupting her thoughts.

'No idea,' she said truthfully. 'What about you?'

He scratched at the white hairs on his chin. 'I don't know, but I'd be willing to bet that with that level of violence there were drugs involved. People do terrible things when they're under the influence. Maybe they took a wrong turn that night and ended up too close to someone's drug crop? It's a small town and it's hard to keep something like that a secret, so maybe someone thought it would be safer if Debbie and Sandra were dead.' He shrugged. 'Or perhaps someone was just planning to threaten them, but when you're high as a kite, you accidentally shoot one of them and then you have to shoot the other one so there's no witnesses.'

'I suspect you're right.' Dana gazed at him with a new respect. 'I can't count the number of cases I've looked at where there's a link between violent crime and drug use. So, what's Debbie's story then?' she asked, realising that she knew a lot about Paul and Sandra, yet the best friend, Debbie, remained a mystery.

'She moved back to Crows Nest from Ipswich a few years back,' he said, as they tore along the highway. 'She's an assistant teacher at the Crows Nest Children's Centre and is very good at her job, apparently. She hangs around a few folk from the Church of Christ, but aside from that I'd say she's always been a bit of a loner. She has this tendency of befriending couples with children, like the Kirbys and Ian Steinmann and his wife, then spending so much time with them that they end up getting sick of her.'

'Has she ever had a boyfriend of her own?'

'She did have a boyfriend, but he *lived in Canada*.' Lachlan mimed quotation marks. 'You know how it is.'

'She made him up?'

'Yes.' Lachlan glanced at her sideways. 'That's exactly what I'm saying, although there was a rumour going around that she was having an affair with Paul, if you believe the good people at the Crows Nest pub.'

'Really?' Dana screwed up her face. 'I wouldn't have thought she'd be his type.'

'I wouldn't put it past him. Hard dog to keep on the porch.' He grinned. 'And that aftershave is something else.'

'Yes, but you also said there was a rumour that Sandra and Debbie were involved with each other,' she reminded him.

'Well, you know what country towns are like, they basically run on gossip.'

As Lachlan sped along the highway, Dana made a phone call to Helen to fill her in on the events of the afternoon. It was half past six by the time they arrived in Toowoomba and Lachlan dropped her at the top of her street.

She strode along the avenue of camphor laurels, the autumn leaves under her feet, and imagined the evening spread out in front of her. She'd return her mother's calls and put her mind at ease about rushing away to Queensland. Then she'd snuggle into her pyjamas and nothing would come between her and an evening of reading her case notes.

As if her mother was on the same wavelength, Dana's phone suddenly rang.

'It's me,' she said, even though Dana would have known her mother's voice anywhere. Dana pictured her huddled on the couch with a Laura Ashley blanket thrown over her legs, watching *Inspector Morse*. 'Honestly, Dana, how've you been? I've tried to call you a dozen times.'

'I'm sorry,' she said, feeling the rough wood of the fence on her back as she looked across the park. 'I've had to hit the ground running in this new job and I haven't had a moment to spare.'

'Well, I do hope you're taking care of yourself. The last time you rushed off to Cairns after a break-up I'm not sure it helped at all – just made us all very worried. And I hope you've been in touch with Doctor Harper?'

'Yes, Mum.' She only just held herself back from reminding her mother that the break-up had been in her first year of university. 'He gave me a script before I left and said I only needed to take the tablets when I'm feeling stressed or anxious, so there's nothing for you to worry about.'

Her mother let out a deep exhalation. 'Well, that's a relief.'

She marvelled at her mother's ability to take her words at face value.

'Anyway,' her mother continued. 'I've had an exciting idea. Lorraine's unit has just lost its tenant and I was thinking that after your little Queensland adventure you might like to come to Melbourne and see what it's like to live here for a while? It would be just like old times. We could go shopping together, catch a movie, visit the National Gallery.' Her mother paused with dramatic flair. 'You'll have to let me know soon though, otherwise Lorraine will end up renting it to someone else.'

Dana considered the proposal as her mother started gossiping about a new neighbour. Her family had always had major reservations that Hugh was only in the relationship for her family's money. But if Dana moved to Melbourne after her job in Queensland was over, she'd basically be admitting that there was no hope of reconciliation. She still wasn't sure what she wanted. She wasn't ready to resume their relationship, but she struggled to envision what moving on would look like.

She finished the call, giving her mother an assurance that she'd think about Melbourne. As she turned into her yard, she noted the unlatched gate and checked the letterbox. At the top of the stairs she unlocked the door and saw that the lounge-room light was on. When she stepped inside, Angus was in front of the TV, sprawled on the Persian rug like a permanent fixture, his head on a cushion.

When he heard the front door close, he leapt up and ran over. 'Can I go on the computer, please? I'll be really careful.'

She smiled at his directness. 'Sure, but only for half an hour. Your nan will be wondering where you are.'

She had no understanding of how he'd come to be inside and had a vision of him slithering through a chimney like a contortionist and ending up in her living room.

In the kitchen she wrestled the stopper from a decanter of Bushmills whiskey and poured a drink. Perhaps she should ask Susan to put a screen on the laundry window? The murders had rattled her and if a killer was on the loose she needed to protect herself. She considered ditching the house and moving into an apartment, with an intercom and security. The more she thought about it, the more worked up she became and her jaw grew stiff.

As the alcohol warmed her throat, she reminded herself that even if she came to harm at the hands of a murderer, surely the worst had already happened. Her beloved Oscar was gone and, although she didn't believe in heaven, she still hoped that in death they'd be reunited.

She took another sip of the Bushmills and tried to refocus. Toowoomba was going to be her refuge. All she had to do was settle in. And get to work.

7

Dana woke early to the sound of birdcall and the low hiss of a sprinkler beyond her window. She pulled on her running tights, tied the laces of her Reeboks and let herself out the front door. The park was golden, wide expanses of green swept in front of her and the camphor laurels swayed gently in the breeze. It was foolish to think she could run a lap of the park when she hadn't exercised for months, but as she jogged through the gates she was so buoyed by the beauty of her surroundings that anything seemed possible.

She ran on the bitumen along the park boundary, up past the bunya pines until she reached the memorial cannon on the northern edge. At the fountain she read the inscription, *The memory of the just is blessed*, and her thoughts turned to Sandra and Debbie. She forced herself to stay in the moment and was soon jogging past an arbour of roses with exotic names. She slowed to examine them, reading the signs staked into the ground beside each of them – *Iceberg 1958 Floribunda*, *White Spray*, *Tamango* and the most beautiful of all, the striking variegation of *Oranges and Lemons.*

She quickened her pace again, reminding herself of her goal as she passed the stone arch and parterre gardens. By the time she'd made it through the playground to Margaret Street her breathing was laboured and her chest tight. She considered stopping at the Park House Café, but pushed on, striding down the hill, across the oval and turning right towards home. With a final burst, she sprinted down the street until she reached her house, where she stood at the gate, gasping for air, her head bent over her knees.

Susan was in her front yard pulling weeds from the flowerbeds. 'Are you okay?' she asked.

'Fine. Just out of condition.' Dana mopped her damp forehead with the back of her hand. 'The garden's looking good,' she added, taking in the lavender bush, small delicate flowers and the newly ripened orange tree. Rainbow lorikeets squabbled on a branch of bottlebrush blossoms.

'I think this will probably be the last nice autumn day before it gets cold, so I'm taking advantage of it.' Susan wiped her hands along the thighs of her muddy jeans and stood up. 'Why don't you come in for a second and I can give you that key for the back gate I was telling you about.'

Dana checked her watch. It was half past six, too early to go into the office. 'Sure.' She followed Susan up the stairs and down the hall to the kitchen where the scent of brewing coffee filled the room.

Susan gestured for Dana to take a stool at the granite island bench and placed a glass of chilled water in front of her. 'I'll be back in a tick.'

Dana sat and drank the cool liquid from the glass. She gazed outside at the manicured lawn and sculpted mock orange tree.

'There you go.' Susan handed her a brass key. 'Can I tempt you with a coffee?' She sensed Dana's hesitation. 'Apple danish perhaps? I've just come back from the bakery.'

'That sounds lovely, thanks.'

Susan returned with a cardboard box filled with pastries and poured hot liquid into fine bone china cups. She sat opposite Dana. 'How've you been settling in?'

'As well as can be expected,' said Dana, hoping she wouldn't have to elaborate.

'That's good to hear. The people of this town can be suspicious of newcomers at times.'

There was silence as Dana bit into her danish and stared at the well-stocked bookshelves in the next room. 'Have you always lived in Toowoomba?' she asked.

'I grew up here, but moved to Brisbane after I met my husband. I eventually brought the kids back here to be closer to my parents, after he died.'

'I'm sorry to hear that.'

Susan looked at her mildly. 'Don't be. He had mental health problems and, in the end, I think he was almost relieved when he was told he had pancreatic cancer. And anyway …' Susan waved the air in front of her as though she was trying to banish the memories. 'Brisbane had been a harsh mistress to me – the place I learnt all my life lessons.' She sipped her coffee. 'And at the end of the day, Toowoomba felt like home.'

She caught Dana's look of disbelief and smiled.

'I know it sounds strange, but there's something about living here. It draws people in.'

'I can see the attraction,' Dana said with more enthusiasm than she felt. A bird chirruped loudly beyond the window. 'Actually, one of the first things I noticed after I moved here was the birdlife. I never noticed them when I lived in Castlecrag.'

'Marvellous, isn't it? Angus has started leaving a piece of meat out for a kookaburra that comes to visit every day.'

'How long has Angus lived here?'

'About a year.' Susan tilted her head. 'A year in August. Sometimes, it feels much longer.' Her eyes glazed over. 'He can be rude sometimes, but he's smart. He had to do an IQ test with his psychologist the other day. His results were off the charts.'

'I did get the sense that he was very clever.' Dana sat up straighter in her chair. 'Actually, I've been meaning to mention that he's been coming over at night. The other day, I woke up from a nap and found him in the lounge room watching TV.'

Susan blinked. 'I'm really sorry. He must have snuck out of the window when I thought he was in his bed reading. He probably used that spare key to get in. He didn't break anything while he was there, did he?'

'No, not at all. He just lay on the rug and watched *Teenage Mutant Ninja Turtles*.'

'He probably really enjoyed himself.' Susan gave a grim chuckle. 'We don't have a TV here.'

'He's very keen on the computer.'

'Yes, he's always had a bit of a gift for technology. And loves to email people, too.'

'Really?'

'Oh, yes. A few months back he was very into birds. He'd drag me to the library and we'd have to borrow these huge volumes on the birds of southwest Queensland. If there was anything he wanted to find out that wasn't in the books he'd just email the people at the state museum and generally they'd get back to him straight away. Very specific questions they were, like: "A hawk has started hunting the feeder birds in my yard. What can I do?" He really enjoyed being treated so seriously.'

'That's very impressive. Actually, speaking of emails, you wouldn't mind if I organise to have the internet installed, would you? I didn't realise how much I relied on it in Sydney.' She discreetly checked the clock on the wall.

'That's fine. Though I wouldn't have the first clue how to organise it.'

'I can do it. It will just be a matter of finding the time.'

'It was a relief to have some peace last night when I thought Angus was in bed. His behaviour has been shocking lately, and he's about a second away from being expelled from school.'

Dana knew she shouldn't pry, but she couldn't help herself. 'What were things like when he lived with his mother?'

'Unbearable, I imagine. She was in the grips of a heroin addiction and he pretty much ran wild. The Department was involved for a while, but they didn't always give me the full details … Anyway, they backed off after I told them I was going for guardianship.' She plucked a stray crumb from the bench and dusted her hands in the bin behind her. 'I should let you get to work. Sorry about Angus. I'll make sure he stays on our side of the fence in future.'

'He's welcome to watch TV, if he enjoys it so much.' Dana said, wondering what she was getting herself into. 'It's nice to have the company, to be honest.'

'Only if you're sure,' Susan said uncertainly.

Dana helped Susan take the dishes to the sink and hurried

home. Once inside, she stripped off her sweaty running clothes. The water from the shower head was either boiling hot or freezing cold and it took the better of part of five minutes to find an even temperature.

When she was done, she turned on the ABC news and towel-dried her hair before pulling on a loose white business shirt and high-waisted pants. Ian Steinmann was giving an interview in front of the Crows Nest police station, a semicircle of microphones capturing his every word as he squinted into the sun.

I think the first thing everyone needs to keep in mind is that Crows Nest has never experienced anything like this before. These killings have paralysed our little town. Hardware stores are selling out of chains and locks and I'm having a hard time getting my men to work nights because it means leaving their families alone. And as I'm sure you've read in the paper, the RSPCA has run out of dogs – which has never happened before. People are terrified.

There are a lot of theories going around about these women's deaths. So, the sooner we're able to find out what happened to them, the quicker we can all get on with our lives.

When the program moved on to the sports update, Dana switched off the TV.

At the office, Dana tried to access the ABC news website to find out if there was any more news on the murders, but a message popped up stating staff needed permission to access the internet.

A strawberry-blonde woman with the sign *Jacinta Verne* on

the wall above her computer turned around and gave Dana a wan smile. 'Trying to get on the internet?' she asked.

Dana nodded.

'Good luck with that.' Jacinta's voice had a nasal twang. 'They make you fill out five forms and then you've got to get them all signed off as well. I've been trying for six months and I still can't find anyone who'll approve the damn things. Just a sec – I'll finish what I'm doing and show you a sneaky way in.'

Dana watched as Jacinta leant over the computer, horrified at how archaic the Department's computer system was turning out to be. What had she expected in a regional town? A top-of-the-line information technology system like the one that she was used to in Sydney?

'Also, is there a practice manual I can look at?' Dana asked, once Jacinta had sorted out the internet.

'A what?'

'A manual,' said Dana slowly. 'So I can figure out how to write up the initial assessment of the family Lachlan and I have been working with.'

'Oh, one of those.' Jacinta smiled. 'We don't have them. Just ask Helen how to do it then put it in a Word document and attach it to the family's file.' She noted the frown on Dana's face. 'We've had people in from the city before and it always takes them a while to realise that they're working in a different context out here.'

'What do you mean?'

'We do things differently in the country. In Toowoomba everyone knows everyone and people are more likely to help their neighbours. That's why we don't use practice manuals and prefer to come up with our own solutions for kids in need.'

'But surely you need guidelines? Procedures, to make sure everyone's on the same page?'

Jacinta gave Dana a sympathetic look. 'That kind of thing sounds good in theory, but in these parts, who you know is often more important than what you know.' Jacinta's phone started ringing. 'Oh well.' She shrugged. 'I'd better get back to it.'

Dana turned once again to her computer, her mind whirring. Surely no practice manual was code for *no standards of practice, no rules, whatsoever.* She wondered what kind of crazy wild-west world she'd wandered into.

She went to the kitchen for a glass of water and when she returned to her a desk, found a slip of paper next to her computer – the school principal had an urgent message for her about Chrystal.

Dana eyed a glass cabinet full of awards and trophies as she walked into the administration block of the school and rang the bell at the counter. While she waited, she stared at the faces of a class from the 1970s. She jumped as the door flew open behind her. Three boys in uniform were led in by a teacher, and told to sit down and wait for the principal. They slumped into chairs against the wall, glassy-eyed and smelling of marijuana. *Were they growing it themselves or was someone selling it to them?*

'Ms Gibson?' Dana turned around. In front of her a turtleneck-clad woman was adjusting a pair of enormous reading glasses.

'Please, just call me Dana.'

'Sue Armstrong.' The principal held out her hand for Dana to shake. 'I'm afraid there's been an incident.'

'What's happened?'

Sue's eyes betrayed a grim look behind thick lenses. 'Chrystal got in a fight with a group of girls before school and she pushed one of them off the side of the grandstand. Says they were picking on her.'

'And were they?'

'What I do know is that the girl she pushed is the daughter of the local solicitor. She'll be lucky if he doesn't press charges.'

Dana's heart sank. 'Where is she?'

'She's in the sick bay down the end of the corridor.' She pointed. 'I know she's been through a hard time, but as she specifically asked to speak to you, maybe you can talk some sense into her.'

Dana walked down to the sick bay and opened the door. Chrystal was sitting up on a wooden bed in a denim jacket that dwarfed her small frame, a cigarette in her hand.

'You know there's no smoking in these buildings,' said Dana.

'I opened a window, didn't I?'

'Please, Chrystal,' Dana said, frowning.

Chrystal looked away before stubbing out her smoke and flicking it outside. She had an old scar on her inner forearm that looked like a series of dots. *Self-harm?*

Dana sat beside Chrystal on the bed. 'What happened?' she asked gently.

Chrystal gave her a sideways glance and hesitated. Dana knew not to break the silence by asking more questions.

'There were three of them. Three against one. I scared the first two and shoved the last one off the side of the grandstand.' She flexed her hand in front of her. 'They didn't know what hit them.'

'What did they say to make you so angry?'

'They said that my sister was killed because she was mouthing off and got what she deserved. And if I had any sense, I should kill myself too.' Her blonde hair was brittle in the sunlight.

'I can see why you were mad. I'll have a talk to Principal Armstrong. See if I can explain things.' Dana paused. 'And how's everything else?'

'Great. I'm living with Carol, copping shit for not having a uniform, it's Billy's birthday and she was in tears all morning. Oh, yeah, and my sister just died.'

Dana breathed in. 'Look, I know you've been through a lot. More than some people go through in a lifetime. Is there anything you'd like me to do?'

'I want to go home to Paul's.'

'My hands are tied, I'm afraid,' said Dana. 'As long as Paul remains a suspect, there's nothing I can do.' There was silence. 'Have you had any more thoughts about what it was Sandra wanted to speak to you about before she died?'

'What?' Chrystal said, looking blank.

'In your interview, you said that Sandra asked to speak to you after school on the day of her death. You thought she was about to tell you something.'

'I've got no idea what she wanted.'

'Had she ever pulled you aside like that in the past?' Dana stared at her intently.

'No.' Chrystal tucked one of her shoes under her leg and stared out the window. 'She was always so kind. Giving me a place to live after Grandad died. I just feel so guilty.' Her bottom lip began to tremble.

'Why?'

'She had so much on her plate with the kids and the problems with the new house. I should have helped out more. I should have been there for her.' Chrystal gave a great hiccupping sob before starting to cry.

'I'm sorry I asked so many questions,' said Dana, digging through her handbag for a tissue. She felt terrible for pushing Chrystal to the brink of tears.

Chrystal was staring at her feet. 'The funeral and the wake are next week … Paul wants me to do a reading, but – no fucking way.'

Dana fidgeted with her wedding ring. 'Funerals are hard enough as it is, without the added pressure of having to do a speech.' At Oscar's funeral the enormity of what she'd lost was so vast words had seemed pointless.

'I don't think Sandy would have cared,' Chrystal said. 'She was never into all that Jesus shit. She just went to church because she thought it was good for the kids.' She blinked rapidly. 'She loved those kids.'

'She really did,' said Dana, feeling the weight of the girl's grief.

'You can come if you want …'

'Where?'

'To the funeral,' said Chrystal.

Dana squirmed on the bed, knowing that Chrystal had asked of her the one thing she wasn't certain she could do.

8

The soothing sounds of organ music wafted through the church where bouquets of purple flowers had been displayed at the altar. Dana's heart stopped when she saw the portrait of a high school-aged Sandra by the casket. She took a breath, fanned herself with the order of service and pushed her way through a media scrum and restless crowd. She scanned the faces of the policemen in navy caps lining the room, trying to locate Connor. He hadn't followed up on his coffee invitation and she could only assume that he'd been busy or had lost interest. She was strangely disappointed. The more time that passed, the more she believed that speaking to him would be the only way to find out more about the Kirby family. The only hope those kids had was that the investigation would be wrapped up soon, so a decision about who was looking after them could be made and they'd have some stability.

She weaved her way further into the church under the exposed wooden beams of the ceiling, until the pews gave way to fold-up chairs. Keely was jammed in the middle of the back row. Lachlan was standing behind her wearing a purple Hawaiian shirt, chatting to Principal Armstrong, who wore a fur-collared mauve coat with shoulder pads.

'You didn't get the memo about Sandra's favourite colour then?' he asked Dana, nodding towards the casket draped in lilac cloth.

'I didn't.' She shifted uncomfortably in her charcoal Country Road suit as a sea of purple-clad mourners filed around them. 'What are you doing here, anyway?'

He raised an eyebrow. 'I could ask you the same question.'

'Chrystal asked me to come.' The memory of the girl's tear-stained face swam into her mind. 'Seriously, why are you here?'

'I've worked with a lot of families around these parts. I wanted to show I care.'

Sue turned to Dana. 'I was just telling Lachlan that I was very glad to see Chrystal back at school this week. I'm just hoping she can get through to the end of the year without any more drama.' She stared pointedly at Dana. 'She has so much potential. I'd hate to see her end up like Alisha. Such a waste, dropping out in her final year.'

'I gather the uniform situation got sorted out then?' said Lachlan.

Sue moved aside to let an elderly man pass. 'It did.'

Lachlan leant in closer. 'Speaking of formal wear, that colour looks lovely on you.'

Sue beamed up at him before arranging her face into a more sombre expression. 'Thanks. I'm sure we'll get to catch up later, Lachlan.' She smiled at him then sauntered away down the aisle.

'I can't believe you're flirting,' Dana hissed once she was out of earshot. 'At a dead woman's funeral. On the most tragic day in the town's history.'

'I wasn't flirting,' he said, taken aback. 'I was just being nice.'

They took their seats and the minister moved towards the lectern in white robes and a scarlet stole. A hush fell over the room as he tapped the microphone and pushed a lock of hair from his forehead.

'We are gathered here to celebrate the life of Sandra Kirby,' he began. Someone let out a howl from the front and Dana stood on her toes to see Paul, in the front row, putting an arm around Billy-Violet.

Dana's eyes stung with tears and she groped wildly through her bag for a tissue. It was a bad idea to go to a funeral so soon after she'd buried Oscar. Why then hadn't she been able to think of an excuse to get out of it? She knew why. Chrystal's desperate face when she'd asked Dana to be there. She stared at a sad little stained-glass window at the front of the church, trying to pull herself together. She was still drawing deep breaths when a woman with red hair and a butterfly tattoo on her bicep leapt onto the stage. She shoved the minister aside and grabbed the microphone.

'When are the police going to get off their arses!' she shouted, casting her gaze wildly around the room. 'When are they going to do something?' She jabbed a finger at Ian Steinmann. 'They need to catch the killer! Sandra deserves that. My friend deserves that. This town has listened to their bullshit for long enough.'

Dana's heart was racing as two uniformed policemen yanked the woman's hands behind her back and led her towards a side room.

Dana felt claustrophobic. There were too many people jammed into the space. Too many colours melting into each other. She struggled for breath.

'I'll see you outside,' she said to Lachlan, and rushed for the toilets.

In the stall, her nose began to bleed, bright red flowers on white paper. When she'd managed to stop the flow, she shoved the bloody toilet paper into the sanitary bin, her hands shaking. Her mind replayed the painful memories: Hugh begging for a burial after Oscar's death when she'd insisted on a cremation. She was certain of her reasoning now – a child-sized coffin going into the ground would have been too much to bear. She grabbed the bottle of valium from her handbag and shoved a tablet into her mouth then forced herself from the cubicle. After wiping her eyes in front of the mirror she went outside and found a quiet spot under an oak tree where she waited for the service to finish.

Eventually, music started inside the church and Sandra's coffin was brought outside by six weeping pallbearers and loaded into the hearse. The rest of the mourners followed, squinting in the cold, bright day as they stood on the grass outside. Groups formed quickly, grasping each other in embraces as they struggled to contain their grief.

'Are you okay?' Lachlan asked. He stood directly in front of her, his body blocking the sun.

'Sorry for accusing you of flirting back there,' she said, not meeting his eyes. 'When's Debbie's funeral?'

He looked at her quizzically. 'It was a private affair. Family only.'

'It's a pity they couldn't have had their funerals together – seeing as they were best friends.'

'They were buried separately as Debbie's mum wanted a private ceremony so the family could mourn their daughter without the presence of a thousand onlookers.'

'Smart woman,' said Dana, as Keely came over and stood next to them.

'And who was the woman who interrupted the service?' asked Dana.

'Kenisha Allenby, the local psychic. When the police want to find out who was responsible for the latest stolen car, they go to her.'

'Seriously?'

He pursed his lips. 'That's probably an exaggeration. Ian's a good policeman, but he doesn't do things by the book. He solves problems in a more pragmatic way. Anyway, let's go and see Paul and Chrystal, pass on our condolences, shall we?'

Paul was standing near a row of metal chairs that had been lined up on the lawn, his arms around Chrystal and Billy. His eyes were shielded by large aviator-style sunglasses.

Dana, Lachlan and Keely stood before them.

'We're so sorry for your loss,' said Dana.

'Thanks,' said Paul. He appeared so choked up that Dana addressed her next words to Chrystal.

'I know you haven't been happy with some of the decisions we've made about where you're living,' she said gently, as Chrystal, clutching a rose, stared at the ground. 'But I thought I'd check in with you to see how things are going at Carol's?'

'They're fine.' Chrystal kept her eyes lowered.

'We want you and your sisters to feel comfortable while you're there, so please let me know if there's anything we can help with.'

Dana turned to Paul, trying to gauge his response.

He surprised her by reaching out and taking her hand. 'Thank you,' he said, squeezing it tight. 'That means a lot.'

The square in the centre of Crows Nest was far larger than required for the town's small population, a memory of early ambition that had long since been forgotten. On one side, Salts antique store stood stalwart in the pale afternoon light, and opposite it, the equally imposing Grand Old Crow Hotel. A group of bikies with paunches overhanging their jeans slouched outside, smoking as they guarded their shiny chrome motorbikes.

One of them, with curly black hair and tattooed arms, she recognised from the funeral. He let out a wolf-whistle. 'Hey Lachlan, does your wife know you're seeing two sheilas behind her back?' The man leant against the brick wall of the pub, his smile full of malicious intent.

'Very funny, mate. I'm here in a purely professional capacity,' said Lachlan. 'These are my co-workers.'

'Great!' the bikie yelled back. 'Looking forward to meeting them later.' His head wobbled from side to side as he spoke, reminding Dana of the inflatable punching clown she'd owned in her childhood.

Keely put a hand over her mouth as she whispered to Dana. 'Tony Mulhain's the leader of the bikie gang and the local drug dealer. I'm surprised we haven't had to visit him lately. We get calls about his two-year-old daughter nearly every second week. Apparently, he's a distant cousin of Sandra's – but don't ask me how that works.'

Dana followed Lachlan and Keely through the pokies to the beer garden, a concrete area where large umbrellas had been erected. An outdoor pizza oven with weeds in its hearth languished in the corner and a sign on the wall advertised *Kids Eat Free Thursdays* and *Sandra's Wake.*

The place was in full swing – a mixture of locals, family members and Paul's workmates. Men in flannelette shirts and boots sat on stools at the bar. Their elbows lined the red and gold counter as they smoked and swigged from schooners of beer. One of them used his terry-towelling hat to wipe the dirt from his face.

Connor was at a table with a group of locals talking and laughing. They crowded around him, hanging off his every word. Dana caught the punchline of the story he was telling as they walked past.

'She let go of the gate and almost broke my bloody leg. You should see the bruise, mate!' Raucous laughter followed and he raised his beer in her direction.

She was relieved to find that the tablet she'd taken had kicked in and any embarrassment she should have felt was non-existent.

Keely handed them schooners of Fourex then led the way to a long table, consisting almost entirely of middle-aged men. They headed for three vacant seats next to Ian Steinmann and his assistant, Gail. Chrystal and Alisha were seated with friends and family on the other side of the outdoor area.

Ian was telling a story and the crowd at the table were captivated. As she sat down, he said, 'Some men have the ability to charm and manipulate women. I can tell you – he has that charisma. There's something about him women like. You get a girl like that, with all that burgeoning sexuality and you've got a problem.'

'Who are you talking about?' asked Keely. 'I'd like to meet him.'

Ian grimaced. 'No-one you'd know.' He gestured to the two men next to him to move over. 'How are you finding our little town?' he asked Dana.

'Very nice.' She ripped large chunks from a beer coaster, gratified at once again being able to rip something to shreds.

Ian handed her a menu. 'You should have a go at the mixed grill,' he said, and winked. 'We don't know anyone who's been able to finish it.'

'He's just being silly,' Gail said. 'That's for men trying to prove themselves. Try the surf and turf. Rump steak, prawns and a lovely sauce. Much more up your alley.'

When the meals finally came out Dana was in no mood to eat. Instead, she excused herself and went up to the bar to get another round of drinks. As she handed over the money, the woman behind the counter with lines around her eyes and a small, hard mouth said, 'You must be the new Family Services officer we've heard about.'

'That's me.' Dana wondered how something as insignificant as her starting work had become a talking point.

'Good luck,' the woman said, handing her a tray of beers. 'Some of the kids in this town need all the help they can get.'

When Dana arrived back at the table and sat down, Ian was on the phone. He slumped visibly in his seat and rubbed his temples as he ended the call. 'I hate to break it to you all, but it looks like you won't be driving home tonight,' he announced. 'I've just had a call from the station – there's been an accident on the highway. No-one was injured, but apparently the fog is like pea soup.'

'But surely if we drive slowly—' Dana started, surprised as she looked out to the street that she could no longer see across the town square, only metres away.

'Don't even think about it. Do you know how many people have been killed on nights like these?' He gave Dana a stern look. 'And don't think you can get away with it because the road's not windy. Most people crash on the straightest stretch.'

Dana took a long sip of her beer, trying to shake the trauma of the funeral from her mind. She bit into a bread roll that tasted like cardboard and finished her drink.

Ten minutes later, a slow warmth was spreading through her body. The walls of the pub were pulsing to 'Eagle Rock' and her mind raced. The volume in the pub rose along with the conversation level and people had to yell over the top of each other to be heard.

She stood up and marched inside to the bar, sidestepping people who'd lost the ability to walk straight. She was on a mission – to find Connor and smooth things over, like she should have done when she first had the chance. She found him by an open fireplace, alone and on his mobile. When he saw her, he ended the call, snapping his flip phone shut and sliding it into his pocket.

Brazenly, she took the beer glass from his hand and took a sip. She held his gaze. 'I knew you were standing there for a reason.'

'Glad to be of service,' he said. 'Can I get you a drink? A chardonnay?' He peered at her closely. 'Maybe you're more of a whiskey woman?'

'I'm fine …' she said. 'Really.'

He leant forward and grinned. 'You must really like me, to have gotten physical with me that day.'

Her eyes bored into his. 'I've told you, I let go of the gate at the wrong moment.'

'That's what they all say.'

'I see that, if nothing else, you've recovered your bravado.' She remembered herself, why she'd come to speak to him. 'Look,' she ran a hand through her hair. 'My behaviour that day was appalling. It should never have happened.'

'Don't worry about it. I've had worse things happen on the job. Besides, makes for a pretty awesome story … I pissed off a Family Services officer off so much that she whacked me.' He smiled. 'Come on, I'll buy you a drink.'

She followed him back to the beer garden and returned to her seat next to Keely and Ian. Keely flashed Dana a pained glance then looked away. *He'll only hurt you*, Dana felt like telling her. She was struck with an image of Hugh, drinking whiskey from a tumbler in his favourite reclining chair. Melinda, beautiful in the firelight as she went to him.

Another schooner of Fourex was placed in front of Dana and she downed it quickly. Unlike the first time, she enjoyed the cold, bitter taste. The others were telling stories. Ian was joking about the time he accidentally fired an officer with pepper spray.

Dana finished her drink and staggered through the crowd to the toilets. Inside a cubicle, the walls swayed and the floor tilted as she sat looking at the graffiti, listening to the chatter of drunk women. The words *Fade to black* had been spray-painted on the door. She checked her phone. There were no messages from Hugh, or anyone else. She felt a stab of pain over his lack of contact, the familiar regret of things being different – if only Oscar had lived. By this age, he would have been at day care and she would have been immersing herself in mother's groups and story time at the local library. More importantly, she and Hugh would still be on speaking terms instead of trapped in a dysfunctional relationship.

She forced herself from the cubicle and splashed water on her face. By the time she'd weaved her way through the beer garden, the lights had dimmed and people were making plans to leave.

Keely came over with a look of concern etched on her face. 'Are you okay?'

'Fine,' said Dana, hoping her mascara hadn't run. 'Where's Lachlan?'

'Snuck off ages ago. He lives in Meringandan so the fog's not a problem.' She cocked her head. 'Don't worry – Ian's booked us into the motel down the road.'

Outside, thick fog rolled through the car park. Drivers in cars and utes skidded into the dark, high beams slicing through blankets of mist. The voice in the functional part of her mind registered the drivers were drunk, as well as the police officers.

'Jeremy's giving you a lift,' she heard someone say, and a second later she was speeding through the night in a police car, freezing air blasting her face.

Somehow, she made it into the hotel room where she collapsed onto a bed. It was a standard-issue suite – a double and a single bed with matching quilted duvets, a tiled area with a desk, a sink and modest tea-making facilities. Her impression of the space was one of maximum function and minimal beauty. Her phone vibrated from the bedside table. Automatically, she picked it up.

How about a nightcap? the text read. *Give you a chance to make up for the other day.*

She scanned her conscience. Since Oscar's death, she'd felt as though she'd died too, but they'd forgotten to bury her.

Was it so wrong to want to feel again?

9

They did not speak when she opened the door. She simply took Connor's hand and led him to the centre of the room where she unbuttoned his shirt and removed her own. She unclipped her bra, letting it fall to the carpet, and he smiled as his hands moved to her breasts. His eyes had a piercing quality, a singular gaze that in other circumstances would have bothered her.

Connor's body revealed itself in glimpses. Collar bones and bare chest. Translucent skin, showing the veins in his arms. Black boxers and a firm stomach, flecked with thick, dark hair.

He sat next to her on the bed. She leant over to kiss him. His mouth on hers was like scalding fire. And it was wrong, wrong, wrong, but she couldn't help it.

'Connor,' she said, pulling away.

He was on top of her in an instant, a condom produced from nowhere. If nothing else, it would be quick. So swift, perhaps it might be like it never happened. They moved together, his body on hers and she orgasmed in a matter of beats, the world obliterating behind her eyes. He rolled onto his back and lay spread-eagled in the centre of the bed. She found a space under his arm. The air conditioner in the window rattled away without warming the room.

She remembered how it was with Hugh. He'd gazed into her eyes, cocooning her until she drifted to sleep. So, this is what they'd come to. Hugh with his midlife crisis and her revenge, sleeping with a toy boy. They were clichés. *Pathetic.* She fidgeted with her wedding band then closed her eyes against the streetlight slicing through the curtains.

Already, she regretted what she'd set in motion.

Connor left early the next morning, mumbling goodbyes and dressing in darkness. Dana was thankful for the quick departure. Nauseous and shaky with a hangover, the thought of small talk was unbearable.

Keely had gone to collect the work car from the pub and was waiting in front of the motel with the engine running. As Dana emerged from her room a plover in a gum tree gave a high-pitched call before swooping a woman as she hurried down the street. Dana slumped into the passenger seat in crumpled clothes, checking her phone to see if Hugh had messaged.

'So, who did you spend the night with?' Keely's voice had an edge to it.

'No-one. I was asleep the moment my head hit the pillow.' She'd always been a terrible actor and the first blossom of a rash raced up her neck.

'Fair enough,' Keely said half-heartedly. 'Must have been someone in another room.'

The air between them grew heavy.

'Shit,' said Dana, suddenly realising she'd left her jacket in the motel room's cupboard. 'I'll be back in a sec.' She rushed into the motel and spoke to the manager, who retrieved it for her.

When she returned to the car, she picked up her phone from where she'd left it in the centre console. Her heart leapt when she saw a text message and then nose-dived when she realised it was from Connor.

Last night was fun. How about dinner tonight? My treat ;-)

Her hands shook with adrenaline and guilt. She glanced at Keely, whose eyes were fixed firmly ahead as she drove out of the car park.

Pockets of mist drifted through the valley creating a scene of eerie beauty as the trees cast long shadows across the road. Dana felt heavy with shame as she reflected on her recent behaviour. Not only had she assaulted a policeman and cheated on her husband, she'd also been seriously in trouble at work and gotten drunk in front of her colleagues.

When they reached the highway, she remembered what Ian had said to her the night before – most accidents occurred on the straightest stretch of road. The same could be said of her own life. Her biggest crash, the loss of Oscar, had happened when her life was on track and she'd been lulled into a false sense of security. If the path had been winding, full of potholes, she might have seen what was coming. Instead, she'd been blindsided and left reeling from the blow.

New cases had been allocated while she'd been out of the office. An eight-year-old whose mother had broken his arm. A family, homeless on the streets and sleeping outside the local IGA. Finally, a toddler with numerous unexplained injuries after the stepfather moved in. She spent the rest of the day going over the cases at home – burying her head in work so she could forget about her troubles. But by the afternoon, her mind was wandering back to the funeral. She pushed the new files aside and returned to the Kirby case. The phone rang.

'We still on for tonight?' It was Connor.

The guilt and self-loathing she'd felt that morning had evaporated and now that it was evening she was ready to see him – if only to find out more about the investigation.

'Sure,' she said. 'Looking forward to it.'

They met outside the restaurant in the main street. Connor wore a chequered long-sleeve shirt and RM Williams boots. He kissed her on the cheek before leading her through the sliding door entrance. A man in a black suit and tie took her coat and showed them to a table by the window overlooking the street. The low-lit room with its classical music and dingy carpet reminded her of a convention centre, but the extensive drinks list soon lifted her spirits.

'What wine do you like?' she asked, as starched white napkins were placed across their laps.

'You choose.'

The buttons on his shirt strained as he fiddled with the cutlery and the pale musculature of his swimmer's chest returned to her in the haziest of memories. Without thinking, her hand moved to her wedding ring.

Dana ordered a Penfolds Bin 407 that was quickly brought

out by the waiter. He poured the red liquid into a fine-stemmed glass and offered it to Connor, who swirled the wine in his mouth then swallowed.

'Lovely,' he said.

The waiter filled both their glasses and placed the bottle on the table.

'It's not wine tasting,' Dana said as the waiter returned to the kitchen. 'You're only supposed to let him know it hasn't gone bad.'

'I know.' Connor tugged at his collar as though his shirt was too tight. 'I was just being nice.'

She was about to apologise for her condescension when there was an explosion from a revving car racing up the street outside.

'What's that?' she asked, relieved to have something else to talk about.

'It's what we call lapping,' he said with a gleam in his eye. 'Where bored teenagers hoon up and down the main drag in hotted-up cars to impress their girlfriends. You don't have that in Sydney?'

She smiled at him. 'Not where I come from.'

The waiter returned, asking whether they'd decided on mains. She took a long sip of wine before ordering. The waiter refilled their glasses and the air between them began to shift and lighten.

Connor leant back in his chair. 'So, why do you work in child protection? What's the appeal?'

'Oh, I don't know …'

'Usually, it's older women in sensible shoes and terrible vests,' he said. 'Or younger women, but still in sensible shoes and terrible vests, like Ally Sheedy in that movie. What's it called? *St. Elmo's Fire*?'

'I think you'll find it was Mare Winningham.' Dana frowned, recalling the character's tragic love life and penchant for knitwear.

'Or that Ratched lady in *One Flew Over the Cuckoo's Nest.*'

'Jesus.' Dana cringed. 'She was a nurse, not a social worker.'

'Alright, go on – name one glamorous social worker. Bet you can't.'

Dana was silent. 'Fine,' she said, 'there are no glamorous social workers in pop culture. Still … it has other things going for it.'

'Like what? The excellent paycheque?' He screwed up his face. 'Social workers are worse off than teachers.'

He was irritating her now. 'You know what they say, Connor – you can't put a price on protecting vulnerable children.'

'Touché.'

'What about you?' she shot back. 'What famous police officer did you want to be growing up?'

'Easy.' He grinned, showing acres of white teeth. 'John McClane. *Die Hard*. Yippee-ki-yay, motherfucker!'

'That's great.' She laughed despite herself. 'I bet you get to say that a lot in Crows Nest.'

The waiter came out with their food and made a show of grinding a large pepper mill over their meals.

'What did you order again?' asked Dana, staring at the roll of meat wrapped in bacon and flanked by kipflers on Connor's plate.

'New England lamb shoulder, but I prefer to think of it as …' He smirked. 'Meat log.'

She laughed until she was wiping tears from her eyes. Was she drunk, she wondered, after just two glasses of wine? Her mind turned to Hugh, the promise she'd made to herself only that morning not to cheat on him again. She tried to pull herself together, concentrate on why she'd come.

'How's the investigation?' she asked.

He ran a hand through his newly washed hair. 'Terrible. I've been doing a lot of long days and yesterday was my only night off, and, as you know, I didn't get much sleep.'

'You must be exhausted,' she said. 'I've been working hard at the Department but it's nothing like those hours.'

'The police report with the autopsy results came back today.'

'Really?' she said casually, not quite believing he was taking her into his confidence. She wondered if it was the wine or simply his youth that led to his complete lack of professionalism.

'The injuries they suffered were horrific.' He dabbed at his mouth with a napkin. 'Debbie was shot in the head and Sandra was shot in the neck and in the chest. It had been raining and Debbie's thongs were found in the mud a few metres from the car. There was blood and brain splatter everywhere and a .22 calibre sawn-off shotgun in the footwell near Debbie. And what's even weirder, there's a few things the pathologist has written that don't even make sense.'

'Like what?' Dana asked, making a mental note to file away everything he was saying.

'Debbie was found without her glasses for a start. One of my mates was sent out to look for them and found them at Sandra's house. I don't think I've ever laid eyes on that woman without those creepy dark glasses ...' He trailed off, a thoughtful expression on his face. 'If there was one thing the autopsy showed, it was that she was a serious liar, that's for sure.'

'Why do you say that?' Dana concentrated on her minimal encouragers. Years of experience had taught her that all she had to do was look as though she was attending to what the person was saying and the floodgates would open. There were times when her clients had spoken for so long, she'd literally had to rise from her chair to end the conversation.

'Ian told us that when Debbie was friends with him and his wife, she always complained about this problem she had with her mouth – osteonecrosis of the jaw, it was called. His wife used to cook her special meals and she even went away for an operation at one point. Anyway, the pathologist does the autopsy and it turns out it was complete bullshit. Her jaw was fine.'

'Really?'

'And another thing she made up was that she'd been married to some Canadian – Will Burgess. She used to tell everyone he'd died in a motorbike accident, but it turns out he's alive and kicking. He lives in Perth and works as a bus driver for a tour company. When we interviewed him, he said they'd been on one date and that was over ten years ago.'

'That is weird. What else did the police report show?' She leant forward, willing him to keep going.

He inched closer, lowering his voice. 'There were absolutely no other car tracks found near the women. So, whoever killed them either pre-arranged to meet them out there and had parked somewhere else or travelled in the car with them and hot-footed it the four kilometres back to the highway when they were done.'

'What's the police theory on what happened?'

'Well, the one we're going with is pretty wild actually. But to be honest, I'm not sure Ian's nailed it this time. When I first heard about what had happened to those women, I thought it reeked of a drug crime. And with the Kirbys' neighbour saying she saw Paul at home that night through her window, being killed by one of the drug dealers seemed even more likely.' He shook himself as though he'd suddenly become conscious of what he was saying. 'Anyway, I shouldn't be telling you this …' He put his hand under the table, caressing the bare skin of her knee. 'How's things with you?'

She flinched. 'Fine,' she said, searching for a way to put him off. 'I'm fine.'

'If you say you're fine one more time, I won't believe you.'

His joke gave her space to regain her composure. 'You know I'm married, Connor.'

He tilted his head towards her ring. 'I'd have to be blind to miss that sparkler.'

'Then you understand, there's no way we can be together.'

'If you say so.'

His petulant look made Dana wonder whether everything else in life had gone his way. 'I hope we'll be friends.'

'Friends with benefits?'

'There'll be benefits.' She smiled. 'Just not the ones you have in mind.'

They stood on the street half an hour later as the old post-office clock struck ten. She marvelled at how quiet the town was, the wind whipping through the lane and the leaves rustling in the gutters. She could have kissed him right then and no-one would be the wiser. But her thoughts had already turned back to the dead women – the loud Sandra and hapless Debbie. Their raucous laughter cut short, their naked bodies in the morgue. A chill went through her and a rogue thought passed across her mind: that a man must have been at the heart of all their troubles.

She placed her hands on Connor's shoulders, brushed her lips against his cheek and ducked into the waiting cab.

10

The office was buzzing when she arrived on Monday morning. A group of admin workers rushed past as she walked down the corridor and a pile of faxes lay on the carpet where they'd fallen. She was almost at her pod when Lachlan stepped in front of her.

'You'd better hurry,' he said in a conspiratorial whisper. 'They've caught the killer. Police are giving a press conference.'

Head whirring, she dumped her bag on her desk and jogged after him towards the packed conference room where a television was set up with the volume on high. Connor appeared on the screen in a crisp white shirt and stood at a podium surrounded by half-a-dozen microphones and a Queensland Police banner with the logo *With Honour We Serve*. He stared into the cameras, his blue eyes blazing.

Lachlan leant over to Dana, hand over his mouth. 'He's good-looking, that young man of yours. Don't you think?'

'He's not my young man,' she hissed.

Jacinta turned around, annoyance etched on her face. 'Shut up, you two. It's about to start.'

Good morning, everyone. My name is Constable Connor Morgan and on behalf of Senior Sergeant Ian Steinmann, I'm here to speak about the deaths of Debbie Vickers and Sandra Kirby. Let me remind you, today's press conference is purely for information purposes. We will not be taking questions at the end.

Dana took in his unruffled demeanour and was impressed.

We believe the women's deaths were a murder–suicide. That Sandra Kirby was shot by her friend Debbie Vickers. The post-mortem examinations have made this obvious and we hope that a sense of calm can be restored to our community now that people know what happened and the case has been solved.

A gasp went around the office and Dana's mind raced back to what Connor had said at dinner about the anomalies of the case. She stared at the screen as he made his way from the podium and wondered what evidence they had for determining Debbie was the murderer. Had he changed his mind? Or was he simply going along with orders? Was there any situation in which Debbie would shoot Sandra in cold blood?

Lachlan nudged her with his elbow. 'Turn up for the books, hey?'

'Murder–suicide,' she spluttered. 'What reason could Debbie possibly have had for wanting to kill her best friend?'

'Unrequited love?'

'You can't be serious.'

He tapped the pocket where he kept his cigarettes. 'Meet me outside for a smoke?'

'I've got work to do.' She knew she was being a spoilsport by not going outside to gossip, but the latest revelation had left her so rattled she needed to think. She returned to her desk, staring blankly at the computer screen, the Kirby case file in front of her.

Her heart rate had only just begun to settle when the phone rang. 'Department of Families. Dana Gibson speaking.'

'It's me,' said a soft, subdued voice.

She knew that voice. 'Chrystal. What can I do for you?'

'Me and my nieces want to go home. Paul didn't do it – the police said so. And we want to go home.'

'Is that so?' Dana tried to pinpoint the source of her disquiet. 'How's everything at Carol's? Is she treating you well?' She felt guilty she hadn't managed to check in with Chrystal since the funeral. 'Has everything been okay at the placement?'

'I guess so …' She trailed off. 'But when Billy-Violet has nightmares, Carol doesn't really do anything.'

'I see.' Dana recalled the anger she'd felt towards the foster carer's lack of concern. 'Look, I'll have a talk to my manager and see what I can do. I'll call you back as soon as possible.'

It pained her to resort to authority as a means of stalling, but she was reluctant to let them return until she understood why the investigation had ended so abruptly. She just couldn't imagine any scenario in which Debbie would murder her best friend.

'Okay,' Chrystal said hesitantly. 'When will you call?'

'Tomorrow. At the latest.'

Lachlan had returned while Dana had been on the phone and the smell of tobacco lingered in the air.

He swivelled in his chair to face her. 'Let me guess,' he said, putting his hands behind his head. 'That was Chrystal and she wants to go home now.'

'Uh-huh.'

'What did you tell her?'

'I'd need to discuss it with Helen.'

'I like it.' He grinned. 'The old, "I'll have to ask my manager" tactic. To be fair, Paul's no longer a suspect, so we have no grounds to keep her. She can go whenever she likes.'

'I know that. I'm just hoping that I can buy some time, make sure they're safe. And put some monitoring in place and organise a youth worker.'

'Possibly,' Lachlan said. 'If Helen goes for it.' He paused. 'You're really not buying the murder–suicide theory, are you?'

'I'm not. I mean, how many murder–suicides, involving two women, have been committed in Australia in the past?'

'I've got no idea.'

'Neither do I, but I plan to find out.'

'Look.' Lachlan stretched his long arms and rested them behind his head. 'They've gone with the lesbian theory and the case is closed. There's nothing more you can do.'

'But it's so implausible,' Dana spluttered. 'Even if they were lovers, and they were having a fight. Shooting someone at point-blank range then turning the gun on yourself … it's not how women deal with things. A woman might bitch about their ex or stalk them in the phone book, but murder seems so extreme. And driving out to the middle of nowhere to execute it, even more so.' She was suddenly struck with an idea. 'Do you know the place where they were found?'

'The crime scene?'

She nodded.

'Sure.' His eyes narrowed. 'A bush track out at Postman's Bluff. Few kays past the pistol club.'

'Can you show me?'

'No way. Helen still hasn't forgiven me for the time Jacinta did some off-the-books investigating and I rolled the car.'

Dana pursed her lips. 'You know those case notes you've been whingeing about not having time to get on file? What if I offered to type them up for you?'

'Well, that's tempting. I bloody hate doing case notes.' He cocked his head in his customary style and smiled. 'You've got a deal.'

They sped out of town in Lachlan's Range Rover. Professionally speaking, this was the craziest thing she'd ever done. The only thing that had come close was the time she'd asked a colleague to give her a leg-up so she could peer into the house of a known drug user. And that was merely overzealousness, rather than going entirely beyond the boundaries of her job.

Lachlan was quiet, his brow furrowed as he drove towards Postman's Bluff. The landscape changed dramatically as they turned down a dirt track. Dana was surprised to see pastures with the desolate stumps of ring-barked trees and an arbour of dead eucalypts. Beyond that, a fallen-down house surrounded by the wrecks of cars and farm machinery.

As they bumped along, Dana thought about the women's journey to this place. Had they met up with someone they trusted and taken a detour on their way to Debbie's aunt's farm? Or had they taken a wrong turn and stumbled across a madman after midnight? And what must it have taken for Debbie to persuade her friend to come to such an unwelcoming place at that hour with a six-month-old baby at home. When Oscar was that age, the only thing Dana had wanted to do after nine o'clock was fall into a blissful slumber. Why sit up chatting and hatch a crazy plan to watch a foal being born? Was Sandra breastfeeding? Or had the baby been weaned?

Hugh had offered no support in those first few months. His favourite trick had been to roll over and pretend he hadn't heard when Oscar woke up crying. Even when she'd had to work the next day, she'd always been the one to bound out of bed to settle Oscar with a bottle. And now, it had been almost two weeks since she'd left Castlecrag and Hugh had made no attempt to call her. Even though she'd asked him not to, he should've known better.

Lachlan veered off the dirt road, jolting her into the present. They drove over uneven ground for a brief period until he braked to a stop.

'Don't want to end up like those two getting stuck in scrub too thick to get out of,' he said.

They walked a few hundred metres until a set of deep tyre tracks came to an abrupt end in the long grass. Lachlan gestured with a sweeping arm at the small clearing, to a fallen sapling near a thin pine tree that they recognised from the crime scene photographs.

'Well, here it is. Not much to see.'

'No,' said Dana, realising the trip had been a mistake. 'I thought, at the very least, the police would have put some tape up to cordon off the scene.'

'Well, the case *has* been solved.' He looked at her sympathetically. 'They're moving on and getting back to the petty crimes and traffic offences that make up their daily lives. What were you hoping to see?'

'Oh, I don't know.' She stared at a rock with a darker patch on the surface. 'I thought that perhaps by coming here, it might become clearer to me what happened that night, but if anything it's raised even more questions.' She knelt and stared at the rock more closely. 'I don't suppose you know what this is?' she asked, wanting him to confirm her suspicions.

Lachlan knelt beside her. After a pause, he said, 'That would be blood.' He pointed ahead of them where the dirt had congealed. 'There's quite a lot of it.'

A light breeze swept around them and she caught a whiff of death. *Body fluids? Surely not after all this time.* More likely carrion or an animal pelt. The crime-scene photos came back to her and she dropped the rock in the grass as she recalled the image of the women stuffed in the front seat of the car. Mannequins in unnatural positions.

She pulled her cashmere wrap around her chest as native grasses shivered in the wind. She looked at Lachlan. 'We should get out of here.'

He stood up, slowly examining something small and metallic in the palm of his hand. 'Check this out,' he said as she stood beside him. 'A spent cartridge.'

'I'm glad to see the police managed such a thorough search of the area.'

'I'll give it to Ian when I see him tonight.'

'Sure thing.' She frowned. 'You and Ian are best mates then, are you?'

'I wouldn't go that far, but I did play a few games of rugby against him. Back in the day.'

'You really are a dark horse.'

He smiled. 'I like to think so.'

Back in Lachlan's car, she asked him all the questions that had been bothering her over the past few weeks.

'So, what's Paul Kirby like? I haven't had the chance yet to form an opinion.'

'Well, he's always had a chip on his shoulder, but he's witty and funny, probably annoyed that his life hasn't worked out better, that he's little more than an air con installer these days. When I first knew him, he was a semi-famous stuntman on motorbikes, then he hurt his shoulder and that put an end to that.' He paused. 'Actually, you'll have to watch yourself working with him, he's got a reputation of being a womaniser and you're just his type.'

Dana restrained herself from rolling her eyes. 'I'll be fine.'

'He's a nice guy, though. I'm hoping that being in charge of all those kids will make him get his act together.'

'In what way?'

'He's been known to indulge in marijuana and the odd bit of coke in the past. Nothing major – though I do worry it might escalate now he's mourning his dead wife.'

'So, given that his alibi has checked out and he's no longer a suspect, do you think he's an appropriate person to be looking after the children? Especially considering that he'll have to work and still look after the baby.'

'Yeah, sure. Those girls seem to really look up to him.'

'But do you think he was acting strangely during the interview?'

He glanced over at her. 'You mean, do I think he's a killer?'

'I suppose so.'

He slid into second gear as they hit rocky terrain. 'I couldn't rule it out, but he's always struck me as being too lily-livered to do such a thing.'

'Lily-livered?' she repeated, raising an eyebrow.

'That's a word, isn't it?'

'If you're from the eighteenth century.'

'What I was trying to say is, I don't think he'd have the stomach for it.'

'But that's what they said about Lindy Chamberlain, isn't it?' Dana argued. 'She behaved strangely after the death of Azaria and therefore she was guilty. I still don't think she did it though,' she added quickly, as they turned off the bush track and back onto the highway.

'Why's that?'

'Didn't fit the profile.' She stared at the road, at the broken centre line that seemed to stretch forever. 'There was no previous cruelty to children, she didn't seem stressed before she put Azaria to bed that night. And she was religious. Her whole life was devoted to helping people, doing her best to please her God. Not to mention, in the *Sixty Minutes* interview she said she'd always wanted a girl.'

'I agree,' said Lachlan. 'I've never thought she did it either, but in a hick town like Alice Springs the local cops end up bungling the investigation and fifteen years later people still don't know what happened.'

As she watched the telephone poles speeding by, he began a diatribe about people being too quick to draw conclusions and she thought about how difficult it would have been to cope with the accusations of society on top of a grief that made it almost impossible to live. Because if she'd thought losing a child was unbearable, jail would certainly have finished her off.

In the early days after Oscar's death all she'd wanted was to be alone, to spend long periods remembering her baby: his murmurings, his touch, his smell, before she forgot altogether. And so it was that Hugh accused her of being cold and unfeeling, of being so obsessed with her work that the entire foundation of their marriage was a sham.

Lachlan was rambling. 'You tell me,' he was saying, 'how's a woman supposed to act after the death of her child?'

'Why would you ask me something like that?' She glared at him, her heart pounding. 'Why would you possibly think I'd want to talk about it?'

'Christ. What is wrong with you?' He looked at her with distaste. 'Just when I think I'm starting to chip away at the ice, you start behaving like a madwoman.'

He'd been referring to the Chamberlain case and not her at all. The chance to apologise floated in the ether around her, but she was too angry. She sank down into her seat.

'You know,' he said, as they made their way back into Toowoomba, 'there's a lot of dark things in this world if you go looking for them.' A shadow of concern passed over his face. 'But there's some bloody good things out there, too.'

'I know.' She gazed out the window at a blazing white sky the sun couldn't permeate.

11

She was tired when she arrived home from work. Bone tired. She sat with her stockinged feet on the table as blood moved through her veins in a sluggish parody of circulation. Her new metallic coffee maker shone on the granite bench top. She'd been quick to discover Toowoomba had no decent coffee and had sought to remedy the situation by buying the best machine available. A pity it was half past eight and too late for one now.

Pink Floyd's 'Time' played quietly in the background. She'd always had a soft spot for *Dark Side of the Moon* and when Dave Gilmour sang about his love of being home, she hummed the melody. After spending all day in conversations with clients it was a relief to return to a quiet house. She was surprised then, when Angus, in an Ansett shirt and navy shorts, suddenly appeared next to her.

'How long have you been here?' she asked.

He held out a scraggly bunch of sweet peas, his face beaming. 'These are for you.'

'Thanks,' she said, smiling. 'Are these from your nan's garden?'

'No. From the park.'

She frowned. 'They're beautiful Angus, but you know you're not supposed to take them from there.'

'I know,' he said without remorse.

'I'll get something to put them in.' She came back with a crystal vase and found him looking at the photos she'd pinned to a corkboard above the coffee machine.

'Who's that?' he asked, pointing to the pictures of Sandra and Debbie she'd stolen from the work file.

'No-one.' She hauled the board from the wall and faced it the other way. 'You shouldn't be looking at it. It's just something I'm doing for work.'

'Bullshit,' he said excitedly. 'It's those dead ladies. I'm not a fucking moron, you know.'

'You're not a what moron?' she asked, hoping he'd replace the swear word with something appropriate.

'You sound just like Nan.'

She wondered how on earth he'd gotten in. Here she was thinking about asking Susan for an upgrade in security and an eleven-year-old was breaking in with ease.

'Anyway, I know what you're doing. It's a crime board, like on TV. Can I help? I've read about it all in the paper.'

She considered for a moment. 'Uh, Angus, I'm not … ah well, I suppose you've already seen it.' She reluctantly turned the cork board back around.

'What are you putting up next?'

'Well, I guess we can put up that map of Crows Nest and mark the journey from the Kirby house to where their bodies were found.' She reached for a red pen from the jar by the window and drew a line between Creek Street and Postman's Bluff.

'Who are these girls?' Angus asked, picking up the photos of Sandra's two blonde-haired siblings she'd copied from the file. 'They're very pretty.'

She took the photos of Chrystal and her older sister, Alisha, and pinned them onto the board. 'They're Sandra's younger step-sisters. They moved in with the Kirby's after their grandfather died.'

'Why weren't they living with their mother?'

'She couldn't look after them.' Dana paused. 'She had problems of her own.'

'You're saying she was like my mum – a bad parent.'

'Possibly … though to be fair, I've never met your mum.'

'She's a bad mum. Everyone says so.' He handed her another photo. 'Who's this angry-looking guy?'

'Now he *is* a bad guy,' she said, staring at a photo of Tony Mulhain when he'd been a pallbearer at Sandra's funeral. 'He's the head of the Crows Nest bikie gang and a drug dealer. He's been in jail and lives on the outskirts of town. I included him because one of my colleagues thinks it's almost certain that drugs were involved.'

'Do you think he killed them?

'Maybe … they say that the best way to predict if someone will be violent is from their past. So, it's possible.'

'Sherlock Holmes always says that when you have excluded the impossible, whatever remains must be the truth.'

'Very true. I see you're something of a sleuth yourself.'

'This guy looks familiar.' He handed her the page of the newspaper with a photo of Paul at the funeral.

'Yes, that's Paul Kirby. You would have seen him on the news. He was the initial suspect, but the police let him go once they realised he had an alibi.'

'What's he like?'

'I like him, actually, and the kids are desperate to get home to him.'

'Are these Sandra's kids?' He pointed to a picture of Billy-Violet and baby Rubi.

'Yes, they're the daughters Sandra had with Paul.'

'Well, there's one thing for sure.'

'What's that?'

'I don't think the baby did it.'

She smiled at his terrible joke.

'Do you want to know the real reason I came over today?'

'Sure.' She humoured him. 'What's the real reason you're here?'

'I installed the internet for you.'

She gasped. 'How'd you manage that?'

'I put in a modem using your phone line then I hacked into the university server to get you connected. It's ready to go.'

The excitement shining from his every pore was so infectious she followed his skinny legs as he sprinted down the hall to the study. He sat at her computer with the glow of the screen on his pale face, his chin dimpled in determination as he tapped the keys. A loud static filled the room.

'So annoying.' He frowned. 'Okay, I set up Netscape Navigator as your search engine because it's the best. And you should get another phone line installed because every time someone rings, you'll get disconnected. It happens to my uncle all the time.'

'Won't I get in trouble for having the internet and not paying for it?'

'They can't trace it. My uncle did a course through the uni so I used his log-in.' He scowled. 'He doesn't even know how to use the internet.'

'Well …' she began, trying to decide whether to reprimand him. 'Thanks,' she said finally.

'It's okay. Now you can find the killers and put them behind bars.'

She was surprised by his faith in her. 'It mightn't be that easy.'

'Yes, it is,' he said matter-of-factly. 'Mum's boyfriend, Wade, killed our dog and they put him in jail.'

'Where does your nan think you are at the moment?'

'In bed. I climbed out the window and jumped onto the water tanks.'

'You'd better be getting back then. She'll be worried.'

'Good-o,' he said, and ran from the room. His feet pattered along the runner rug then the front door slammed. She walked back into the kitchen feeling strangely bereft.

The crystal vase gleamed from the table and she gathered the sweet peas and laid them on the bench. She thought about Angus as she trimmed the stalks. The freckles on his nose, his mischievous grin. She was warming to him, she realised, filling the vase with water.

She'd just finished arranging the flowers and set them on the table when her mobile rang. A sudden panic set in when she saw it was Hugh. The moment had finally arrived for them to talk and she had a sudden, desperate need to be in control of her emotions.

She gazed at the drinks cabinet then picked up the phone. 'I'm in the middle of dinner,' she lied, trying to stall for time. 'Can I call you back?' She hung up and, after a steadying glass of scotch, dragged the doona from her bed and sat on the Chesterfield. She draped the doona over her knees before dialling his number.

'Dana,' he said.

She noted the absence of their pet words – sweetie, sweetheart – and followed his lead. 'Hugh.'

'How's Toowoomba?'

'Cold. I thought about lighting the fire, but I don't have any kindling. What's happening?'

'Not much. I ran into Antonia the other day when I was getting my coffee.'

The hairs on the back of her arms prickled. Antonia was his ex-wife. 'How is she?'

'Seems fine. Having a whinge about taking her father to a doctor's appointment.'

'Nothing's changed then.' Antonia had always been one to complain about the most minor of issues. 'And how's work?'

'I've started in the new office, but I'm working with Ivan and all we've done since the first day is argue.' He chuckled. 'Not a good look, being the new guys in the team.'

She'd hoped to find him contrite, apologetic for what he'd put her through, but he was speaking as though she was away on one of her work trips. She didn't know whether to be relieved or worried. Perhaps Melinda was still showing interest or perhaps he was fresh from a one-night stand, a repeat of what had happened in the early days of their relationship. She couldn't bear to ask.

'How's your job?' he said. 'Hey, you weren't involved in that murder–suicide were you? I was reading the paper this morning and saw this story about a mother from Queensland …'

'I was actually.' She had no intention of telling him she was still working with the family.

He took a deep breath. 'Jesus, Dana.'

'What?'

'What do you mean, what? I'm worried about you. You're up there alone. You don't know anyone, and some gruesome murder takes place and you're right in the middle of it.' He paused. 'What is it with this self-destructive impulse? You see danger and then you run towards it. You never used to be like that.'

Dana had a flashback to what Jimmy, the tow-truck driver, had said about the kangaroos. Dazzled by headlights and leaping into oncoming traffic.

'I'm fine,' she said. 'I was in the field with other workers, there were policemen around and I can handle myself. I'm not some delicate flower who's going to run back to Sydney at the first hint of trouble. And the idea that you'd suggest otherwise is offensive.'

'Fine, but there's no need to do a Helen Reddy.'

He launched into an out of tune rendition of 'I Am Woman Hear Me Roar' and by the end she was laughing so much that she almost forgot that things had been bad between them. This was their relationship at its best, their shared sense of humour and a history that went back years.

'How long will you be away?' he asked.

She hesitated, repositioning herself on the couch and hauling the doona back over her legs. 'I need time to process everything.'

The heaviness of all that lay unsaid returned, the question of the other woman, the death of Oscar. All the arguments they'd had over the years, back and forth, until all that was left was sorrow clawing at her heart.

After they'd said their goodbyes, she went into the study and sat down in front of the glowing computer screen. She began to shiver. The temperature had started to drop to single digits in the night-time and the Queenslander felt like a hut compared to the warm stone of her house in Sydney. She was about to rush back to the lounge room for the doona when she had a thought. The night Sandra and Debbie had disappeared they had dressed lightly. If they had planned to be in an open paddock watching a foal being born late at night, why, then, were they in thin jackets and thongs? Her fingers hammered the keys as she opened Netscape and looked up the temperature in Crows Nest the night they died.

It was freezing.

Dana had trouble sleeping that night. She dozed off in the early hours of the morning, but her mobile rang at six, shattering her slumber like an axe. She tried to will the sound away, but after a few rings she relented, rolling over and dragging the phone to her ear.

'It's Helen. Sorry to ring so early, but I've just had a call from Crisis Care, about Chrystal.'

The after-hours centre was in Brisbane and generally only contacted the Toowoomba office in an emergency. She braced herself. 'What's happened?' She switched on the bedside light and reached for her notebook.

'Chrystal didn't return to the foster carer's house last night. Carol went to pick her up from school and she wasn't there and didn't come home afterwards. To be honest, I'm a bit surprised the kids haven't been returned to Paul yet.'

'I'd been planning to drop them back,' said Dana, racking her brain for places Chrystal might have gone. 'I was just hoping to organise a youth worker to help out a few days a week. Paul hasn't been a sole carer and if the state of the house is anything to go by, he's going to need help. I'm meeting the youth worker this afternoon.'

'You might have to reschedule, because I also have a priority-one notification that's come in. A report from the day care saying that the child of ex-criminal Tony Mulhain has shown up with suspicious-looking marks on her arms.'

Dana wondered what her chances were of doing both.

'I'm not sure if you're aware of this,' said Helen, filling the silence. 'Our office has a high backlog of cases at the moment. Three hundred and fifty-one, to be exact.'

'Jesus.' Dana let out a long breath. 'I had the sense things weren't running smoothly, but three hundred—'

'Yes, well,' Helen said irritably, 'the idea when we hired you was that you'd be able to do the assessments, close as many cases as possible and hit the ground running.'

'Is that a euphemism for not having an induction?'

'Lachlan's been your induction,' Helen snapped. 'But what I'm trying to say is – you need to close the Kirby case because I've got fifty more to allocate.'

'I'm not closing it until I've visited the home and can be assured those children aren't at risk.'

'Fine.' Helen sighed. 'I'm afraid you'll have to locate Chrystal and do the assessment yourself. Lachlan's kids have the flu and Keely's down as well. One of Ian's officers can go out to the Mulhain house with you. Let me know how you get on.'

12

The windscreen was spotting with rain as Dana drove into Crows Nest. Trees on the median strip bent in the wind. She went to the school and waited outside for half an hour before checking out the local parks. Eventually, she drove back towards the centre of town where two fair-haired girls emerged from the Grand Old Crow Hotel. Dana slowed the car. One of the girls was wearing black eyeliner, white make-up, ripped stockings and a ratty jumper. With a jolt of recognition Dana realised it was Chrystal. And the other girl was her older sister, Alisha, who Dana remembered from the photograph in the paper.

She watched as the girls crossed the road in front of her car and entered the village square. Alisha, the taller of the two, was keeping stride with Chrystal, shouting and throwing her arms in the air in anger. Dana skidded into a nearby car park, got out and rushed towards them, the wind whipping her hair.

'How could you be so fucking stupid?' Alisha was screaming. 'How the fuck could you?'

Chrystal was pale, a look of shock on her face, her arms folded across her chest. The girls looked up and saw Dana at the same time. Chrystal nodded in Dana's direction then bolted behind the pub towards the supermarket.

Dana thought about chasing her, but knew the chances of catching her were minimal. Alisha shot Dana a filthy look as she got into the driver's seat of a nearby ute. It backfired before careering down the street.

Dana trudged towards her car and leant against the cool glass of the window. She reached into her handbag for her phone. 'Lachlan, it's Dana.'

'Hey.' There was a volley of coughing down the other end of the line.

'How are you?'

'Terrible.' He sniffed. 'I've got this shocking flu.'

'That sounds awful.'

'Not only that, but my eighteen-month-old and three-year-old daughters are both down with it, too.'

'Your kids are that young? How did I not know this?'

He laughed. 'You never asked.'

'Anyway,' she said, remembering why she'd called. 'I was hoping you might know where Alisha Lawrence lives? You know, Chrystal's sister?'

'Last time I spoke to her she was living in the tourist park – on the highway as you're driving in from Toowoomba. There's a windmill you can see from the road.'

'Okay, well, I hope you feel better soon. Maybe you can hire a babysitter to give you a break?'

'Fat chance.' There was a crash in the background followed by screams. 'Gotta go.'

~

The sign at the tourist park boasted luxury ensuite cabins and a sparkling swimming hole. Dana drove through the gates, past a row of corrugated-iron cabins and a tepid dam. The scene reminded her of visits she'd made to the Parramatta Caravan Park where some of her former clients were so wary of government workers, they'd run for the hills the moment she arrived.

She stopped at the last cabin and saw Alisha out the front strumming a guitar, her hair wet as though she'd just had a shower.

'What do you want?' Alisha said and placed a cigarette in her small mouth. She had delicate features, a sharp nose and porcelain skin. Her hair was parted on the side in a loose plait that hung next to her cheek. A long-ago sadness was etched into her expression. Despite this, it was a beautiful face. A face that could cause trouble without parents or family to keep an eye on her.

'I just want to talk.' Dana pulled up a plastic chair and smiled as she sank into it. 'What were you and Chrystal fighting about?'

Alisha scowled. 'None of your business.'

'Is she here?'

'God, no. As far as I know she's been staying with that foster carer lady.'

'Unfortunately, she didn't stay there last night. Do you have any idea why she decided to run away? Where she might have gone?'

'Nope.'

'I'm sorry to ask,' Dana opened her arms in a conciliatory manner, 'but I need to look around to make sure she's not here.' She was fully aware that, under the Act, Family Services officers had the authority to enter a place where a child could reasonably be in danger.

'Be my guest,' Alisha said sarcastically, waving Dana into the cabin.

Dana tiptoed across the linoleum flooring, her senses on high alert. She took in the brown curtains, tired kitchen and patterned bedspread in the corner. The walls were adorned with a black and white photograph of a group of cyclists and a painting of dogs playing pool. A glass cabinet filled with bottles of Oban whisky was by the door and, in a drawer below the kitchen sink, she found a utility bill addressed to Richard Beutel. In the second drawer she found a photo of a silver-haired man at the beach with two dogs, a woman and two teenage children.

When she was outside again, she dragged the plastic chair across the concrete to be closer to Alisha. 'Who pays the rent on this place?'

'I do.'

'Not the décor I would have expected.'

Alisha shrugged.

'You like fishing and expensive single malt whisky, do you?'

Alisha's eyes glittered with annoyance. 'Sometimes.'

Dana took another tack. 'So, before you came here, you lived in town with Sandra and her kids?'

'Uh-huh.'

'Why did you move out?'

'I wanted to.'

'But why?' Dana's patience was wearing thin.

Alisha tapped the end of her cigarette. 'I hated living there. And it's not as though I had some fairytale family to return to in New South Wales. My grandfather died and my mum was pretty much useless. Okay?'

'Okay,' said Dana, feeling like a diver needing to go deeper.

'Well, what would you say about the kids going back to Paul's?'

Alisha stared into the bushland on the other side of the road and took a long drag on her cigarette. When she met Dana's eyes her gaze was unwavering. 'I wouldn't recommend it.' She sipped her coffee. 'The house is disgusting. Paul's never figured out how to use a dishwasher and he's always working.' She paused. 'The only good thing that prick ever did for me was teach me how to shoot.'

Dana raised an eyebrow. 'Really? When was this?'

'He used to take me with him to shooting practice. You know, targets and stuff. I ended up being a pretty good shot actually.'

'I see.' Dana relaxed, relieved the shooting lessons had taken place in a controlled environment. 'Anyway, getting back to what I was saying, in all likelihood the girls will be going back to Paul's.'

'Why did you ask me about it then?' Her coffee cup made a loud clink as she banged it on the table. 'Honestly, you people are all the same. You come in and fuck things up even more.'

Dana waited for Alisha to continue. It was clear she wanted to get something off her chest.

'The police saying Debbie killed my sister. It's the dumbest thing I've ever heard. Debbie couldn't kill an ant – literally. Once, she had an ant plague at her unit and instead of spraying them she'd scoop them up on a paper towel and put them on the grass. So, for them to say she killed Sandra. It's bullshit.'

'When was the last time you saw your sister?'

'The day before she died.'

'Tell me about that.'

'It was pretty normal. I saw them at lunch. Debbie took me out to the car to show me the Power Ranger she'd bought for

Billy-Violet's birthday. She had to hide it so Billy wouldn't see.' Her face was pained. 'We had sausage rolls and then her and Debbie went into Sandra's room. I don't know what they were talking about, but they told me it wasn't for my ears.' She paused. 'It pissed me off. They used to include me in everything. But now ...' Alisha shook her head as though trying to remove the image of what had happened. 'I just wish I knew what they'd said.'

'How would you describe Sandra and Debbie's relationship?'

'You want me to say they were like' – she rolled her eyes – 'carpet lickers or whatever. They weren't. They were besties. Debbie used to come over every day and bring us treats – lollies, hot chips.' A smile passed across her face. 'We called her Aunty Debbie.'

As the high morning sun cast its light on Alisha's face, Dana was struck by how much Chrystal resembled her. She sat back and rested her arms behind her head. 'What do you do out here with your spare time?'

Alisha picked up her guitar and adjusted the tuning pegs. 'Loads of stuff. I go into town and do the shopping. Make tea for Chrystal and her friends. On the weekends a bunch of us go to the pub, to check out the live music.' She frowned as though the sum of her life sounded meagre.

Dana bit back an urge to ask whether she'd considered enrolling in Toowoomba TAFE or the Darling Downs Institute of Adult Education, knowing it wasn't the right moment.

'If you ever need anything,' she said instead, 'anything at all, feel free to give me a call.' Dana handed the girl her work card.

Alisha squinted at it. 'I can look after myself.'

Dana gathered her bag and rose to leave. 'I've no doubt you can.' She took a few steps in the direction of her car, then stopped suddenly and turned around. 'Where were you the night of the twenty-eighth of April. At midnight?'

'You don't think I had something to do with it, do you? That I killed my own sister?'

'I don't know what to believe, but I know you haven't been honest with me today.'

The girl's face turned cold as she stared at Dana, challenging her to continue.

Dana shrugged, gave her an apologetic smile and headed back to her car. She sat in the passenger seat and watched as Alisha went inside the van. Her intuition told her not to start the ignition. Not yet. Fifteen minutes passed and she was just beginning to doubt herself when a lycra-clad figure on a bike zipped past and pulled into the carport. The man from the photograph dismounted and removed his helmet revealing a crop of silver hair. *Richard Beutel.*

The sliding door opened and Alisha, teary even from a distance, wiped her eyes and fell into his embrace. He soothed her for a moment, rubbing his hand in circular motions on her back. As he glanced in Dana's direction she sank lower into her seat. Her heart hammered as he led Alisha inside.

After a quick lunch at the bakery, Dana drove to the police station so she could get someone to accompany her out to the assessment with the drug dealer's daughter.

'Your car or mine?' Connor's eyes twinkled as they stood in the car park in the drizzling rain.

She felt the weight of his gaze like a burden. Yes, she was physically attracted to him, and sometimes she found him amusing, but he was too young for her, too cocky and far too caught up in his own imagination. She'd have to do something, nip it in the bud, but just how remained unclear. He was her only link to inside information and she was curious about why the case had changed direction. At dinner he'd been sceptical, but within days had declared it a murder–suicide.

She aimed for a formal tone. 'Your car's fine, thank you.'

When she got into the passenger seat Connor adjusted the rear-view mirror and gazed over at her, grinning. 'Would you like the sirens on?'

'That won't be necessary,' she replied stiffly. 'It's hard enough bringing the police along as it is.'

'Well, you were wise to call.' His expression darkened as they headed for the centre of town. 'Tony Mulhain is a major grub. Just after I started here, he got in a pub fight where he beat the other guy to a pulp. There wasn't one inch of the victim that wasn't purple.' He stopped at the traffic lights before driving on. 'About two years ago, the old lady who lives next door to him called up in tears because she'd seen Tony beating the shit out of his ex. Apparently, he was laying into her on the driveway and the only time he stopped was to run inside for his boxing gloves because he was hurting his hands.'

They turned down a dirt road where the surrounding houses grew thin and the bushland took over.

'This new one seems more capable of holding her own, though,' he said. 'The old one never seemed to get it. It was like he'd dish it out and she'd keep coming back for more.'

Dana sighed. 'It can be very hard for women to leave violent relationships. Their partners are often controlling, cutting off finances and isolating them from friends and family.'

'Yeah, by the time he was finished with her she was so skinny she was wearing her kid's clothes.'

Dana flicked a glance at him, wondering if she could ask him what was really on her mind. 'Did the police ever make any headway confirming that a foal had been born at Debbie's aunt's farm on the night Debbie and Sandra died?'

'Yes, we confirmed with the aunt, Nancy Frecklington, that a foal was born at three in the morning and that Debbie had told Nancy earlier that evening that she and Sandra might head over there later that night. They just never made it. As well as that, both the aunt and her mum, Betty Vickers, told us that Sandra and Debbie had visited the farm in the early hours of the morning one other time when one of the mares was giving birth.'

She shook her head sadly. 'Do you ever wonder …' she trailed off, staring at the passing trees. 'Was it possible for someone, or multiple people, to force them off the road with a gun, or a promise of something, shoot them and then make their way back into town under the cover of darkness?'

'Easily. Except that thirteen kays is a long way back into town without a vehicle.'

Dana rubbed her temples. 'And what about the murder weapon? Did it have Debbie's prints on it?'

'Yeah, but that doesn't mean much – anyone could have placed her hand on the gun after she was dead.'

He slowed the car and they drove up the dusty gravel track to the isolated property. Bunya pines huddled against the dark sky beside an A-frame house. Dana noticed the lower windows boarded up and paint peeling from the timbers. As they set off across the yard, a man with a black mullet, who Dana remembered from Sandra's wake, appeared on the verandah. Tony.

'Who the fuck are you?' he said, before Dana could reach for her ID.

His powerful shoulders and black eyes reminded Dana of the Rottweiler her cousin owned. 'Hi, Tony, I'm Dana from the Department of Families. And this is Connor from the police. We—'

'Who sent you here? What do you think you're doing?' There was danger in his voice. Dana's pulse quickened as she inched across the lawn.

'If we could just come inside—'

'Not without a bloody warrant!'

'Look, mate.' Connor passed Dana and strode up the stairs. 'We don't need one. We just need to come in and go through some information we received about Amber.'

Connor flashed his badge and Tony relented, waving them through and glaring at Dana as she squeezed past him in the doorway.

Dana and Connor filed into the sparse living room where a samurai sword hung in the hallway and a rust-coloured stain, reminiscent of blood, had leached from the nail on which it hung. They sat on a couch that smelt of cigarettes and beer, a box with a half-eaten pizza on the coffee table in front of them.

'Why have you barged into my house then?' Tony addressed Connor from the cracked leather recliner opposite.

'We've received information that Amber has welts on her upper arms,' said Dana.

Tony avoided her gaze. 'That happened ages ago. She got tangled up in Chopper's lead.'

'I'm assuming Chopper's the dog?' she said. Tony nodded. Dana looked at the paperwork in front of her. 'The information here says it happened yesterday.'

'See for yourselves, then. Nenita, Amber!' he called, turning his head to the rooms behind him. 'Come out here, would ya?'

A nervous-looking two-year-old with a grubby face and her thin mother appeared and stood beside Tony.

'This is me wife,' he said, tilting his head towards Nenita, who smiled, flashing a row of braces on her teeth. Tony shoved Amber towards them. 'See? There's absolutely nothing wrong with her.'

Amber stood blinking with fright as Tony turned her by her shoulders in a full circle in front of them.

'Can I get back to my day now?'

Dana was stunned. Everything she knew about men like Tony made her feel certain he'd whipped Amber in a moment of anger. In her experience, the day care centre, a professional organisation, could usually be relied upon to provide accurate information.

'That's fine,' she said cautiously. 'But I will need to inspect the house before I go, including Amber's bedroom.'

Connor shifted in his seat then glanced out the window. He lowered his voice. 'Is that necessary?'

'Yes,' she said, annoyed. It was standard practice to review a child's bedroom and he should have known it. 'Perhaps you can take Tony outside while Nenita shows me around. Is that okay?' she asked Nenita.

An electrified look of panic skittered across Nenita's face, but she nodded. Dana followed her down the hall and into the main bedroom where Jim Beam and Hells Angels posters hung from the wall. An overflowing ashtray sat on the bedside table. Opposite there was a smaller bedroom, presumably Amber's, with a cot in the corner and a change table against the wall. Next was the bathroom.

When she opened the door, the smell hit her first. On the tiles beside a bin of soiled nappies was an ominous brown smear. Dana yanked the door shut and retraced her steps down the hall and into the lounge room.

Dana called Tony and Connor back inside and they resumed their positions in the lounge room with Nenita hovering behind Tony's recliner. The adrenaline rush she'd had when they first came had subsided and Dana found herself feeling drained when she thought about the lecture she'd need to give the parents about their lack of hygiene.

'So, at this point it would appear that the concerns about Amber having welts on her arms are unsubstantiated,' she said. 'But you need to clean up the bathroom. There are faeces on the floor and flies hovering around the food that's been left out.' She gestured to the pizza. 'Those same flies will be attracted to it and Amber is sure to get sick.'

Tony leapt up. 'Are youse saying that we're unclean?'

She gave him an icy smile. 'Those are your words, not mine. But, yes, unless you clean up, I'll be forced to call the health inspector. And I'll be back at some point to check.'

He glared at her. 'We'll see about that.'

She stood up, nodding to Connor to indicate she was ready to leave. Connor led the way through the house and out into the sunlight.

'Well, that was weird,' she said to him as they walked down the stairs.

'The complaint was probably malicious,' said Connor.

'Does he have any enemies?'

He gave her a sideways glance and hit the button on the key fob to unlock the car. 'Only half the town.'

Dana fastened her seatbelt and watched the house through the side mirror as they were driving away. She mulled over the fearful expression she'd seen on Nenita's face and wondered what had happened to the woman to make her look so terrified.

When they were back on the road, Dana called Helen and let her know the concerns about Amber Mulhain were unsubstantiated, but she still hadn't found Chrystal. After Connor dropped her back at the station, Dana decided to make one more phone call.

She dialled Paul Kirby's number. 'It's Dana from the Department of Families. Chrystal left her foster placement last night and hasn't returned. I don't suppose she's with you, is she?'

'No, she's not. I haven't seen her since the funeral.'

A weight dropped in Dana's stomach. If Chrystal wasn't with Alisha or Paul, then where the hell was she? An image rose in her mind. Sandra and Debbie lying side by side in a blood-splattered car. A murderer on the loose and Chrystal unaccounted for.

'Let me get this straight,' said Paul, his voice thick with irritation. 'You lot take my kids because you say I'm a crap parent. Then you put them and my neice with a foster carer and she ends up on the streets?'

Dana remained quiet, struggling with the truth of what he'd said.

'Must make you feel pretty powerful,' he continued, 'getting to decide who gets to keep their kids and who doesn't. How would you feel if you woke up one day and the kids you loved with all your heart weren't there anymore because I'd stolen them from you?'

'I can understand why you'd be angry, Paul,' she said, avoiding the question. 'But we can discuss your concerns in the morning when I come to do my visit.'

The leopard tree at the Kirby house had sprouted new branches since Dana's first day on the job. Dana followed Keely up the path and almost collided with her when she stopped abruptly. Keely wrenched a tissue from her pocket and spluttered into it. She put her head in her hands and sighed loudly.

'Are you sure you're okay?' Dana asked.

'I'm fine,' she said curtly.

Dana followed Keely up the stairs, wondering why she was giving her the silent treatment.

Paul was waiting to greet them on the front porch. He waved them down the hallway and into the lounge room where a photo of Sandra in her wedding dress grinned down at them. Dana looked away, staring at the shiny surfaces of the kitchen benches, the uncluttered carpet.

'The place is looking good,' she said, recalling the previous disarray.

'The school's P&C sent round a clean-up crew to help out.'

'That's nice.' She smiled at him. 'I don't suppose Chrystal's turned up?'

'She's not here,' he muttered, fiddling with a blue bandana around his wrist. 'Have you asked Alisha? She normally keeps pretty good tabs on her.'

'I have, and unfortunately she has no idea where Chrystal's been staying either.' Since starting work that morning, she'd made enquiries with the school, the church and the newsagency where

Chrystal worked. No-one had seen her. Dana was worried. It was a small town. Someone had to know where she was, didn't they?

'Have a seat.' Paul gestured to the couch opposite.

Dana opened up her notebook and jotted down the date. 'We've organised a youth worker to come to the house once a week, to help out when the girls return home and anything else you might want assistance with,' Dana said, trying not to look rattled.

'No,' said Paul, his mouth curling downwards.

'We discussed this,' she said firmly. 'A condition of the children returning was that a youth worker would visit once a week to monitor the situation.'

He shook his head. 'I've been through hell, and now you're telling me that some stranger is going to be coming in and telling me my business.' His voice was rising. 'It's not happening.'

Dana couldn't believe what she was hearing. 'I was very clear about this,' she said, exasperated. 'The youth worker will be here once a week for a few months and if everything goes well, we'll be out of your lives.'

'But I just told you,' he said. 'I don't need one! The house is clean. Chrystal's going to help with the baby. I don't want a youth worker.'

The hallway door slammed in a gust of wind and Paul startled in his chair. When he sat back in his seat he gave them a self-deprecating smile and held his palms upwards. 'I promised the girls that once they came home, things would return to normal. And when I say normal, I mean the normal we used to have – before Debbie came into our lives.'

'How's that?' Dana asked.

'She was always here.' He stood up and paced the lounge room. 'Eating our food, drinking our drinks. And now, even though she's dead and has taken my wife with her, it's like she's having the last laugh.' He walked over to the window, beckoning them to join him, and drew back the curtain. 'See that shed over there?' He pointed to a small brick building with a peaked roof. 'A couple of years ago she was going to have it turned into a granny flat. She'd even had a draftsman out to do the plans.' He let out a harsh laugh. 'Imagine how much fun that would've been!'

A cat darted into the yard and disappeared under the back fence.

'You hear what happened to our other cat, did you?'

'No.'

'Soxy used to have this lovely habit of lying in the sun on the driveway. Liked to indulge himself, he did.'

'I see.' Dana worried about where the story was going.

'So, one day, Sandra asked Debbie to nip to the shop for some milk. Well, she skidded out of the driveway and damn well flattened him. Oh, she put on an act of crying and whimpering. But it was all for show. When she thought no-one was watching she gave me this evil look, right out of her devil eyes.'

Paul was standing so close to Dana that she could smell the cigarette smoke on his shirt, the nicotine on his breath. He reached into a cabinet behind the couch and produced a framed photograph. The picture was of the two women at a party, both in black, both with heavy eyeliner, their arms around each other. He handed it to Dana.

'People used to think Debbie was this mild-mannered kindy teacher, but she wasn't. And they'd go on and on about how religious she was, all the prayer meetings she went to. But yeah, even though they were going to church all the time, Sandra and Debbie used to laugh at those people. Called them Bible bashers.'

The cat returned to the yard and stretched out on the grass, licking its paws.

'Not only that but she was into witchcraft and the occult. That's the real reason she wanted to go out that night. They'd taken their Bibles and were having a black mass. Performing all sorts of satanic rituals.'

Dana handed back the photo and stepped away. 'For god's sake, Paul, why didn't you tell the police this?'

'I didn't have to,' he said. 'Ian knew what Debbie was like. He'd known for a long time that she'd led my wife astray. Sandy was never into voodoo and disappearing all night. That was Debbie's influence, through and through.'

Dana couldn't believe what she was hearing; Paul was clearly still harbouring a great deal of anger about the death of his wife. 'So, Paul. The youth worker?' she said, feeling as though his rant had gone on long enough.

'Fine, I guess,' he relented. 'As long they're only here once a fortnight. And they give me lots of notice of when they'll be dropping by.'

'Once a week. And the visits are unannounced.'

'You drive a hard bargain.' His eyes narrowed, then creased with mirth. 'But I like that.'

'Great,' she said bluntly. 'I'll let him know your address.'

As they walked outside to the car, the weak sun on their backs, Dana turned to Keely with curiosity. 'What did you make of all that?'

Keely's eyes reflected the purity of the sky. 'Those women,' she paused, gazing back towards the house as though she might be overheard. 'They were bad.'

13

Dana and Keely drove around Crows Nest for the remainder of the afternoon searching for Chrystal. After an hour in the car, Dana realised they'd passed the school, an aged care home and a soft drink factory, and had barely seen a living soul. They were just about to update Helen when they caught sight of two figures up against the tree by the Jimmy Crow statue. Dana slowed the car.

'You don't think …' Keely said to Dana.

Dana nodded. 'It's definitely her.'

They skidded into a park and jogged over to the couple. Their display of passion was still in progress by the time Dana and Keely reached the statue.

'Sorry to break up the party,' Dana said loudly.

The couple went on kissing, their mouths mashing into each other. Chrystal slowly raised her middle finger in their direction. Dana put a hand on Chrystal's shoulder.

'Stop it you pervert,' she yelled.

Dana looked at her sternly. 'I have no desire to know anything more about your private life than I have to.' She glanced at the boy, a pimply youth with overlapping front teeth and a scowl. 'Aren't you going to introduce me to your friend?'

'Mick Richie,' the boy said, and Chrystal shot him a filthy look.

'Nice to meet you. Chrystal, can I talk to you. Alone?' She took Chrystal gently by the elbow.

Chrystal yanked her arm away. 'You can't manhandle me. I know my rights.'

An elderly man walking his dog stared at them.

'No, I can't.' Dana lowered her voice. 'But I do need to know where you're staying. You're still in the care of the Department and we have parental responsibility for you.'

Chrystal pouted. 'It's none of your business.'

'She's living with me,' Mick volunteered.

Chrystal sighed with exasperation.

'Really?' said Dana. 'Where's that?'

'At my parents' place, in a caravan my buddy Tony lent me.'

'Tony Mulhain?' Dana's heart sank.

'Yep,' he said, oblivious to Dana's dismay. 'I've got it looking real nice.'

'I see.' Dana turned slowly to Chrystal. 'You mightn't realise this, but myself and a number of the teachers from your school have been searching everywhere for you. There's a lot of people who really care for you – including me. I've been worried sick.'

Chrystal's eyes glazed over. 'Your point?'

'Well, I wanted to let you know that we've decided that you don't have to stay with Carol anymore and that you can return to Paul's. If that's what you want,' she added cautiously.

Chrystal leant against the sandstone base of the statue. For the first time Dana felt as though she had her full attention.

'I'll think about it,' said Chrystal. 'I probably won't though,' she added. 'It's been good not having people telling me what to do.'

'I'm sure it has.'

'Come on.' Chrystal gestured to Mick. 'Let's get out of here.' She grabbed his hand and they set off across the road in the direction of the supermarket.

As they walked across the square, Keely shot Dana a sideways glance. 'Well, that went well.'

'At least we can tell Helen we saw her,' Dana said, ignoring the sarcasm, 'and that she's self-placing with this Mick guy, but she knows that she can return to Paul's whenever she likes. And we'll continue to encourage her to go back to school and link her in with supports.' Dana's words sounded unconvincing, even to her own ears. The wind blew across the square and she pulled her scarf tighter around her neck as they headed for the car.

'Do you mind if I stop for a smoke?' Keely asked. 'I feel like shit.' She pulled a packet of Winfield Reds from her handbag without waiting for Dana's reply. Her eyes were red-rimmed and her face was pale.

'You look terrible,' said Dana, as they walked into the nearby rotunda and huddled on a seat inside. 'Why don't you let me give you a lift home?'

'Sure.' Keely sniffed and wiped her nose before inhaling on her cigarette and blowing a puff of smoke that was immediately whisked away by the wind.

'Where do you live?' asked Dana.

'Pechey. Country girl from way back.'

'I had no idea you were a local.'

Keely paused for a moment, gazing across the park in the same direction Chrystal had taken. 'When Chrystal was on Lachlan's caseload, I remember him telling me about how open and chatty she was. How much she loved school.'

'I'm yet to get her to really open up, but there's definitely been a change in her behaviour since Sandra's death – which is understandable.'

'I don't know if anyone has ever told you,' said Keely, 'but Crows Nest has a massive drug problem.'

'I did hear something along those lines,' said Dana.

'My best friend from high school fell in with the druggie crowd in the last six months of Year 12 and thought she was some cool skater chick.' Keely rolled her eyes. 'When I saw her two weeks ago, she said that the drug community in Crows Nest is terrified of Tony Mulhain after he drove out to some crop and chopped some dude's finger off who owed him money.' She sniffed again and tilted her head backwards as though she was trying to clear her sinuses.

The pieces of the puzzle began to come together in Dana's mind. 'Your friend didn't happen to mention where this crop was, did she?'

Keely cocked her head. 'Out the in the bush, past Rocky Creek somewhere.'

'Near where Sandra and Debbie were found murdered?'

'Possibly.'

Dana's heart beat faster. She was onto something now, she knew it. 'Do you think they might have stumbled upon a drug crop on their late-night drive and were murdered for it?'

Keely shrugged. 'Sandra was famous for having blabbergitis. If someone did kill her for finding their drugs it was probably because they knew she'd never be able to keep her mouth shut.' Keely took a final drag on her cigarette and stubbed it out with her shoe. 'If I were you, I'd tell Chrystal to get the hell away from those losers before she ends up regretting it.' She shoved her hands deep into her pockets. 'There's a reason why everyone in Crows Nest leaves Tony Mulhain and his druggie friends alone – he's an animal.'

Dana opened the car door and started the engine. She thought about her visit to Tony, his face contorted with rage when they questioned him about Amber. The way his strong jaw and cold eyes made the hairs on her neck stand on end.

Had the lethal combination of Tony's explosive temper and his drug dealing brought about the deaths of two innocent women?

14

On Friday night Dana took Angus to a local diner, George's, which had a train that circumnavigated the restaurant. Jacinta from work had said it was sure to be a hit with a ten-year-old boy and so far this had proved true. Angus was kneeling on his seat, his eyes glued to the locomotive, as he slurped a milkshake through a red and white straw.

Dana sipped her tea. 'How's your mum?' she asked tentatively. According to Susan, Angus's mother had been dropping around unannounced and asking for money.

'Okay,' he said, fixated on the train. 'I wanted her to take me to the LEGO show, but she had to go to Brisbane.'

She'd read Angus's child protection history in a quiet moment at work – an action that could have brought about immediate dismissal. But while her conscience troubled her, it was impossible to help him unless she had an idea of what he'd been through.

His was a story she'd read a thousand times over. The unsettled, drug-affected mother. The absent father. Parenting that was loving and rejecting in turn. After a stint with the paternal grandparents, his mother changed her mind and took him back. She then asked for help because of his wilful behaviour, until desperation led her to the local DOCS office. Finally, she'd said something that was bound to prompt action: that she was planning to put her methadone into his cordial – unless someone took him off her hands, which they did with expedience. Despite this, Angus was steadfast in his loyalty, running back to his mother at every opportunity. In the end, Susan got involved, shepherding him away from looming caseworkers, delivering him to the loving home that should always have been his.

Angus slurped the last of his milkshake and began arranging toothpicks in a complicated geometric pattern. 'I wrote to Professor O'Sullivan about your question,' he said.

She was bewildered. 'What question?'

'I saw your diary. You wrote: *How many Australian murder–suicides in the past twenty years have involved two women?* It must have been important. You underlined it three times.'

She stared at him.

'I checked the computer when I got home from school and Professor O'Sullivan wrote back and said *zero.* There have been no cases like that on record.'

She closed her eyes and took a deep breath. 'Angus, we've talked about this. Please, please, please don't touch my private things. I was hoping you got the message last time.'

'But you left it open and the question was right in front of me,' he said, his voice raised. 'What was I supposed to do? Unsee it? It's a bit hard, you know.'

'Okay, okay,' she said. The other customers were beginning to stare.

'I wanted to help you.' His face was sullen. 'I'm not a sneak, you know.'

She felt strangely as though he'd read her mind. 'I know,' she said slowly. 'Just make sure it doesn't happen again.' He was starting to clench his jaw.

'So, who's this professor you emailed?'

'I looked him up on the University of Melbourne website and it said, *Terence O'Sullivan is an expert in suicidology*.' He said the words precisely, as though he was quoting the sentence verbatim.

'He sounds impressive,' she said grudgingly.

'Yeah, he knows all about suicide. The signs are' – he began to tick them off on his fingers – 'depressed, no plans for doing stuff, bad mood and you can't cope with normal life like other people do.' He scratched his head. 'Something like that anyway.'

'And you just emailed him?'

He nodded. 'He answered me straight away.'

'Who did you say you were?'

'Angus Fitcher. I told him I was interested in research and that a lady I knew was a federal policewoman investigating a miscarriage of justice.' A dimple formed on his right cheek. 'I know it's bad to tell lies, but I thought he might help us if he thought you worked for the feds.'

She massaged her temples and stared at the other patrons as they gazed at their menus deciding what to order.

'What's wrong?' he asked.

'It's just that—'

'I've figured out what you need to do.'

She sighed. 'What's that?'

'You have to go back to Crows Nest and talk to Debbie's mum. She'll be able to tell you if Debbie was depressed and if she had any plans for the day after she died. And if she had plans, you'll know she's not the murderer.'

'That's all well and good,' Dana replied. 'But if that's the case, how do you suggest I catch the real killer?'

'I don't know.' He gave her an impish grin. 'You work for the feds. You'll figure it out.'

Dana strode down the sunlit corridor of the Church of Christ Nursing Home towards the Banksia Wing just as the grandfather clock was striking one. She came to a room with a sign: *Betty Vickers*. The door was ajar. Inside, an elderly woman with a soft grey perm and a brooch on her cardigan sat in a reclining chair, her head bent over a crossword puzzle. Her mouth opened with surprise when she looked up and saw Dana.

'Sorry to bother you,' Dana said, stepping closer. 'I'm the social worker for Sandra and Paul Kirby's children. I was wondering if we could have a chat?'

'Sit down, dear.' Betty gestured to the hospital bed beside her. 'I've had hardly any visitors lately. After they closed the case and all the media attention died down, it was like she never existed.' She nodded sadly towards photographs of Debbie lined up along the sideboard.

'Do you mind?' Dana asked. Betty nodded as Dana picked up a picture of kindergarten-aged Debbie smiling shyly against a backdrop of finger paintings. 'She was a beautiful child,' Dana said, as she moved on to the next photo of Debbie, this time in jodhpurs and a riding cap, sitting astride a chestnut pony.

'She was.' Betty put her crossword puzzle aside and brushed the invisible lint from her lap.

'By the looks of it, she loved horses.'

'Oh, yes. She was horse mad. When she was about ten, she'd get up at five o'clock every morning to ride that pony. Buster, his name was. She just lived for him.'

Dana examined the rest of the photos of Debbie in her youth. It was apparent this was how Betty liked to remember her daughter – in her innocence, before the ravages of adolescence had set in.

At the end of the cabinet was a large blue bottle of Harveys Bristol Cream, surrounded by four crystal glasses.

'My nan used to love sherry,' Dana said wistfully. 'When I was little she'd let me stay up late and have a sip of hers while we watched TV.'

'Fancy one now?' Betty gave Dana a sly smile, then hesitated. 'You're probably not allowed, seeing as you're working.'

Dana smiled back. 'I've never been afraid to bend the rules.'

Betty struggled to get out of her chair.

'I'll get them,' Dana said, quickly pouring shots of the liquid into two glasses. She handed one to Betty and took a sip of the sherry. It was both sweet and tart. She was about to ask about Debbie's childhood when a woman with her hair pulled back in a scrunchie came in.

She stopped abruptly, staring at the bottle. 'What's going on here?' she asked in a clipped New Zealand accent.

Dana leapt from her chair. 'I'm Dana Gibson. We were just having a little chat.'

The woman stood with her hands on her hips, a look of disbelief on her face. 'Has this been authorised?'

'I spoke with a lady in your office who told me it would be fine.' Dana checked her watch. She'd told Connor to meet her here at one o'clock just in case she ran into any problems. *Where was he?*

'Well, I've not heard about it, so you'll have to come to the office so I can verify that.'

'For god's sake, Merryn.' Betty banged her glass down on the side table. 'We were just having a friendly chat – which is more than you lot provide. I've been sitting here for the last two hours and I haven't seen another person all morning. It's almost half past one and I haven't even had lunch yet.'

The worker ignored Betty and examined Dana more closely. 'How am I supposed to know that you're not another one of those media tarts?'

Betty straightened in her chair. 'Don't be ridiculous, she's one of Norma's kids.' She looked at Dana, nodding her head encouragingly. There was a clarity in her eyes, which Dana hadn't noticed before. 'How is she these days?'

'Oh, she's great,' Dana said, not missing a beat.

'I suppose it's fine,' the carer said reluctantly. She filled a tea cup with water and splashed it onto a single mauve orchid by the sink. She made a mess of it and wiped the excess dirt and water up with a rag. 'You wouldn't believe it, but ever since the murders the media people have been hanging around the place like flies. And the *Sixty Minutes* woman was the worst one of all.'

'I can imagine,' Dana said, the old jealousy flaring inside her. There was a story here and her old high school friend, Isabell, knew it as well as she did. 'I know Betty's been through a hard time. That's why it would mean a lot to me if I could take her to the café down the road. Get her some nice sandwiches and tea.'

'It's not possible, I'm afraid. We've been given strict

instructions that no-one's to take Betty off the premises. Only family members.'

'But she is family,' Betty piped up. 'She's one of cousin Norma's kids. Second cousins. That's what you call them.'

The carer's eyes narrowed, looking Dana up and down.

Dana suddenly noticed that Connor was standing in the doorway. She had no idea how long he'd been there. His smile was in full wattage as he strode into the room.

'Sorry I'm late. Got caught up trying to arrest a drug dealer. He told me he was growing marijuana for medicinal purposes. Can you believe it?' He ran his hands through his hair. 'Anyway, I'm here on official police business. I need to wrap up a few matters on the murder investigation.' He flashed the woman his police badge. 'I can accompany them into town.'

'Fine, then.' Merryn shook her head. 'I'll go get the forms you'll need to fill out and a wheelchair for Betty.'

After she'd closed the door behind her, Connor leant towards Dana. 'Christ, woman. You let Betty say you were a family member? You're completely ruthless.'

'She was never going to let me—'

'Don't apologise.' He laughed flirtatiously. 'I love it.'

Dana turned her attention back to Betty, who looked over at them, removed her glasses and rubbed her watery eyes.

'Every day since it happened, I've been praying he'd send someone like you.' Betty smiled sweetly at Dana, then noted Connor's baffled expression. 'Don't worry, I know she's not Norma's kid. I just made that up so they'd give me the chance to speak to someone. I knew who you were, the minute I saw you,' she said to Connor. 'You're one of the policemen who handled the case. Am I right?'

'Yep,' he said.

'And you've come to tell me there's been a mistake?'

'Not likely.' He shot Dana a look of annoyance.

Dana bent down to Betty's level and took her hand. 'I'd like to hear your side of the story.'

They pushed Betty in the wheelchair down the street to the Raven's Roost. The café had a rusted corrugated-iron awning and was perched between Wigget's Plumbing and a travel agent. They placed their orders for scones and tea, which were brought to the table by a clearly bored teenager.

'What happened in the lead up' – Dana stumbled, searching for the least brutal words – 'to your daughter passing away?'

Betty took a sip from her steaming cup of tea and set it down, her hand trembling. 'On the night Debbie was killed we had dinner at her place with my brother, Arthur. She made a lamb roast and she was completely normal. One thing about Debbie was I always knew when she had something on her mind.'

'How did you know?' Dana asked.

'How did I know? Because she bloody well told me. Debbie was quiet with strangers, but once she got to know you, she'd tell you anything and everything. And a whole lot more than you asked for.' Betty blinked, wiping away sudden angry tears. 'She told us that the next morning she had to get up at five o'clock to finish a scrapbook for work. And then she was driving to Toowoomba for some sort of health and safety training. She said she was looking forward to it because her work was paying for them to have lunch at The Spotted Cow. She was always a big one for food, my Debbie. She loved to eat, but she was always trying to lose weight, too. Once she joined this belly dancing group and I thought to myself – maybe she'll jiggle that fat off her.'

Connor looked at Dana with a smirk and she booted him under the table. She thought about what Professor O'Sullivan had said about people with suicidal ideation losing interest in their favourite things and having no plans for the future, and found it hard to reconcile with Betty's description of Debbie.

'What was Debbie's childhood like?' Dana asked, sneaking a glance at Connor, who had stopped listening to the conversation and was gazing out the window.

'I'd say it was happy, right up until the point where her father died in a car crash.' Betty reached into her bag for a handkerchief and began to dab at the stream of tears running down her face. 'She was only twelve. It was hard for her. She'd become very introverted, would go into her room for days on end and only come out when I forced her to.'

'What did she do in her room?' Dana asked.

'She wrote in her journal.'

'She kept a journal?' Dana leant forward.

'Yes,' said Betty. 'She was meticulous about it. Ever since she was a kid, she'd write down the cost of things and how much she'd spent at each shop. She was always thinking about money. One day she wanted to own a big house.'

'Did she still keep a journal as an adult?'

'She had a hiding place. A compartment under her desk at the back. Her brother, Martin, read her diary once when she was a kid and, my word, didn't I have a fight on my hands. She never left it lying around after that.' Betty picked at the chequered tablecloth with her weathered fingers. 'I tried to escape the nursing home and go and get it myself.' She frowned. 'I would have made it, too, except the head nurse caught me trying to jump the fence.'

Connor and Dana looked at one another, each trying to suppress a smile.

'There was no diary,' Connor said, swiping a large dollop of cream onto his scone and taking a bite. 'We searched Debbie's flat for evidence with a fine toothcomb.'

Betty began to weep. 'I'm sorry. It's just that every idea I have to prove my Deborah wasn't a murderer comes to nothing.' She took deep breaths to steady herself. 'And for anyone to think that Debbie killed Sandra then shot herself. It's madness.' She sniffed. 'She loved Sandra and her girls. And she finally had so much to look forward to after all these years.'

'What do you mean – after all these years?' Dana asked, as Connor excused himself to go to the toilet.

'Debbie had a long history of befriending couples, making' – she hesitated – 'a nuisance of herself. She wanted some children and a family of her own, but she didn't seem to know how to go about it. Instead, she'd go to all these church events and become friendly with the couples. And then she'd go too far. People got sick of her. But just lately, all that was starting to change. She'd met someone. Rocco, his name was.'

Dana frowned. 'And did you meet this Rocco?'

'Not really. She pointed him out once, as we were leaving church, and told me he was the one.'

'And did you ever see him at church again?'

'No. They only met about two weeks before she died. After that I wasn't allowed to go anymore. I couldn't take two steps out of the nursing home or the news people would come at me. Like vultures, they were.'

'So, this man,' Dana said. 'Did you know anything else about him? Where he lived or worked?'

'No, I didn't make too much of it. I told her I'd wait for her to introduce us. You know' – Betty's eyes slid away from Dana's, then back to her, begging her to understand – 'to make sure it was real.'

'Do the police know about this?' Dana asked Connor as he returned to their table. 'That Debbie had recently started a relationship?'

'Not that I'm aware of.' He shrugged his shoulders, dismissively.

She looked at him, incredulous. 'Just that it seems incongruous for a woman who wants to kill herself?'

'To be fair, Debbie was known for being a bit of a liar. And do I need to point out—'

In that moment Betty's head dropped to her chest and she began to sob. She covered her eyes with her hands. Eventually, she looked up. 'I always knew Debbie was a liar, but she didn't mean it. She just couldn't help herself. But for you to say she was capable of cold-blooded murder. It's not …' She choked and only just got out the word. 'It's not … possible.'

'Okay, Mrs Vickers.' Dana signalled the waitress for the cheque. 'I'm so sorry we've upset you. I really think we should be getting you home.'

Betty wiped her eyes and glanced at Connor. 'I know you've made up your mind, but please,' she said, turning her attention to Dana. 'Try to find that diary for me. If you can just tell me you'll do that, maybe I can start sleeping again at night.'

'I will,' said Dana, knowing full well she'd counselled her workmates on the folly of making promises they couldn't keep.

The sky began to look ominous after they dropped Betty home. Dana and Connor stood outside the nursing home beside a row of shrunken pines as Dana searched through her handbag for her keys. 'Could you have been any more insensitive back there?' she asked, the wire in her veins coiling tight.

'I'm not sure what you're playing at, trying to give hope to a woman whose daughter's a proven killer. Dragging me out here when the case has already been solved. If anyone saw me, my arse is grass.'

'Well, clearly it hasn't occurred to you, but the more I look into this the more I'm convinced the police made an absolute balls-up.'

'Bullshit,' he said angrily. 'What I don't understand is, why are you even interested? The case is shut. *Closed.*' He put his hands on his hips. 'Are you just trying to prove how smart you are? Because, newsflash' – he gesticulated wildly – 'I don't like you for your brains.'

'And, newsflash' – her fingers tingled with rage – 'there's no way I'll be going out with you again after your abhorrent, insensitive behaviour.'

'Get stuffed.' His eyes glazed with disgust. 'Once again, you got what you came for and I've ended up with nothing.' He stalked away into the black afternoon as the bell clanged from the nearby school.

Dana was relieved she'd restrained herself from slapping him, but as the first drops of rain sank into the pavement, so too did her chances of finding the diary.

At home, she went straight to the study, where the screensaver of her computer glowed brightly. In the desk drawers she found a sheet of white cardboard and a pair of Susan's dressmaker shears, which she used to cut a perfect square. On it, she wrote one word: *Rocco?*

She stood back, her mind working overtime as she pinned it to her makeshift evidence board. It was an unusual name, perhaps too fanciful to be real. Debbie had a proclivity for lies and exaggeration. Surely Rocco was another of the men in Debbie's life with whom she'd had little contact or made up. But what if he wasn't?

She opened the desk drawer to return the scissors when she noticed Isabell's business card underneath the invitation to her high school reunion. She'd been asked to give the opening speech, but hadn't responded yet.

Isabell's face was larger than life next to the *Sixty Minutes* logo, with her helmet hair and a smile that never reached her eyes. Dana cringed when she remembered their meeting in the mall. Isabell had beaten her to the punch and had already done the groundwork on the Kirby–Vickers case. But what if she checked in on her old friend when she made the trip back to Sydney?

15

Winter was in the air and it was getting colder by the day. Leaves dropped from trees and the branches were getting bare. A lone pigeon shivered on a telephone wire, its feathers ruffled by the wind. Dana walked with Angus through the car park to the indoor swimming pool. She'd offered to take him to his swimming lesson to give Susan the day off, and was hoping to get get some laps in for herself.

Over a month had passed since she'd crashed her car on the highway and she was now almost halfway through her contract. Soon her time in Queensland would be over.

She made herself comfortable in the grandstand as the children lined up along the edge of the pool. The thick smell of chlorine rose from the water. Angus smiled up at her from the concrete below, a thin freckled boy among his peers. She was glad she'd decided to go back to Sydney. It was high time she confronted her demons and made a decision about whether she and Hugh had a future together.

Angus held his hands above his head, ramrod straight, and checked to see if she was looking before he dived into the steaming water. She applauded as he surfaced and he returned her gaze with a coy smile. His face beamed with angelic light and she smiled at him, realising that over these past few weeks he'd somehow managed to wheedle his way into her heart.

After she'd watched him for a few minutes, she headed for the change rooms and then to the lap-swimming lane. She pulled on her goggles and swam freestyle up the twenty-five-metre pool. Down below, the water was calm and silent, the stresses of the outside world forgotten. By the time she'd finished ten laps she was buzzing with endorphins. She pulled herself up the silver ladder at the shallow end where she saw Paul Kirby giving Billy-Violet a piggyback ride.

'Paul,' she said, surprised. 'What brings you here?' She bridged the awkwardness of appearing in her speedos by lunging for a towel and tying it around her waist.

'Bringing Billy for a swim. I didn't have to work this morning so I thought, why not?'

His beard had grown since she'd seen him last and there was something unsavoury about the coarse hairs that curled around his chin.

Billy let go of Paul's back and went headfirst under the water. She resurfaced with a toothy grin. 'Hey, Dana,' she said.

'Hi, Billy.' Dana looked across to Angus in his swimming lesson, then back to Paul. 'Long way to come for a swim, isn't it?'

'Crows Nest's pool is terrible,' he said. 'It's basically impossible to swim at this time of year because it's freezing.' He smiled at her. 'You look a million bucks in that swimsuit. Do you work out here often?'

'Not especially,' she said, trying not to cringe. 'How's Chrystal?'

'She's fine – and I've got the neighbour looking after Rubi this morning just in case you were wondering.'

'Okay, well, I'd better let you get back to it.' She waved at Billy. 'See you soon.'

As Dana passed the wading pool on the way to the change rooms she saw Helen was heralding two fair-skinned toddlers from the water.

'Wow, this really is the place to be on a Saturday morning.' Dana nodded to the girls by Helen's side. 'I didn't realise you had kids.'

'These are my sister's daughters, Jessica and Ashley. I bring them every Saturday to get them out of their mother's hair.'

'That's very kind of you.'

'It's good for me, too. Sometimes in our job we need a reminder of why we do this work.' A look of amusement passed over her face. 'We've never really had a chance to check in on your progress since you started, have we?'

'That's true,' said Dana. Her pulse increased. She wondered what she'd be in trouble for this time.

'Well, what do you say we have a catch-up before work on Monday? Say, seven-thirty?'

'Sounds good,' said Dana, summoning a smile.

Helen wrapped a multicoloured beach towel around herself and said her goodbyes.

When they were back in the car, Dana put the keys in the ignition and turned to Angus. He was banging his ear, trying to remove the water lodged inside. 'What do you feel like doing for the rest of the day? Your nan's not back from her sewing group till late this afternoon.'

He wiped his hand across the side window to clear the condensation. 'I keep thinking we're missing something.'

'Like what?'

'In the murder mysteries, people always go and look at the old files to see if they can discover something from the past. Can't we look at some old stuff, too?'

'Look, you shouldn't be thinking about that. Leave it to me. I suppose I could request the archives on the family from when they lived in New South Wales.' She looked at him, thinking about how sweet he looked with his tousled blond hair. 'Anyway, you still haven't answered me. What do you want to do this afternoon?'

'I think we should drive out to Crows Nest and find Debbie's boyfriend. The guy you told me about that no-one's ever met.'

'Rocco?'

He nodded.

'And how do you suggest we do that?'

'We start by talking to the minister of the church. I saw a picture in the newspaper of him at Sandra's funeral. I reckon he'd have to know just about everyone in town.'

She glanced at him sideways. 'You're a kid. You shouldn't be be involved in all this. Also, he might not be at the church. He might not be working today. We might drive all that way and not even get to talk to him.'

'That's okay. If he's not there we can drive to Crows Nest Falls and you can help me find some birds I've been reading about.'

'Seeing that we drove all this way, I may as well just quickly pop in and see Chrystal, while we're here,' said Dana, pulling up outside the newsagency. 'I know she works every weekend, so I think it's a fair bet that's where we'll find her.'

'Good idea,' said Angus, as she turned off the engine.

'Will you be alright to stay here?' she asked him.

'I've got the street directory,' he said holding it up. 'I'll find the quickest way to the church.'

'You really are thinking ahead.'

He smiled. 'I know.'

She strode into the newsagency to where a woman with black hair and a white stripe down her part line was standing behind the counter snapping rubber bands around notes and separating them into the till.

'Is Chrystal around?

'She's just on a break. Out the back.' The woman gestured behind her shoulder and then suddenly stopped counting and gave Dana a dark look. 'You're not with the media, are you?'

'No,' Dana said, wondering whether she should keep Chrystal's status as a child in care confidential, before deciding her boss would surely already know. 'Her caseworker.'

The woman appeared satisfied with Dana's response and returned to counting her money.

In the car park out the back, Chrystal was sitting on an overturned crate, smoking. She eyed Dana warily before smoothing her blue work dress over her knees. 'Hey,' she said.

'How's things?' Dana dragged another crate over and leant back against the brick wall.

'I've got to go back inside soon,' said Chrystal.

'No worries,' said Dana. 'I was out this way so I thought we could have a quick catch-up … I've been worried about you.'

Chrystal shrugged. 'Yeah, you and everyone else.'

'I don't really understand what's been going on. You seemed so keen to get back to living with Paul and then the next minute you're running away to Mick's?'

'I don't know.' Her bird-like shoulders slumped as she kicked at the gravel at her feet. 'Mick seemed so nice to start with and we were going to take the caravan to the Gold Coast and hang out at the beach for a few weeks. But then everyone, including Tony, started dropping round at all hours and from that point on everything became about selling pot.'

'Maybe next time try not to shack up with the local drug dealer's friend?'

Chrystal's face held the hint of a smile. 'Yeah.' She took a drag of her cigarette. 'Anyway, now I'm back at Paul's things aren't that great either. He keeps expecting me to do all this stuff. Clean the house, get up at night to feed Rubi, shop for food. But not just do it … like, he wants it all done perfectly. He starts pecking me, like this giant hen – the kitchen stuff goes in the kitchen, the toilet paper goes this way … I just want to be a kid again.'

'Look, I can talk to Paul, if you'd like? Tell him you're taking on too much responsibility.'

'No,' Chrystal said quickly. 'Anyway, it's fine. I think I gave him a real shock when I had a huge tantrum about it the other morning. He's much better now.'

'Well, let me know if that changes.'

'Chrystal!' said the owner, popping her head out the back door. 'Break's over. Get your butt inside.'

Chrystal jumped up and stubbed her cigarette out in the dirt with her foot.

'I'll talk to you again soon,' said Dana.

Chrystal gave Dana a dubious look but nodded. She seemed sad and Dana felt the urge to hug her. Instead, she settled on rubbing her arm in what she hoped was a bolstering way.

When Dana returned to the front of the newsagency Angus was still waiting in the car. 'Can we go to the church now?' he asked.

'Sure thing,' she said, still thinking about Chrystal and the lost expression on her face.

The church was a pentagonal-shaped building in the centre of town beside a hall that was inscribed with the words: *Jesus Born For You*. As they got closer to the hall, they could hear yelling from inside and were taken by surprise when two boys burst through the front door, pushed past Angus and leapt over the gate.

The minister, who Dana recognised from Sandra's funeral, came charging out after them as they sprinted down the street.

'Next time you steal the collection money,' he shouted, 'try taking it out of the tin.'

He turned back to Angus and Dana. 'Sorry about that,' he said. 'I've been having some problems of the teenage variety.' He paused, looking up the road in the direction the boys had disappeared. 'I'm William, by the way. How can I help you?'

Dana hesitated. The ruckus had thrown her off guard and now she struggled to decide the best way to approach the situation.

'I wanted to talk to you about a woman I knew, Debbie Vickers. And what happened to her,' Dana said.

'Oh, no, no, no.' He held up his hand. 'The only person I spoke to about that was from the police and that is the only time I intend to talk about it.'

'But I'm worried—'

'No,' he said.

Angus managed to jam his small arm between the door and its frame as the minister tried to push it closed. The minister had no choice but to open it.

'I want to get baptised,' Angus insisted.

'Really?' The minister's eyebrows shot up.

Dana tried to hide her shock.

'Why, may I ask, do you want to get baptised?'

Angus gave him the benefit of his big brown eyes. 'It would make my nan happy.'

The minister still looked dubious. She had to give Angus credit. He'd clearly anticipated the scenario and given it far more thought than she had.

'She wants me to be good and, if I did it, it would show her I've changed.'

'And would it make you happy?'

'I think so.' Angus nodded slowly. 'I'd like to get some information or something. So I can think about it.'

'I'm sure I've got a brochure in the office somewhere. Why don't you follow me and I'll get it for you?'

Angus winked at Dana as they followed the minister past rows of pews and went through a door beside the altar. Inside was a small office with a desk in the corner, overflowing with loose papers. The minister took a seat and gestured for them to sit in the two chairs opposite.

'What's your name, young man?' he asked, as he opened his desk drawer and started rifling through it.

'Angus. Angus Fitcher.'

'And is this your mother?'

Angus laughed nervously. 'No. This is Dana. She works for

the Department of Families, helping kids to be safe. She knows Sandra Kirby's kids and she's worried about them because she doesn't think Debbie did it and the murderer's still out there.'

The minister looked over at them. 'Well, I'm sorry I can't help you with that.'

Dana drummed her fingers on her knee. 'Well, can you tell me if the name Rocco rings any bells for you. Whether he's a member of the church?'

'No, definitely not. I'd remember a name like that.'

Why, then, had Debbie told her mother that he was the love of her life? The answer reverberated deep in Dana's bones. *To shut her up.* How many times had her own mother asked if there was anyone special in her life? If she was going out on Friday night. Whether there were any nice men at work.

'Look, from everything I know about Debbie,' she said, 'I don't think she did it. And if you knew her as well as her mother Betty says you did, I don't think you'd believe she was a murderer either.'

He removed his glasses and rubbed his eyes as Dana continued. 'I'm not asking you to disclose what they told you in confession. I'm just asking about what was happening with the family before the women died. General observations.'

'You have no idea what kind of trouble I'll be in if anyone finds out I've been talking to you. I'm supposed to be above reproach.'

'Surely any kind of just God could not abide the travesty that's been committed against this woman. And her mother, Betty Vickers, attends your sermons every Sunday. I know because I saw the St Thomas's notepad in her room. It says, *You matter to God.* Did Debbie matter to God? Did she, Minister?'

He crossed his legs and stared out the window. 'If you ever

feel like a change of career you could do worse than becoming a minister. We're welcoming women into the fold these days.'

Dana stared at him. He still hadn't answered her question.

'Alright, alright. General observations. Well, one thing that stood out was that Sandra and her family started coming to church more often.'

'How often?'

'They suddenly started attending at every opportunity. Sunday services, midweek prayer meetings, garage sales, kids' club, you name it they were here.' He stroked his beard. 'It was strange. Prior to that, I would have only described them as E and C Christians.'

'E and C?' Dana frowned.

William looked sheepish. 'That's church terminology for people who only come at Easter and Christmas.'

Dana laughed. 'You made a joke.'

His eyes were full of mirth. 'We Christians do that sometimes.'

She leant closer. 'So, what do you think brought on their sudden interest in religion?'

'You know, I pondered it for a long time and it didn't occur to me until one day when I saw the youngest daughter – what's her name. Billy-Joe? Billy-Bob?'

'Billy-Violet?'

'That's the one. Anyway, the minute the Sunday service ended at ten o'clock, she raced into the hall to the refreshments table and started piling her plate with sandwiches and cakes and wolfing them down. It was like the poor child hadn't eaten in a week. And then it finally occurred to me. The reason that they'd been coming to church so often was that we put food on at most of our events. And they were broke. Literally starving.'

'I don't get it. Paul has a good business with the air conditioners and Sandra could have gone back to hairdressing. They had enough money – at least to feed themselves.' Dana looked at him quizzically. 'What went wrong?'

'I think it might've had something to do with the new house.'

'The house?'

'Yes, the one they bought at Chestnut Drive and were planning on moving into.'

Dana had a flashback of Paul reversing out of his driveway on his way to see the builder the very first day they'd met.

'What makes you think that?'

'Just a comment he made after I'd given a sermon on John 14:2.'

She was confused. She'd attended Mass as a child, but since then she'd become a lapsed Catholic.

William smiled at her kindly. 'The one about, *In my Father's house are many rooms.* When I spoke to him at the end of the service and asked him what he'd thought, he said, "My house also has many rooms, but they're fucked." He had to apologise to me for swearing.'

Dana's pulse quickened. She reached for her handbag and stood up. 'Thanks, Minister. You've been an enormous help.'

He rose from his seat and smiled at her. 'Please come and see me again if you'd like to talk about Jesus.'

She beamed back at him. 'I will.'

Angus jogged down the pathway behind her, trying to keep up. 'Are we going to see it?' he said.

'Yes, it's a good idea to corroborate any information people give you,' she said, as they hurried through the church gate. 'Besides, I think it could be a clue.'

She handed Angus the street directory when they got back to the car. Five minutes later they were at Chestnut Drive.

They stood on a strip of grass in front of a house in a new residential development. A red and blue tarp stretched across the front patio gave it the unsettling air of a circus tent. A sign had been staked into the lawn: *Dangerous, KEEP OUT.*

'I think you should have brought your jumper,' she said to Angus. The wind stung her eyes. She drew her scarf across her chest. 'The first day I went to visit Sandra I asked her how things were going financially. She told me how amazing the house was going to be. She never mentioned this.'

A shadow passed over his face. 'Back when we lived in Brisbane, Mum never had any money for my lunch and stuff, but she said that I could never ever tell anyone – I had to say that I'd lost my tuckshop money or I'd already eaten. I asked Nan about it and she said Mum was probably embarrassed.'

'So, that's it. You think they were ashamed?'

He shrugged. 'Maybe.'

As they walked back to the car, Dana wondered whether the trip to Crows Nest had been worth it. They knew that Sandra's family was under financial strain when the women died and that Rocco might not have existed. But had it brought them closer to the truth? It seemed like she now had more questions than answers.

When they arrived home, Angus headed straight for the study.

'I'm just writing the email for you to send the interstate person when you're at work tomorrow,' he yelled out. She heard the sound of the computer booting up.

A smile formed at the corner of her lips. She opened the

lounge-room blind and watched the mock orange tree sway in the breeze outside. 'You do like a good email, don't you?'

His fingers raced across the keys, logging in with her password, opening her emails and typing *DRAFT* in the subject line. 'Dear Interstate Liaison Officer.' He screwed up his nose. 'Does that sound good?'

'Sure,' she humoured him.

'What should I say?'

'I'll type in the names and dates of birth for the children later, but just say something like:

I'm the caseworker for the Lawrence family and would like to request the hard copy files for the family from 1980 until Alisha and Chrystal moved to Queensland in 1994. It's my understanding that the family lived in the Blacktown area during this period. Please contact me if you require any further information in relation to this matter.

Kind regards,
Dana Gibson
Department of Families

Dana sat on the single bed next to the computer and read over what he'd written. Two lines formed between her eyebrows when she reached her signature block. 'I should probably get my manager's approval before I go around emailing other states for files.'

He saved the message to her drafts folder. 'You could just say you didn't know the protocol and that when you worked in New South Wales you used to request files all the time.'

'I'm hardly going to lie, Angus. You'd really make a great

private investigator though,' she said, another smile curling at the corner of her lips. She paused, her expression suddenly serious. 'I've been meaning to mention this – but I have to go back to Sydney next weekend.'

He crossed his arms and stared at the carpet. 'Will you be coming back?' he asked softly.

'Of course,' she exclaimed, moving closer. 'It's just for a few days. I'll be home before you know it.'

'Okay,' he said, his gaze returning to the computer screen.

He was quiet that night as they watched *Seinfeld* and at eight o'clock he said a hurried goodbye before tearing down the hallway and slamming the door behind him.

16

Dana trudged into the office at twenty-five past seven on Monday, relieved to find the security alarm had already been switched off and the building lights had been turned on. She resented the fact that she'd missed her morning coffee, but knew the folly of caffeine before a stressful meeting.

The door was open. Helen was unwinding her scarf and hanging it on the coat rack. 'Have a seat,' she said, gesturing at the couch by the window. 'Tea or coffee?' Helen asked, heading for the kettle that sat on a bench in the corner. 'I'm having one.'

'Tea, thanks,' she replied. Maybe she was just here for a heart to heart, there wasn't going to be a staunch interrogation. At least, not yet.

'So, how are you finding everything?' Helen asked. It was the social work equivalent of *How are you feeling, within yourself?* The question Dana had been asked endlessly since Oscar's death.

'I'm good. I've settled into my house and I'm getting to know the neighbours.'

'That's nice.' Helen reached for an old-fashioned silver bowl and scooped a spoonful of sugar into her cup, stirring with concentration. 'What's been happening with the Kirby file? I would've imagined you'd have closed it now the case has been solved.'

'I will,' she said, relieved the conversation had turned to work. 'The youth worker's been out and hasn't noticed anything untowards. He said that Chrystal's doing more than her fair share of housework and caring for the baby more than she should, but I was planning to talk to Paul about that.'

'So, you'd say that, essentially, it's as good as closed?'

'Essentially.'

Helen brushed her fringe from her eyes and leant in closer. 'So, it's not closed.'

'I just think it's pertinent to keep it open for a few more weeks. So I can keep an eye on things and make sure Chrystal stays at school.'

Helen sat back in her chair. 'What I don't understand, Dana, is why you have such a fixation with this case?'

Dana had a sense of déjà vu, as though the conversation she'd had with Hugh was taking place all over again. She looked into Helen's open face. 'Honestly?'

Helen nodded.

'I don't think those kids are safe. And I don't believe Debbie was any more likely to have murdered someone than …' She swept her hands in the air as she searched for an example. 'Rubin Carter.'

'Well, it's all well and good that you believe there was a miscarriage of justice, but a coroner signed off on the case, so it's impossible for me to go against that. Even if what you're saying is true, if Debbie didn't do it and the murderer is still on the loose, why are those children at any more risk than any other child in the community?'

It was a good question, one Dana couldn't answer, except to voice her intuition that something was wrong.

Helen stared at Dana from under her eyebrows, an earnest, pained expression. 'Look, I don't want to ask you this, but I have no choice, I have a duty of care. Is the reason you're so wedded to this case because of the baby? Is there some misguided attachment?'

'No.'

'Good,' Helen said. 'Because now you can shut it and I can allocate you five new cases.'

'There's just one more lead I need to look into, before I can do that.'

'What's that?'

'There's a man. Richard Beutel. He has Alisha holed up in his cabin. He pays the rent and has a wife and children at home. Don't you think that's strange?'

Helen's eyes flashed with anger. 'Why have you, an experienced practitioner, allowed yourself to be led astray by small-town gossip. You should leave it alone. Richard's a good teacher. I will not have you dragging his name through the mud.' She flicked her fringe again. 'I notice you've put in for leave to go to Sydney on Friday?'

Dana nodded.

'Well, I think you need to consider your future while you're away. Decide whether you want to finish your placement with us, or whether you're too distracted by whatever's going on in your personal life.'

Dana's cheeks were burning as she trudged back to her desk. Why on earth was Helen so against her speaking to Richard?

She did her best to concentrate on her other cases, but by half past eleven she'd had enough. She gathered her case files and shoved them into her briefcase. She took the lift to the ground floor, the meeting with Helen still grating on her. Why was Helen so eager for her to close the case? There were alliances in this town she knew nothing about, a lack of context that gave her a huge disadvantage in figuring out what had gone on that fateful night in April.

She was deep in thought as she went through the glass doors and out to the Bell Street Mall to get an early lunch. When she looked up, Paul Kirby was walking in step beside her.

'Hard day?' His expression was sympathetic.

She grimaced. 'How can you tell?'

She recalled seeing him at the pool on Saturday and feared that Lachlan had been right. Paul was interested in her and now she was seeing him everywhere. She sighed inwardly, wishing the extra complication would disappear. He wore a white collared shirt and his thinning hair was combed back, as if he was on his way somewhere important.

'What brings you to Toowoomba?' she asked.

'Just in town to pay a few bills, pick up my tax return.'

'Sounds like an exciting day then.'

'Not really,' he said in his thick Scottish accent. He grinned, revealing a silver tooth in his upper gum. 'What do you say we walk up to the Shamrock and I'll buy you a drink? We could have a counter meal, shoot the breeze.'

'I can't,' she said, marvelling at how her day was going from bad to worse. A miniature whirlwind gathered up the leaves and dust from the pavers and sent them spinning around their feet.

'What, not good enough for you?' he said in mock outrage. 'Oh, I get it. You'd rather go somewhere fancy. Gipps restaurant or Weiss's on the range. We can go there if you want?' He was still smiling.

'It's not that.' She paused. 'It's just that, I don't date clients.' She stopped at the intersection at the top of the mall, waiting for the lights to change.

'C'mon, Dana. Just a quick drink. You might enjoy yourself.'

'Sorry, Paul. The answer's no.'

'No worries.' He smashed the pedestrian button multiple times with his fist, making her jump. When she looked over at him, she realised his eyes were glassy and she wondered if he'd descended into the drug use Lachlan had mentioned, now that he was mourning a dead wife and caring for three children. 'Enjoy your lunch.' He spat out the words as though he was not used to having his advances rejected.

The lights changed and he crossed the road.

The next few days passed in a blur of activity as Helen delivered on her promise to hand over five new cases. On Thursday evening, the night before Dana was heading for Sydney, she fell into a haze of scattered dreams. Dreams that turned into nightmares where she had to defend herself and Angus against a dangerous assailant, where she was racing through the park under a blood red moon, screaming his name.

She was just coming to from the lastest nightmare when the window exploded with a smash and she woke up. She got out of bed, grabbed her dressing-gown around her and switched on the bedroom light. Shards of glass glittered on the carpet. A brick was by the dresser. The roar in her ears grew louder as she tiptoed to the broken window, her back against the wall. She drew back a curtain and peered into the yard.

The garden, bathed in streetlight, was still. She considered rushing to the kitchen for a knife, though deep down she knew it would only make things worse. She crept along the hallway to the other end of the house. As she looked out the kitchen window, she caught sight of the back gate closing.

Her skin prickled. Why was someone trying to scare her in the middle of the night? Possibilities rushed through her mind. The interview with Betty? The investigation of a wrapped-up case? Visiting a crime scene without authority? Or more likely, rejecting a man who wasn't used to people saying no?

When she returned to her room her hands were shaking. She called the police, but was told they were unlikely to send someone out until morning. How could she have forgotten that one of the enduring benefits of marriage was never being alone at night? She hauled a chest of drawers over to block the bedroom door and thanked the heavens she was leaving for Sydney in the morning. She lay down again and closed her eyes, tossing and turning until the soft light of dawn ebbed through the curtains.

At eight o'clock the next morning two uniformed officers arrived. One was young and fit with a buzz cut, the other white-haired with a moustache. Dana opened the door to let them in. As she watched them taking up space in the hallway the threat to her safety was suddenly all too real.

She showed them to her bedroom where the breeze came unfiltered into the room. The older officer frowned as he glanced at the jagged hole in the window and the debris of brick and glass glittering on the carpet.

The younger one pulled a palm-sized writing pad and pen from his breast pocket and began to take notes.

'What time did this happen?'

'About one o'clock.'

'Did you hear anything beforehand? Any unusual sounds?'

She shook her head. 'I was asleep.'

'Anyone you suspect might have done this? Someone with a grievance? Problems with the neighbours?'

Dana tilted her head, considering the endless possibilities. 'I work for the Department of Families, so there are a number of people who are annoyed with me at any given time.'

The older officer gave his colleague a knowing look. 'In that line of work you've got to expect that people will be pissed off at you sometimes.' He gazed at her sympathetically. 'I'll tell you what we can do, we'll fingerprint the brick and see if it matches anything on the database. My feeling is, it was probably just some teenage kids thinking they were being funny, so I don't like our chances.' He clicked his tongue with disapproval. 'In the meantime, I'd consider letting the neighbours know what happened and asking them to keep an eye out for you. And call us back if anything like this happens again.'

A few minutes later, Angus and Susan turned up, asking about the police car.

Angus was in his school uniform and Susan stood beside him surveying the damage. 'Holy shit,' he said, his face lit up with awe. 'Who do you reckon it was?'

Susan gave him a sharp look. 'Angus. Have some manners.'

'He's fine.' Dana tousled his hair and blinked to keep the

tears from her eyes. 'I don't know who did it. Probably some parent who wasn't happy with the work I'm doing.' She gave Angus a hard stare, pleading with him not to tell Susan about their investigating.

'It's absolutely terrible.' Susan shook her head. 'This used to be such a quiet neighbourhood. Now you've got cars hooning up and down at all times of the day and night. Don't worry, I'll make sure that window is replaced before you get back from Sydney. It's the least I can do.'

Dana glanced at her watch and suddenly felt dizzy. 'Oh, my god. I'm going to miss my flight. I have to be at the bus in ten minutes.'

'Come on,' said Susan. 'I'll give you a lift.'

17

Dana's eyes were dry and sore as she stared out the window of the plane. After the incident with the brick she'd failed to get back to sleep and now she was exhausted. Had she angered someone with her questions about the Kirby case, or was her smashed window pure coincidence?

The plane flew through dark clouds as she flipped through the in-flight magazine. A real-estate advert featuring a striking man with a shaved head in a suit stared back at her, reminding her of the waiter at the café she had frequented in Castlecrag. The one she'd come to rely on after Oscar's birth and the sleepless nights of those first few months. It had been one of life's simple pleasures to duck out of the house, skid up to Bean Scene and order a double-shot latte.

'Here you go, beautiful,' he'd say, and she'd laugh and say thank you. Because she'd craved the attention from this stranger. Affirmation after the trauma of childbirth that had left her with a stomach she barely recognised. As they flew out of the clouds, it suddenly dawned on her that things between her and Hugh hadn't been right for quite some time.

At the Channel Nine offices in Willoughby, she signed the visitors' book and was told to wait in the foyer. A group of television personalities entered the building and a woman Dana recognised from the morning show flashed her a smile. She felt guilty about using her North Shore connections to gather information, but before she could give it further thought, Isabell was marching towards her in a loud red business suit.

'Hi Dana,' she said and ushered her into an elevator. They went up to the twenty-second floor. 'I was so glad you called,' said Isabell, looking Dana up and down. 'You're looking good.'

Dana didn't know what she was talking about. She felt dishevelled and the drops she'd bought from the chemist hadn't worked; her eyes were more irritated than ever.

The lift chimed and Isabell used her security pass to swipe them through the glass doors. Dana followed her down a light-filled corridor to an open-plan office, with lush greenery and reporters on phones yelling over each other.

Isabell's desk was jammed with photographs of schoolchildren and a super-sized jar of Moccona. The man at the next desk was screaming into his receiver, demanding to speak to the manager.

'We can go somewhere quieter if you'd prefer,' Isabell said.

'No, it's fine.'

Isabell opened her compendium, removed a pen and began to write. 'Should I start? Or do you want to?' she asked, not looking up.

'I think we need to establish the ground rules of this little chat before we begin.' Dana looked around. 'I'm fairly sure I'm putting my career on the line just by being here.'

'Sure,' Isabell said, undeterred. 'What do you want?'

'If you use this interview in the program, you can't mention me by name – I'll lose my job. I need you to be absolutely clear about that. And everything I say is strictly off the record.'

'Can I at least say where you work?'

'No. No way.' A muscle in her jaw tightened. 'Toowoomba's much too small. Just say I'm an unnamed source.'

'Alright,' Isabell said, sighing. 'Since the prospect our little fact-finding mission is making you so jittery, I'll go first. Shall I?'

Dana nodded.

'So, as you know, my source said that the Crows Nest police absolutely butchered the Kirby–Vickers case. There was a policy in place at the time about not paying anyone overtime, so instead of cordoning off the scene when it was getting dark and calling in more senior detectives from Brisbane, the two morons out there declared the case a murder–suicide before they'd done a thorough job of gathering physical evidence.'

Dana stared at Isabell wondering if that was all she had to offer. 'Thanks, but to be honest, I'm well aware that the police botched a major investigation.'

'Not only have they botched it, but now the police commissioner in Roma Street is having a major panic trying to figure out how to bury it entirely.'

'That's hardly surprising either.'

'Okay. So, you know about the police. Did you know that one of the main people of interest was Tony Mulhain, who has a criminal history for manslaughter?'

'I wasn't aware of that.' Dana frowned. 'I knew he'd been in jail, but I had no idea that the charge was so significant.'

'And on the night of the murders, he was supposed to be having dinner at an ex-girlfriend's house, but when I interviewed her, she told me that she lied to the police so he'd leave her alone. He's been known to intimidate the women in his life, old Tony.'

'I see,' Dana said, shivering at the memory of how angry he'd been when she'd gone to his house. 'You think he did it? You think he's the murderer?'

'I don't know. But the Mulhain family is so dysfunctional it doesn't take much for me to picture Tony wanting to kill someone. I was also told that there was so much violence in Chrystal and Alisha's extended family that they were put in foster care for a year when the family lived in New South Wales – you probably already knew that though.'

'I didn't,' Dana said. Queensland and New South Wales were separate organisations. 'The interface between departments is surprisingly poor,' she said, her mind racing.

Isabell's phone rang loudly, making Dana jump.

Isabell yanked it from the receiver. 'Thanks, Jenny,' she said. 'Can you put him off again? I'm going to need at least another half hour.' She slammed the phone down.

'So, essentially, what you're saying is that Tony had some sort of feud with Sandra and killed her and Debbie,' said Dana. 'What were they fighting about though? What would make him angry enough to kill her?'

'Honestly,' said Isabell, reaching for her mobile and tapping out a message, 'I think it was about drugs. In my experience, if things aren't adding up, it's always drugs. And apparently Crows Nest has a thriving drug community. One man I spoke to told me that it's very possible they took a drive that night and just ended up in the wrong place at the wrong time.'

'How do you know this? Who's your source?'

'One of the locals – guy called Jimmy. He was into the drug scene, but he's cleaned himself up in the last few months to get access to his kids.'

'Jimmy?' Dana let out a strangled laugh. 'The tow-truck driver?'

Isabell nodded.

'It can't be the same guy that I met. That's ridiculous.'

'How many tow-truck drivers called Jimmy do you think there are in Crows Nest?'

'Regardless,' Dana said. 'The man is a lunatic. I had to sit with him for two hours when he towed my car to Toowoomba and he couldn't even last that long without lighting up a joint.'

'People change. That's what your business is about, isn't it? Working with people and hoping they improve. And so far, everything he's told me has turned out to be spot on.' Isabell's eyes narrowed as she leant back in her chair. 'So … I've told you everything I know about the case. It's your turn. Spill.'

Dana's mind was reeling from everything Isabell had told her, but she concentrated on summarising what she knew. 'Okay. So, on the night Debbie and Sandra were murdered, they were dressed lightly in skirts and thongs and it was freezing outside.'

'Your point?'

'It doesn't make sense. If they were planning to be outside all night to see the foal being born, wouldn't they have dressed accordingly? It's like they hadn't been planning to even get out of the car. It makes me think that someone was in the car with them, directing them where to go. And it was against their will.'

'Interesting.'

'Also, there's no evidence that Debbie was suicidal. She had concrete plans for the future. There was no indication of her being depressed, and she held down a respectable job at a local kindergarten, which I'm told she enjoyed enormously. From the research I've done, those qualities are completely incongruent with someone wanting to kill themselves. Not only that – she has no history of violence. She was so anti-violence that she didn't even like killing insects. And there hasn't been a single female murder–suicide in this country in the past twenty years, if ever.'

Isabell's phone chirped insistently and her face flashed with anger as she picked it up. 'I'm not speaking with him. I'm busy. I'll call back later.' She slammed the receiver down again. 'I've got to wind this up. Is there anything else?'

'There's a few people in Crows Nest who seem to think the women were devil worshippers. That they got their just desserts.' Dana paused. 'And of course there's Paul, but his alibi is airtight. The neighbour saw him through the window and Chrystal said she talked to him for half an hour that night – about her plans for when she left school. She was very specific about that.'

Isabell sat back in her chair, her arms behind her head. 'So, it would appear that there are a number of different angles with regards to what could have happened. There's the murder–suicide theory, being in the wrong place at the wrong time, the husband, and of course a violent drug-dealer with a criminal history.'

There was a pause in the conversation, a sudden dip in energy levels as they realised their options were limited.

'Are you going to the reunion?' Dana asked.

'Yes. And you?'

'Yes,' she said with the merest hint of a sigh. 'I've got to give the speech.' On the bookcase to her left, a dozen golden trophies and plaques were on display. 'Given you're on TV,' she added, 'they'd have been better off asking you.'

Isabell smirked without malice. 'I wouldn't have said no.'

Dana smiled back, for the first time wondering whether there might be more common ground between them than she'd imagined. 'Great,' she said. 'I'll see you tomorrow night.'

As Dana stepped out of the rental car and gazed up at the terraced garden and the sandstone of her Castlecrag home, she felt a mix of emotions – happiness, anticipation and a tangle of memories tied up with losing Oscar. She hurried up the shrub-lined path and cupped her hands over the front window into Oscar's bedroom. The white sleigh cot, change table and Winnie the Pooh print were still there. Towards the end of her pregnancy they'd put the finishing touches on the nursery and spent an entire weekend sticking glow stars on the ceiling and arranging cloth nappies in a hanger behind the door. What she wouldn't give to go back to that happier time.

Her finger hovered above the doorbell, but she was unable to press it. She'd behaved so badly towards Hugh before she'd left – accusing him of cheating then rushing to Queensland in a fit of madness. She pulled herself together then pushed the door open and walked down the hallway. Hugh was in the kitchen arranging water crackers onto a platter. Her last thought before she collapsed into his arms was that his paunch, which betrayed his weakness for beer and fajitas, was gone. She buried her face in his chest and felt the warmth of his arms around her. She breathed in the scent of his woollen jumper, the cologne she'd bought him last Christmas.

When he released her from the embrace he'd still not spoken and confusion seeped through her like cold mist. She stood back, taking in the neatness of the lounge room, the aroma of roast meat. The folding glass door to the garden was open and, when she looked outside, she understood. Antonia, his ex-wife, was sitting at the wrought-iron table, china skin and curly silver hair fluttering in the breeze.

'Hello, Dana,' she said regally. 'Would you like to join us? We're about to start on the cheese.'

'I'm fine,' she sputtered. She turned and took in the Art Deco lamp of a nude woman on top of the piano. A new addition. Her back was still to the garden as she looked to Hugh for an explanation.

His expression was confused. 'You could have told me you were coming.'

'I was going to,' she said, 'but I wanted to surprise you.'

It had been folly to leave him alone for so long. He was always going to find someone to take her place. Hugh and his endless neediness.

'How long are you here for?'

'Not long.' She glanced outside again. An empty bottle of champagne sat beside two crystal flutes that were so close to each other they were almost touching. Dana struggled for breath.

'Come on,' said Hugh. 'It wouldn't kill you to stay, would it?'

Antonia gave her a smug wave and Dana lifted her chin defiantly.

'Sure,' she said. 'It's not every day I get to spend time with your ex.'

Hugh collected the plate he'd prepared and she followed him outside.

'How's Toowoomba?' Antonia asked after they'd sat down.

'Wonderful.' She gave Antonia a generous smile. 'I've had some interesting cases to work on.'

'She's been working on that murder case,' Hugh said. 'The two best friends who were lovers. And one of them shot the other one.'

'Hugh!' Dana shook her head. 'You know that's confidential.'

'I didn't know!'

'Everything I work on is confidential.'

'I just hate how those women have been portrayed in the media. Like they're these murderous lesbians.' Antonia picked up the cheese knife and stabbed it into the pâté. 'It's fucking pathetic.'

'How is Philippa?' Dana asked.

Antonia's cheeks flushed pink and she shot a look at Hugh. 'We're not together anymore. She's focusing on her career.'

Hugh's face gave nothing away.

'It's been hard. We've had to sell the house, separate the business. And, of course, my father's been sick.' Antonia toyed with her hair. Her gaze suddenly turned on Dana. 'Will you be staying here tonight?'

'I was planning to. Why?'

Hugh fumbled around for a cracker, not meeting her eyes. 'I should have mentioned this a few weeks back, but Antonia's staying for a while.'

'What?' Her chest tightened. 'Which room is she in?'

'The spare room.'

That was something. At least she wasn't staying in Oscar's room. The thought of her son brought on a depression so intense it was all she could do to stagger from her chair.

'Dana—' began Hugh.

'Can I see you for a moment? Inside?'

She barricaded herself between the corners of the kitchen bench as Hugh stood by the table. 'Honestly, Hugh.'

'She was struggling. I gave her a place to live. End of story.'

She raised her eyebrows. 'Clearly she's hoping for a little bit more than somewhere to rest her head.'

'I'm not interested. I just thought – I'm rattling around in this enormous house. It's not going to cost me anything to help her.'

'Don't be so sure.'

'What's that supposed to mean?'

'All it's going to take is a moment of weakness and you'll be fucking her again in no time.' Her cheeks were burning, her voice starting to tremble. 'When you've been in a relationship and you're under the same roof, it's too easy. You're not paying attention and suddenly you've crossed the line.'

'I'm glad you hold my morality in such high regard.' He stared at the ground, then back to her. 'When I married you, I was committed. I was up to the challenge of living with this … this workaholic, and nothing was going to stop me. But you never asked me about leaving. You took that job in Queensland and there was nothing I could do. I had to lie to our friends and family. I had to pretend it had all been planned when, in reality, you packed up and left me.'

'Well, after that incident with Melinda, I had no choice. Not to mention that fling you had when we first started dating.'

'Jesus Christ. You're still going on about that? It's embarrassing.' He paused. 'What you need to understand is that you and I are no longer together.'

Dana crossed her arms, cocooning herself. 'You don't mean that.' She searched his eyes. 'Something bad happened to us. Something terrible. And all I wanted was some time and space to process it.' She paused. 'Soon, when some more time has passed, we'll be together again.'

He laughed bitterly. 'This is exactly what I mean. You've been gone for over a month and I've got no idea when you're coming back? Are you coming back?'

'Not yet.'

'Why? Is there someone in Toowoomba? Or is it this god-awful case you keep talking about?'

'I'm still working on the Kirby case, and until those kids are safe, I need to be there.'

'You need to get some perspective on your job – it's not healthy.'

'Oh, and fucking the nearest person because you're lonely is?' She closed her eyes, knowing she was hardly one to talk about fidelity. She stepped closer and reached out to him. 'Please, Hugh, nothing has changed.'

He held her at arm's length. 'Our chance of happiness ended after Oscar died and you stopped talking to me.'

She slumped against the bench. When she looked at him again, she realised that this was the most honest they'd ever been with each other. 'Please, Hugh.'

Her phone rang, startling them both. The Toowoomba office number came up on caller ID.

Hugh looked at her. 'You should get that.'

'They'll call back.'

'Pick it up. You clearly want to.'

She hesitated, her finger hovering above the green button. The call rang out.

Hugh shook his head. 'I always knew you cared about the battered children, the tired mothers. What I was never sure about was whether you ever cared about me.'

Antonia burst into the kitchen, taking the dishes to the sink in a flurry of activity. 'Everything alright in here?'

Dana gazed out at the lights of Darling Harbour from the window of her hotel room. She searched the minibar for something edible and settled for a Snapple and packet of Smith's crisps.

Despite being exhausted, she lay awake wondering why the fight with Hugh somehow felt more permanent than the others. After all, they'd had many arguments during their marriage and most of them had no greater effect on their relationship than bad weather. So much so that she struggled to remember one fight with any specificity. Only the themes stood out. Their separate bedrooms and her working too much. Hugh not helping out enough and her constant battle to maintain the house. And how she'd felt after Oscar died. Like her throat was burning with sorrow, her body's deepest expression of sadness. She yanked the wedding ring from her finger and placed it on the bedside table, fighting the urge to fling it from the window.

Sleep didn't come. By two that morning she'd reached the second of Kübler-Ross's stages of grief with impressive swiftness. She seethed, thinking furiously about the ridiculous things Hugh had said. They were no longer in a relationship, she only cared about her clients and, worst of all, he was just friends with Antonia.

~

On Saturday night, after a day holed up in her hotel room, she sat in the back seat of a taxi, the window down as it swept up the circular driveway of her old school grounds. It had taken her an age to put on her make-up and she'd finally chosen a black dress with a silk scarf draped around her shoulders. She paid the driver and trudged up the driveway, cool air on her face as she lingered by the oval.

At the glass-doored entrance to the hall she was given a name tag, which she carefully pinned onto her dress, avoiding the delicate material at her neck. Inside, air conditioners had been installed beside archaic-looking fans and small groups were gathered by the stage.

She took a glass of champagne from a passing waiter and said hello to two women from her form class. When it was time to give her speech, Dana was surprised by her lack of nerves. With everything that had gone on recently – losing Oscar, the murdered women and the attack on her house – making a fool of herself in front of people she hadn't seen for years was suddenly the least of her problems. She thanked everyone for coming, and in particular the teachers for putting up with them, made some references to the music they'd all loved and encouraged everyone to have a wonderful night. When it was all over the first person who came up to her was Isabell, in a glittery top and skirt.

'Dana! Great speech!' Isabell's voice echoed through the hall, making Dana wonder if she'd already had a few wines at home. 'Where's the hubby? I'm dying to meet him.'

An aching sadness settled in Dana's chest. 'He couldn't make it,' she said quickly. 'Migraine.'

Isabell pouted. 'That's a shame. Mark's around here somewhere. He's the local candidate for Willoughby this year, so he's probably schmoozing some party member.' She craned her neck in search of him. 'Tell me, what's it been like living near Crows Nest? Honestly, with some of the people I met there, I don't reckon I'd last two minutes in that place, let alone a few months. Doesn't it freak you out?' Isabell grabbed a glass of champagne from a nearby table and bolted down her drink.

'To be honest, I have started to feel pretty scared the last few days.'

'Really?' Isabell's eyes snapped into focus. 'What happened?'

'Someone threw a brick through my window the other night.'

'Wow, that's really serious.'

A woman who'd become a High Court judge swept past in a backless gown and Isabell waved. 'Julia! You look stunning! How've you been?'

As Isabell moved away, Dana felt her mobile vibrate in her handbag. She was almost relieved to return through the glass doors to the fresh air outside to answer it.

'Lachlan,' she said with surprise. 'It's a bit late for you to be calling, isn't it?'

'I've got to go into work to finish an affidavit tomorrow and I don't remember the security code for the office. You were the first person who came to mind.'

'It's 324 892,' she said, nodding at an ex-teacher as he went through the door. 'Sorry you had to give up your weekend.'

'You know what Helen's like. I swear our office isn't half as busy as she makes out, but she can't seem to help herself, has to micromanage every detail. Anyway, how are you liking the big smoke?'

She hesitated, not wanting to talk about the argument with Hugh. 'It's been nice to get a decent coffee and to see everyone again. But I have to say, I've been a bit worried about what's happening in Toowoomba while I've been away.'

'Why's that?'

'Two nights ago someone threw a brick through my bedroom window,' she said, wondering whether she'd get more sympathy from Lachlan than she had from Isabell.

'Jesus. Did you report it to the police?'

'They told me they were unlikely to get a match with the fingerprints, so the chances of finding the person are slim.'

'I can't even imagine …'

She pictured him grimacing on the other end of the line. 'As well as that, I've developed a bit of a friendship with the boy next door and I got the sense that he wasn't entirely happy about me leaving for Sydney.' She paused, realising how strange she must sound. 'He was in foster care before he started living with his grandmother and he's a sweet kid, so I've been spending time with him.'

'Fair enough.'

There was a moment of silence.

'Anyway,' she said, trying to move on. 'I'd hoped that being away might give me some perspective on Crows Nest and some of our clients who live there, but I'm not sure it has.'

'Well, if you ask me, I'd say it was like that town in *Wake in Fright* where everyone has a gun, gets real drunk and tries to kill things.'

'And that's it?'

There was a pop and a fizzing down the end of the line. It sounded like Lachlan was mixing a drink. 'I don't know.' He paused, and she heard him take a sip from his drink. 'I guess people usually end up as products of their environment, and in

Crows Nest, the women end up becoming victims – usually by being trapped in dysfunctional relationships. And the men metamorphosise into something else.'

'What exactly?'

'They end up hard. They take shortcuts to deal with their pain and most of it, like the drugs, the violence and the criminal activity, is highly immoral. But it's almost impossible to be a moral person when you're trying to survive from day to day.'

'You really think so?'

He laughed. 'Probably just my late-night rambling.'

'Sorry.' Her cheeks flushed. He'd rung for the security code and she'd ended up giving him her life story. 'I should let you go. Good luck with that affidavit. I'll see you on Monday.'

Back inside she circled the room, taking in the memorabilia on the walls, pictures of smiling schoolgirls, the high school orchestra and hockey teams.

The moon was high in the sky when she found the school captains' honour board. A deep nostalgia washed over her as she remembered the heady days of her final years. The hopes and dreams she'd had for her future. The friendships she'd never quite managed to replace. The family she'd hoped for. With a sinking feeling, she located her name – *Dana Gibson* – in thin gold leaf. The last time she'd seen it, she was on the up and up. Her captaincy a crowning glory after years of achievement. Now the inscription seemed small and insignificant. Lost in the sea of those who'd come before and those who came after.

18

Her flight was delayed and by the time Dana arrived back in Toowoomba it was one o'clock in the afternoon. An eerie silence hung over Godsall Street as she stepped out of the taxi. The birds were quiet and there was no sound from the children in the park. Susan was on the front step of Dana's house, her head in her hands and her normally neat hair in spikes over her head.

When she spotted Dana, she called out. 'Angus is gone.'

A panicky sensation rose in Dana's chest. She dumped her bags on the path. 'When did you see him last?'

'When he went to bed, at about eight last night.' Susan's face was pale with anxiety.

'Did you call the police?'

'No. They're not interested. They said that the next time I called, I needed to be really sure he's missing.'

Dana searched her mind. 'Had you had an argument?'

'No. He was his normal self. I let him read a book for an hour and then he went to bed.'

'Any friends he could be with?'

Susan gave a grim smile. 'We both know he doesn't have any – that boy he sits with in the library, but that's just safety in numbers.'

'Look,' said Dana, a sinking feeling gripping her stomach. 'It hasn't been very long, so we shouldn't report him missing yet, but if you've got a photo of him, I'll drive into town and ask if anyone's seen him.'

'He used to do this all the time, you know, a few years back, when he was with DOCS. They used to call him a runner because it wouldn't matter what foster home they put him in, he'd always return to his mum. But he's been so good lately. I thought he'd gotten over it.' Susan searched Dana's face. 'Should I come with you?'

'It's best if you stay here. That way if he turns up someone will be home.' Dana put a hand on Susan's shoulder. 'He's a young boy. In all likelihood, he's probably gone to the park, then lost track of time.'

Susan managed a weak smile. 'Thank you. Call me if you hear anything.'

Dana dropped her bag inside and waited for Susan to retrieve the photograph of Angus. She got into the car and reached for her phone. As soon as it was in her hand it started ringing. She sighed when she saw the caller and immediately felt guilty.

'Hi Mum,'

'Dana.' Her mother sounded breathless. 'You have to let me know about Melbourne. Lorraine said she can't keep the unit any longer than a month. She's thinking of letting it to one of her daughter's friends.'

'Sorry, Mum. It's a bad time. There's a missing kid and we've just started searching. I'll get back to you soon. I promise.'

She hung up and called Lachlan.

'Lachlan, it's Dana.'

'Dana,' he said. Children were screaming in the background. 'How are you? How was the reunion?'

'Not bad,' she lied. 'Sorry to call on a Sunday, but I was hoping you could help me. My neighbour, Angus, is missing. And I'm trying to find him.'

'That boy you hang out with?'

'That's the one. I'm afraid my trip might have set off his abandonment issues.'

'Okay, okay,' he said. 'What do you want me to do?'

'If you could do a bit of a search around Toowoomba, check the park, the Bell Street Mall. Have a chat to Ian Steinmann to see if he's heard anything. I'll drive to Crows Nest and see if he's there.'

'Why would he be in Crows Nest?'

She hesitated. 'He's become very interested in the Kirby–Vickers murders … I may have let him do some investigating with me.'

'Oh, Dana …'

'I know. If you can just help me find him I can sort the rest out later.'

'Alright,' he said. 'I'll drop these lunatic kids off with my wife and then I'll get onto it.'

'Great. Maybe try the library first. He's been known to hole up there for hours. And Lachlan,' she said, taking a breath, 'thank you.'

'You can repay me by typing some more case notes. I've got a whole pile on the go.'

'Consider it done.'

She hung up and sped past Highfields, Cabarlah and Hampton in record time, flying down the hill past the cow paddocks and deserted tourist park to the township of Crows Nest. She passed the police station and considered going in, but remembered Angus's mistrust of authority and went to the newsagency instead.

Inside, the same raven-haired woman with a white stripe along her part line was behind the counter sifting through magazines.

Dana took Angus's school photo from her handbag and held it out over the counter. 'You haven't seen this boy around this morning, have you? His name's Angus and he's been missing since last night.'

The woman reached for her reading glasses and squinted at the photograph. 'No. He looks like a sweet little fella though.'

Dana felt a panicky sensation rise in her chest.

'You know what I can do?' The woman smiled sympathetically. 'My brother's a cabbie. He starts his shift in an hour. I'll get him to keep an eye out for you. And why don't you give me that picture and leave your number. I can make a copy of it and ask anyone who comes in.'

Dana's heart swelled with gratitude. 'That's so kind,' she said, giving the woman her phone number and handing over the photo for her to copy.

'My name's Tracey,' she said. 'I don't think we've met.'

'Dana Gibson.'

'Is he in care, like Chrystal?'

'No, nothing like that.' Dana remembered the kindness of country folk was often equalled by their curiosity. 'His grandmother's a friend.'

'Well, I'll keep my ears open and let you know if I hear anything. Try not to worry yourself too much. They usually show up.'

Tracey handed back the photograph. Dana was turning to leave the shop when something at the rear of the store caught her eye, a banner pinned up against the back wall announcing a stocktake sale. Something twigged in her memory.

'I can't believe it's that time of year again.' Dana nodded in the direction of the sign.

Tracey looked up at her from over her glasses 'Copies of the *Women's Weekly* are going cheap, a heap of the stationery's on sale, too.'

'I'm fine,' Dana said quickly. Her heart hammered in her chest. 'I remembered Chrystal telling me how she helped you prepare for the stocktake.'

'Chrystal said that?'

'Yes.'

'Really?' Tracey's eyes narrowed. 'She's never helped with the stocktake. My husband and I do it ourselves. Years ago, we used to let the juniors help, but it always came back to bite us. They'd start daydreaming and lose count of the inventory they were supposed to be keeping track of.' She frowned. 'So we gave up on that practice. She told you we let her help?'

Dana nodded.

'That's strange,' she said, punctuating her words with the slap of the pricing gun firing a label onto a magazine.

Dana dawdled back to the car and mulled over the conversation with Tracey. In her interview with the police, Chrystal had said that Sandra wanted her to stay home from work the day she and Debbie died, she said Sandra wanted to tell her something important, but Chrystal was needed at work for the stocktake. The next day they were dead and Chrystal's only hope of finding out what was on Sandra's mind had turned to dust.

Dana was doing up her seatbelt in the stuffy car when it hit her. There was only one explanation for what the woman in the newsagency had told her.

Chrystal had lied.

But why? Why lie about something so mundane as doing the stocktake?

She started the engine, bringing herself back to the task at hand. She had a vision of Angus on a reconnaissance mission, spying on the Kirby family. But when she passed the Creek Street house, the curtains were drawn and the carport empty.

She drove on to the church and then to the nursing home where Betty Vickers lived. Then later, to the square, the pub and Raven's Roost café. All places they'd talked about.

Nothing.

A tightness prickled her chest. She was running out of places to look. Where would she go if she was a young boy researching a real-life murder mystery? The idea that came to mind made her sick to her stomach. He was obsessed with Debbie Vickers, with the idea that she'd been hard done by. Dana sped up the road to Debbie's flat. She'd only made it past the rotunda at the top of the square when she saw him, trudging along the street with a backpack and a bandana around his head. She skidded over to the kerb and yanked on the handbrake.

'Angus,' she yelled. 'What are you doing?'

He stopped walking. His cheeks were apple red and his forehead shiny with sweat. He looked spooked, as though he'd seen something that wasn't meant for him.

'Jesus Christ,' she said. 'Where have you been? I've been driving for hours and your nan's at home worried sick about you. You've scared everyone to death.'

Her words were harsher than she'd intended and when his bottom lip started to quiver, she knew she'd gone too far.

'It's okay,' she said, feeling terrible. 'Hop in the car and I'll drive you home.'

Once they were back on the main road, Dana glanced over at him. 'So, where'd you go?'

'I don't want you to be angry with me.'

'Uh-huh.'

'I broke into Debbie Vickers's house.'

She gripped the steering wheel tightly. 'I was afraid you'd say that.'

She pulled over at Crows Nest Soft Drinks, an old brick factory with a slanted green roof and awnings over the doors. Inside, they stood in front of a refrigerator containing old-fashioned bottles in every colour of the rainbow.

'What flavour would you like?' she asked him.

'That one.' He pointed to a cerulean-blue bottle of lemonade.

She chose a double sarsaparilla and settled Angus at a table before going outside to call Susan and then Lachlan.

Lachlan exhaled down the phone. 'That's a relief.'

She leant against a telephone pole. A motorbike cruised down the street. 'You don't feel like coming over for dinner later?' she asked. 'I need to bend your ear about work.'

'Sure. Seven sound okay?'

'See you then.'

She returned to Angus, handing him the sandwich she still

had in her handbag from the flight. The food and drink seemed to revive him and he chatted about his nan and the plans they had for his birthday.

'Angus,' she said gravely, bringing him back to what they needed to talk about. 'What were you doing at Debbie's place?'

'Investigating.'

'And what happened in there?'

'I didn't like it,' he said.

She was worried he'd shut down again, but he looked at her, blinking rapidly.

'It was so messy,' he continued. 'All her things, these crystal figurines she had in her bedroom. They were all broken.'

Dana remembered the similar state of the Kirbys' house after the police had searched for evidence. 'So, you went into the bedroom,' she said cautiously. 'Where did you go next?'

He sipped his drink and his eyes under their furled lashes were as wide as she'd ever seen them. 'I didn't go anywhere else, because someone came into the house. A man, I think. I was so scared. I shut myself in the wardrobe and made myself invisible, like I used to when Mum and Wade were fighting. But it was so hot in there. There were so many clothes.'

'Was he there long, this man?'

'A while. I could hear him stomping around and pulling all these papers out of the drawers.'

She nodded for him to continue.

'He couldn't find what he was looking for so he started yelling and banging on everything. I was worried he was looking for the diary and that made me even more scared.'

'Why?'

'Because I had it.'

'And where is it now?'

'In my backpack.'

She shifted in her seat. She'd been holding her breath. 'Angus, I need you to listen carefully to what I'm about to say.'

His brow creased with consternation.

'This whole investigation we've been doing has gone far enough now. We both need to stop what we've been doing and let the police do their jobs. I think you need to give that diary to me, and I can decide what to do with it – which is likely to involve giving it straight to the sergeant.'

'Why? The police will just ignore it. Or not pick up any of the clues it contains and just stuff up again like they've done with everything else.'

'Angus,' she said firmly, 'I really need you to trust me on this. Withholding evidence is a criminal offence and is not something I want us to be involved in.'

He put the soft drink bottle down on the table. 'Fine,' he said sulkily. He removed a floral-covered A5-sized diary from his backpack. 'Don't blame me if the mystery is never solved.'

She slipped the diary into her bag and reached across the table. She put her hands over his. 'Angus, what you did today was very brave, but also very dangerous,' she said, trying to appeal to his pride. 'And in many ways that's my fault. I encouraged your interest in this case and I let you help me, when I shouldn't have.' She increased her grip on his hands. 'So, please promise me – no more investigations and no more running away.'

'Okay,' he said, holding her gaze just long enough for her to believe him.

~

By the time she'd driven back to Toowoomba and dropped Angus home it was almost six o'clock. From the moment she opened the creaky gate and hurried through the dark garden there was only one thing on her mind. She put the kettle on and threw some soup ingredients into the crockpot. Once she was at the table with a steaming cup of tea, she snapped on a pair of pink kitchen gloves and removed the diary from her bag.

Inside the front cover was an inscription.

This journal belongs to Deborah Vickers. If lost, please return to 21 Darling Street, Crows Nest.

Dana's hands were trembling as she turned the page over. The first entry was dated 1 January 1996.

Dear Diary,

This is the first time I have ever written 1996 as a date! The dawn of the day is here and so is a fresh new year! This year I would really like to do a fun run and lose twenty kilograms. I know I can do it. Mum's always said that when I put my mind to things I've got the determination to do anything.

Dana pictured the thirty-five-year-old Debbie writing in her brand-new journal and couldn't help but feel cynical. She skimmed the first few pages, which were mostly about new year's resolutions, until she came to a ledger that detailed how much money Debbie had earnt during the month of January and how much she'd spent. Betty had been right about Debbie's note taking. She'd been meticulous.

There were a few journal entries of mundane details, but then on 29 January 1996 there was one that caught Dana's attention.

Dear Diary,

Something truly horrible happened the other day. Me and Sandy went to the Old Crow last Friday. Everything started off as usual with the bikies doing drug deals while Rocco sat at the bar, but then the night ended with us doing something really bad … something I can't believe I did. It was raining so we

The entry stopped mid-sentence.

Dana imagined Debbie being interrupted as she wrote in her journal, the phone ringing or the doorbell chiming. A cliffhanger that would never be resolved, Debbie had not explained who the mysterious Rocco was or the terrible event that had occurred that Friday in January. The next few entries were a rumination on romantic love and why she'd been so unlucky.

Dana was starting to wonder whether she was actually going to find anything of interest when a folded card slid from the pages. When she opened it, the hairs on the backs of her arms stood on end. A scarlet pentagram had been carved at the top of the page above an inscription in handwritten calligraphy. Golden tendrils curled around the borders. A knife dripped with blood.

Satanism Certificate of Authenticity

Let it be known, that on this day Tuesday the thirteenth of February 1996, I hereby proclaim Deborah Vickers to be a member of our Satanic Worship Order.

I support her claim that she has previously undertaken supremacy rituals to align herself with the Order of Satan. As a high priestess of this Satanic Worship Order established in January 1996, I welcome you to be empowered to act in the capacity of Satan and to attend any rituals, worship sessions or congregations which may be held in the glory of Satan.

I also welcome you to be a satanic, sadistic and sexual ritual partner.

Dana's heart hammered in her chest. She dropped the card back into the diary and snapped it shut. She had a vision of Sandra and Debbie working on the certificate together. The hours they'd spent finely crafting its design.

Could it be that the murder–suicide theory held water? That Debbie had killed Sandra in a satanic ritual gone wrong?

19

Lachlan was standing on the front verandah in a soft, brown cardigan when she opened the door. Dana was still shaken from reading the diary and wanted to hug him tight. Instead, she took the cake he'd brought for dessert and led him down the hallway. The rich aroma of pea and ham soup filled the house.

'Something smells good,' he said, as she ushered him into the lounge room.

'Thanks,' she said. 'I was just about to put the fire on.'

'Good idea,' he said, kneeling by the basket of pinecones and kindling. 'I can do it, if you like?'

'That would be great,' she said, before ducking into the kitchen to check on the soup. When she returned, he was sitting on the Chesterfield, entranced by the darting and flickering flames.

'I love these old Queenslanders,' he said, gazing up at the roof as she sat down next to him. 'This one's a cracker. Pressed-metal ceiling, beautiful breezeways. Vj walls.' He turned to her. 'Who owns it?'

'The lady next door, Susan. This one and the house she lives in have been in the family for years. Her father bought them in the 1940s for ninety pounds or something ridiculous.' She got up and stood in front of the grate, letting the heat warm her body. 'The soup should be ready if you want to come into the kitchen.'

Lachlan stopped abruptly when he saw the evidence board. 'What's this?'

She cringed. She'd grown so accustomed to seeing it, she barely noticed it was there. 'It's for the Kirby case. I've been using it for work.'

'Christ. That's not half creepy.' He stared closely at the photo of Sandra's casket being lowered into the ground.

'It helps me to see things visually.'

'I guess I can be thankful there's not one in your bedroom.' He looked worried. 'There's not, is there?'

'No.'

'Phew.' He sat down at the table.

She ladled the soup into china bowls and placed a crusty loaf of sourdough in the centre of the table.

'Like some wine? I've got a nice red I've never gotten around to drinking.'

He grinned. 'Now you're talking.'

She took the large balloon glasses from the cupboard and uncorked the 1987 Beringer cabernet sauvignon. She poured the deep cherry-coloured liquid into them and sat down opposite him.

'Cheers,' he toasted her, raising his glass.

'What are we toasting to?'

'Saving the world,' he said with an ironic smile. 'One kid at a time.'

'Speaking of which,' she said, sipping her wine, 'I feel like I've been quite ineffectual since I started this job – case in point being Chrystal. She's transformed from an innocent girl into a traumatised teenager within a month or so and there's nothing I can do.' She indicated behind her. 'There's two spare rooms in this house. I'd like to be able to take her in.'

'Chrystal!' He choked on his wine. 'Living with you?'

'What?'

'She'd drive you nuts. She'd be having boys over. Doing lines off the vanity.'

'But she's a young girl at a fork in the road.' She paused. 'I'm her social worker. Someone has to do something.'

His smile was grim. 'Like you say – you're a social worker. Not a bloody magician.' Lachlan tasted his soup and gazed at Dana with amazement.

'This is divine. What's in it?'

'Ham from the hock and pepper to taste,' she said, still frustrated about Chrystal. 'My grandmother used to make it for us as kids.' She buttered a slice of bread. 'I've been trying to get to the farmers' market in the park on Saturdays. The produce is unbelievable.'

There was silence as they ate.

'I probably need to tell you that I've ended up in possession of Debbie Vickers's diary – the one that Connor told me didn't exist because the police had gone through her flat with a fine toothcomb.' She held her breath and waited for his reply.

He looked at her, chewing his bread. 'How'd you come by that?'

'I'd rather not say.'

'Protecting your source, hey? Well, what's the goss? Is there anything interesting in it?'

'Well, if anything it supports the police theory – that Sandra and Debbie were lovers and that their deaths may have been the result of some sort of satanic ritual.'

'See! They're not as stupid as you think.'

Dana sighed, unsatisfied by the explanation.

'What do you plan to do with it?'

'The diary?'

He nodded.

'Hand it over to the police, I suppose.'

'I'm seeing Ian tomorrow. I can give it to him?'

She retrieved the diary from the study and Lachlan put it in his satchel.

'Would you like some more wine?' she asked.

'Sure,' he said, and she rose to pour him a glass. 'You're not having one?'

'I've still got some left,' she said, gesturing to her half-full glass.

Lachlan smiled at her, his blue eyes twinkling. She took a deep breath, reminding herself he was married, that her last dubious decision had ended with Angus running away and Susan almost having a breakdown.

They went into the living room and she sat in front of the fire. The wind outside rustled the leaves in the camphor laurel trees, whipping through the branches. The rhythmic sound was like waves crashing against the shore. Lachlan was at the mantelpiece examining a clock before moving on to a china figurine of a sparrow.

'Susan's, I assume?'

She nodded as he sat down.

'So, what did you want to be when you were at school? Did it all turn out as you'd planned?' he asked.

'No.' She smiled. 'After I first came up here to summer school, I had all these delusions that I was going to be a musician.'

He looked at her thoughtfully. 'I can picture you doing that.'

'I couldn't cope with the lack of job security. And social work annoyed my father just the right amount.' She gazed at him tentatively. 'How long have you been married?'

'Eight years. Rachel and I met at a fancy-dress party after the death of my first wife, Kate.'

Dana sipped her wine trying to hide her shock. 'How did she die?'

'Cancer.' He paused. 'A terrible business. One minute she was diagnosed then two months later, she was gone.' He raised his glass to his mouth, but didn't drink. 'I should be grateful really. That it was swift.'

'Have you ever managed … to move forward?'

'In the beginning it was hard. CS Lewis said that the death of a loved one is like having the same leg cut off time after time, and after everything I went through, I tend to agree.' He stared into the fire, not meeting her eyes. 'I heard you had a little boy who passed away.'

'Oscar.' She tried to control her emotions. 'He was eight months old.' She stoppped, not trusting herself to speak.

'And has being back at work made it easier?'

She shrugged. 'It's been slightly better in this new job where nobody knows me, but back in Sydney people used to approach me with this look in their eyes. As though they were deciding whether to say something.' She smiled ruefully. 'What they didn't know was that talking to me about it wouldn't have made any difference … I'd hate them if they did and I'd hate them if they didn't.'

He got up to stoke the fire. 'How've you been settling into the job?'

'The entire office hates me. They still call me Princess Diana behind my back, so I presume they think I'm an enormous snob. No-one ever talks about the good things I've done. The time I worked twenty-four hours straight. Stayed out after dark searching for Chrystal.'

There was silence for a moment and he looked at her thoughtfully. 'And how are you finding the work itself?'

'I don't know.' She removed a speck of dirt from her glass and shook her head. 'I mean, how am I supposed to live in a world where people inflict the most heinous atrocities on children and my own child drops dead without warning. Just – what the fuck? And just when I think I've witnessed every combination of horror and evil that could befall a child, someone comes up with something new.' Tears were streaming down her face and she had no idea how they got there. 'I don't know if it's a good thing I've never managed to desensitise. Or just pathetic.'

'It's not a sign of weakness that you're traumatised from work. It's an occupational hazard. Inevitable if you stay around long enough.' His expression shifted to one of concern. 'Did you ever consider getting counselling after Oscar died?'

She wrapped her arms tightly around her, shaking her head.

'Maybe you should go and see someone.'

'Maybe,' she repeated, wondering what on earth would be the point.

He clicked his tongue. 'It's tough alright. Did the relationship between you and your husband survive?'

She laughed, breaking the sombre mood that had fallen over the room. 'You don't shy away from the hard questions, do you, Lachlan?'

'I can but ask.'

'The last time I saw him he said that he needed a break. That he still loves me, but … it's too hard.'

'And Connor?'

'No way. That was a mistake.'

'Well, if you ever want to join us at the Irish Club for trivia we can invite you along? Plenty of single men there.'

'I haven't completely given up on Hugh,' she said, surprised she'd finally admitted it. 'Sometimes, I think if he was just willing to move out of that house, with all those memories … and if we could just forgive each other for what happened next.' She thought of Melinda, Connor.

'Even if you weren't there looking for a man—'

'I'm fine, but thank you.' She felt like a recalcitrant teenager. Knowing he was right, yet digging in her heels.

'Up to you,' he said good-naturedly. His eyes landed on the record player in the corner and the shelf of records next to it. He walked over and ran his finger over the spines, a wistful look on his face. 'These your neighbour's, too?'

She nodded.

'Mind if I play one?'

'Go ahead.' She sipped her wine, feeling sleepy, yet somehow lighter than she had in a long time.

He removed an Eagles album, *Their Greatest Hits (1971–1975)*, from its sleeve and placed it on the turntable.

She chuckled. 'You really are an old man.'

He returned to the couch. There was crackling followed by a simple piano melody as 'Desperado' began.

He gazed over at her with an almost imperceptible smirk. 'This song could have been written for you.'

'I need to let somebody love me?'

He raised his eyebrows as though it was obvious. 'Before it's too late.'

She laughed, resting her head in her hands as a wave of exhaustion swept over her.

'My father used to love these guys,' she said, her voice unsteady. 'It pained him, because he liked to believe he was part of the aristocracy … but every now and then, when he thought no-one was looking, he'd put it on.' She lay her head on the back of the couch and closed her eyes.

'Tired?'

'I can't remember the last time I had a full night's sleep. All the talk about the murders has gotten to me.'

'Maybe you should take tomorrow off?'

She shook her head. 'I'd rather work. Keeps my mind occupied.'

He moved over and placed a cushion beside him, gesturing for her to rest her head.

She lay down. 'I'm not like that song – not really,' she said. 'And if I was, I'd be the Queen of Hearts not the Queen of Diamonds.' She was dimly aware she was no longer making sense.

'Course you would.' He patted her shoulder gently.

20

When Dana woke her mobile was ringing. Shrill and insistent. She was still on the couch, a woollen blanket pulled over her. The clock on the mantelpiece read ten o'clock. Dana reached for the phone.

'Dana.' Lachlan's bewildered voice was on the other end of the line. 'Where the bloody hell are you?'

'I just woke up.'

'Helen's on the warpath. She wants you in her office. Now.'

'I'll be there in ten.'

Twenty-five minutes later, she knocked on Helen's door.

Her boss glanced up briefly, then continued typing. When she finally finished and looked up, Dana couldn't miss her expression of distaste. 'There's a rumour floating around that you interviewed Betty Vickers under false pretences?'

'Yes,' said Dana flatly. There was nothing further to add.

'So, let me get this straight,' Helen said with a piercing stare. 'You took her out of the nursing home pretending to be a relative, wheeled her downtown and gave her a cup of tea. All on work time, did you?' She looked incredulous. 'How did you manage that?'

'Betty told the staff I was her cousin's daughter. I went along with it.'

'And apparently you upset her so much that by the time she got back to the nursing home she was in tears.'

Dana was taken by surprise. 'I didn't upset her.'

'Then who did?'

Dana was unable to meet Helen's grim look.

Helen stood up and walked over to the window, gazing out at the rain and a thin sliver of mist that hung across the city. 'Every weekend I take multiple folders from this filing cabinet and load them into the boot of my car until I can barely shut it. And I triage them on my lounge-room floor according to the age of the child, the severity of the injury and the child protection history. So, I rely on the integrity and hard work of my staff to get through them as quickly as possible.' She turned to look at Dana. 'Since you've been here, you've only finalised three cases and have spent an unusual amount of time on the Kirby case.' She shook her head and said almost imperceptibly. 'It's unbelievable. You've left me no choice but to suspend you for a week. Effective immediately. Hand in your ID and Keely will have to take over your cases. When you return to work, I expect you to close the Kirby case and say goodbye to those girls.'

Helen ushered Dana to her office door. They stood face to face as Helen opened it. For the first time, Dana sensed the steel beneath the floaty layers of Helen's clothing.

'For what it's worth,' Helen added, 'if you'd have been honest with me I could have worked with that.'

Dana felt a surge of guilt as she realised that what Helen was doing gave her no joy.

The door closed and Dana was left in the corridor as though she'd been banished from the principal's office. She silently thanked the gods she'd been suspended in another state, that this wouldn't go on her job record back in New South Wales. But at the same time, she bristled. She was so close to finding out what had happened to Sandra and Debbie. If only she had more time.

Dana took the long way home. A thick fog had drifted into town. She reached the intersection and trudged across the park, cutting a direct route through an area thick with pines. The trees were sinister, their branches like hands twisting in the gloom. As she looked over her shoulder, she could see a lone figure behind her.

The fog swirled around her and she felt like she was being swallowed by heavy white vapour. A wail of sirens started in the distance. Her pulse quickened and she picked up her pace, striding to what she thought was the edge of the gardens, but the mist confused her sense of direction and suddenly she was in a playground, having lost her way on a path she'd walked a hundred times before.

Sandra and Debbie swam into her thoughts. She imagined a fog, like the one she was in now, drifting over them as they fought for their lives. Their panicked screams. The sounds of gunshots in the bush. Debbie hitting the ground and being dragged into the passenger seat. Begging. Pleading for mercy.

She heard the dull thud of footsteps speed up behind her, as real as the cold air on her face. She broke into a run. Fuelled by adrenaline, she bolted off the path through the trees, their branches grazing her face. The laboured breath of her pursuer drawing ever closer. She burst onto Godsall Street, every sinew on high alert. There was a break in the mist and she caught sight of her neighbour up ahead.

'Susan!' she called out.

Susan turned with surprise from the mailbox. 'What's wrong?'

'There was a man,' Dana gasped, out of breath. 'Following me across the park. I had to get away.'

Susan placed a steadying hand on her shoulder. 'Come inside. I'll make you a cup of tea.'

Dana smoothed the frizzed mess of her hair. 'I'm serious. He chased me from the playground.'

'It's okay.' Susan guided Dana through the front gate. 'You can relax now.'

Dana's mind raced with possibilities. The police hadn't followed up with her about the night her window was smashed in. Could it be the same person who followed her? Her first thought was of Paul Kirby. Had she hurt his feelings by turning down a date? Could he really be that pissed off? And then there was Tony Mulhain, who'd clearly been angry with her when she'd questioned him, but no more than any other parent she'd had to interview. The only other man she could think of with a grudge against her was Connor. She hadn't heard from him since they'd argued at the nursing home. Still, she reasoned, stalking wasn't his style. He'd be more likely to give her the silent treatment.

And the worst-case scenario, one she'd barely allowed herself to consider, was that her mind was playing tricks on her. She glanced over her shoulder as Susan led her up the front stairs of her house. A minute ago, she could have sworn someone was following her. Now, she wasn't sure of anything.

There hadn't been time for breakfast, so she did something that she hadn't done since university – she dressed in tracksuit pants and a City2Surf t-shirt from the 1980s and ordered a large supreme pizza and coke from Pizza Hut.

She tried to distract herself by watching *Oprah*, but fifteen minutes into a heart-rending show about orphans she switched it off. Instead, she spent the afternoon scouring Netscape. She typed the words *Crows Nest*, *bikie gangs*, *drugs*, *occult* and *deaths of Debbie Vickers and Sandra Kirby* into the search engine and various chat rooms. What came up were endless conspiracy theories, from the women running away *Thelma and Louise*-style to being killed by the leader of a cult named Eye of Darkness.

By nightfall she had no new information about the case. For the first time since starting her research it occurred to her that the question of what had happened to Sandra and Debbie might never be solved, that it might remain just that. A mystery.

She made herself a cup of tea and looked across at the evidence board she and Angus had been adding to. She leant in to examine the photo of Sandra and her sisters, as if by staring at them they might be able to tell her what had happened.

Ironically, Sandra, a big talker, was now silent. It was what Dana hated the most about cases like these. The silence of women. Women who'd been murdered because they had something to say.

Aside from that, something else was bothering her, but she couldn't put her finger on it. It was only later, as she was climbing into bed, that she finally realised what it was. In the photo, Sandra's smile had been forced. She was looking at the camera, her arms around her stepsisters, like a lioness protecting her cubs. Chrystal and Alisha didn't look happy either. They glared at the camera with hollow grins, in an imitation of happiness that could more accurately be described as guarded.

The next morning Dana established her non-working routine: collecting *The Chronicle* from the lawn and reading it while she had breakfast. As she sipped her coffee and browsed the paper, her mobile on the kitchen table vibrated.

'Hey, Dana,' said Jacinta, her voice screeching down the line. 'A few boxes arrived today and I wasn't sure if it was work stuff or personal, so I thought I'd give you a buzz.'

Surely she knows about the suspension? Then she remembered that Jacinta had only just returned from a week's holiday. Dana couldn't believe her luck.

'Just some personal stuff I had sent up from Sydney,' she said quickly, knowing that the files would have a New South Wales postcode.

'Cool. Should I leave them for when you're in next?'

'Sounds great. Is Helen around?' Dana asked.

'No, she's out for most of the day. Some meeting in Ipswich.'

Dana looked to the ceiling with gratitude. 'Okay. If you leave them by my desk I should be able to pop by at some point and grab them.'

She brushed her hair and threw on a coat and some mascara. By the time she was done the taxi she'd called was waiting out the front.

'It's only a short trip,' she said in an out-of-breath voice to the driver. 'I need to collect something from work, so if you leave the meter on, I can pay you for your time.'

'Sure,' he said. 'It's not exactly busy.'

When they arrived at the office Dana directed him to the underground car park and raced up the fire escape to the third floor. Her heart was in her throat as she walked in behind a couple of the admin staff she recognised. When she crept into the pod, Jacinta was playing solitaire on the computer in the corner.

'Just collecting these boxes,' Dana said casually. She stood in front of her desk, sizing up the archive boxes and wondering how on earth she was going to get them downstairs.

'Oh, hey,' said Jacinta, swivelling in her chair.

Dana hoped she wasn't going to be up for a chat.

'Want some help with those?' Jacinta offered, but she remained seated.

'I'm good,' said Dana, as she struggled under the weight of the first box. She staggered into the foyer and left it inside the door of the fire escape.

When she got back, Jacinta was in the same spot with a look of confusion on her face. 'Aren't you working today?'

Dana made a grab for the second box. 'I'm, er … having some time off. See you next week.'

She hauled the final box into the stairwell and carried them down to the waiting taxi one at a time. She was back home in under thirty minutes. Once inside, she heaved the three boxes onto the kitchen table.

The files on Chrystal and Alisha Lawrence were a mess. There were case notes, authority to care forms, notifications, concerns reports and initial assessments all thrown in together with the court work. In Alisha's files there were a number of blank pages, where evidently the printer cartridge had run out of ink. Dana set about arranging the pages in chronological order and making notes.

The case notes started in the 1980s, when Chrystal and Alisha's mother, Rosalyn, was living in Bankstown. Alisha was born in 1978 when Rosalyn was thirty-one and Chrystal arrived shortly afterwards. There was no mention of the girls' father, just a stepfather named Darryl. Sandra and an older sister had been left in the care of their father in Crows Nest.

Dana started constructing a genogram, a hand-drawn diagram of a family tree that displayed detailed information on relationships and allowed an analysis of hereditary patterns and psychological factors that characterised those relationships. She'd always found them helpful when reading child protection histories, as the visual representations made it easier for her to see where issues within a family originated.

The relationship between Rosalyn and Darryl was rocky from the start, with police call-outs to the house for incidents of domestic violence between the parents, including Rosalyn and her young children being locked out of the house and Darryl giving Rosalyn a black eye. There were a number of raids – though nothing was ever found. In the background was the general neglect of the girls, severe nappy rash, decaying teeth, endless bouts of head lice and the parents' refusal to engage with support services to help them meet the children's needs.

Reading between the lines of the patchy casework, Dana was sure that something else was going on, something that no caseworker had managed to put their finger on. When Rosalyn and Darryl broke up, after he slept with one of Rosalyn's friends, she moved to Blacktown and things really went downhill.

In Blacktown, Rosalyn and her daughters moved into a one-bedroom unit. According to the notes taken by the social worker, they all slept on a mattress on the floor in the lounge room. The flat soon became a hub for all-night parties, loud music and endless comings and goings. The neighbours complained.

Things came to a head in January 1983, when Chrystal was found wandering the streets at one o'clock in the morning in only a nappy and crying inconsolably. It had taken the local Juvenile Aid Bureau hours to locate her address and, when they finally did, they found Rosalyn passed out on the couch and a naked Alisha in the kitchen eating honeycomb.

Dana had been reading through the files for most of the afternoon when Angus came over and called out to her through the open window. He looked into the kitchen as though he was gazing into a lolly shop.

'What's that?' he pointed to the cardboard boxes.

'Just some files I'm reading through for work.'

His face lit up. 'Is it the archives we asked for in my email?' When she didn't respond, he added. 'Can I help? Please, Dana.'

She sighed, fighting the urge to set him up next to her with a Milo as she worked her way through the files. 'I promised your nan that after the last time there'd be no more investigating, but you can help yourself to some chicken fettuccine and watch TV if you're bored.'

A wave of guilt swept over her as he helped himself to a bowl of pasta and trudged through the sliding door into the lounge room. The reason he'd loved delving into the case was because solving the puzzle of Sandra's and Debbie's deaths had given him something to look forward to – a bright light in a life filled with sadness and disappointment. With a jolt, Dana realised that she was the same. Without the case, her life would be in freefall, a black hole threatening to swallow her up. With the case to focus on at least her nightmares had stopped.

Angus had nothing.

She got up from the table and opened a box of Roses chocolates. She offered one to Angus then made a coffee to have with the sweets and returned to her reading.

Initially, there was a struggle to find foster carers for the girls and they had been placed separately. But after Chrystal stopped talking, the caseworker pulled out all the stops to ensure the girls were placed in their grandfather's care. Once they were reunited, they refused to sleep unless they were in the same room and often fell asleep holding hands.

Dana had a flashback to her job in Parramatta, where she'd had to remove two little girls from their parents with substance misuse issues and place them with separate carers. The next morning, when they'd seen each other at day care, their eyes lit up with joy. Dana had never forgotten that special moment, and it brought home to her the importance of keeping siblings together.

She leant back in her chair. So, Chrystal and Alisha had been inseparable when they were younger. But were they close now? Dana didn't think so. The last time she'd seen them together, Alisha had been yelling at her sister: *How could you be so fucking stupid?* What had happened to drive a wedge between them? She made a mental note to ask Chrystal about it when she was back at work.

She was still mulling over the rift between Chrystal and Alisha when it occurred to her that the TV wasn't on. She found Angus in the lounge room, holding a small photo of Oscar she'd hidden in the study.

'Put that down, Angus,' she snapped.

He looked up with surprise before placing it on the bookshelf. 'Sorry,' she said, taking a deep breath. He perched on the couch and took a tentative bite of his food. 'Nan said you had a little boy.'

'Yes,' she said.

'What happened to him?'

She took a long sip of her coffee. 'When he was eight months old, I put him to bed one night and when I checked on him in the morning he'd passed away.' The well of emotion began in her chest and radiated outwards. *Would it ever get easier?*

'I get sad sometimes, too,' he said.

'Really? What about?'

'My mum.' He paused. 'I'd like to live with her, but Nan says it's not practical.' He sounded as though he was repeating what Susan had said.

'Well, your nan's probably right. But it's okay to feel sad.'

'Anyway, it's not too bad – I like living here and being able to visit you.

'What do you like about it?'

He smiled at her, revealing flecks of parsley caught between his teeth. 'The computer.'

She gave him a wry smile. 'Well, that's something.'

It took two days to finally work through Chrystal's and Alisha's case files. Now she was slumped at the kitchen table reading the paper and sipping coffee with a sense of defeat that bordered on depression. The files had proved no more enlightening than the information she had access to at work. Just as she was about to give up and turn on the TV, she noticed an article towards the back of the paper advertising a psychic expo that was taking place in Toowoomba that day. As she perused the list of locals taking part, one name stood out – Kenisha Allenby. The tattooed woman who'd made such a scene at Sandra's funeral and accused the police of not doing their jobs. The one Lachlan had told her was the local psychic. She rushed to her bedroom to get changed, thankful for an escape from the endless self-doubt.

At the convention centre she wandered between tables covered in purple and red fabric, adorned with books and jewellery. The walls were plastered with charts on astrology, aura readings and crystal healing. A fake palm tree swayed in the breeze from an upright fan. In the far corner, Dana spotted the woman she'd been looking for sitting at a table.

Kenisha Allenby was in her early thirties with tattoos of a rose and a butterfly on each shoulder. Her long, hennaed hair had been pulled back from her face to reveal gold hoop earrings. Dana sat down opposite her, a lava lamp glowing between them.

'What can I do for you.' Kenisha eyed Dana's tailored blouse with curiosity. 'We don't normally get businesswomen at these things.'

Dana smiled. 'It's not the type of event I'd usually come to.'

'So, what can I help you with today? Palm reading? Tarot cards? An aura assessment?'

'None of those actually.'

Kenisha's eyes narrowed.

'I'll pay you for your time,' Dana said quickly to reassure her.

'I just wanted to ask you about the Kirby and Vickers murders.'

'Well, you wouldn't be the first.' Two lines formed between her eyebrows. 'What exactly do you want to know?'

'For a start, how did you know them?'

'I was at school with Sandra's older sister Denise. We were a few years ahead of her at school. So, I'd always known her, but not real well. Then when I had Kayden, who is the same age as Billy-Violet, I used to see Sandra hanging around the school gates and after I talked to her a few times I realised we were on the same vibration.' Her frown deepened. 'Course, that was a few years ago. I left that shithole as fast as I could. Couldn't handle the bullshit people used to say about me one minute longer.'

'Which leads me to what I wanted to ask you about next,' said Dana, picking up a lump of jade from the table and turning it over in her hand. 'There's a rumour going around that you know about the dark arts.'

Kenisha looked at her blankly.

'You know, Satanism?'

'Oh, that.' Kenisha rolled her eyes. 'When I was living out at Crows Nest, all these birds died on my property. Indian mynas, honeyeaters and so on. About a hundred of them. I called the Department of Agriculture and when they came out to investigate, they told me it was probably toxic algae or pesticides that killed them. It was just the strangest thing.' She shook her head in wonder. 'Anyway, after that, the dickheads at the pub – Jimmy Cullens and that lot – said I was a devil worshipper. That all the dead birds fell out of the sky and were the work of Satan or something ridiculous. Thing is, I'm just a single mum who runs a café and reads a few palms on the side. Not very glamorous, is it?'

'So, what's this then?' Dana pushed the Satanism Confirmation Certificate across the table.

'Oh, shit.' Kenisha put her hand over her mouth and laughed. 'I made one of those for Sandra's birthday. As a joke, after we'd had a few. I told her to burn it a few days later, for luck.' She grimaced. 'Sandra and I used to joke that I was a devil worshipper and she was my apprentice. We'd both had a few run-ins with a group of bitchy mums at the school and it was our way of just laughing at it all.'

'So, what was Debbie doing with one?'

Kenisha rolled her eyes. 'You know what it was like – wherever Sandra went Debbie was there, too. So, I did her a certificate so she wouldn't get jealous.'

Dana sat back in her chair. It all made sense. 'So, to your knowledge, Sandra was not a Satanist.'

'No, if anything, what both of those women believed in was God.' Kenisha crumpled as though she was about to cry. 'I just hope they're up there in heaven right now laughing at all those losers in Crows Nest.' She leant forward across the table. 'I've never told anyone this, but after they died, Ian Steinmann paid me a visit and asked me what I thought happened to Sandra and Debbie. I said to him, well, I can tell you one thing, it sure as hell wasn't murder–suicide.'

'What do you think happened?'

Kenisha sat back in her chair. 'I think that they had a run-in with some bikies, like the ones that hang out in the pub, and were unlucky.' She paused for a moment. 'Just very, very unlucky.' She blinked suddenly, as though something had just occurred to her. 'I bet you don't know what the collective noun for a group of crows is, do you?'

Dana humoured her, as though she hadn't heard it all before. 'What is it?'

'A murder.' Kenisha's face was incredulous. 'They call it a murder of crows.'

Dana paid her fifty dollars and left the convention centre knowing it was over. This case was never going to be solved. Instead of wasting hours, days, falling down rabbit holes that led nowhere, she was going to stop. A phrase her music teacher had once used came to mind: 'When you find yourself in a tug of war, let go of the rope.'

21

The week-long suspension passed quickly and, before Dana knew it, she was back on the road with Lachlan heading out to see the Kirby family one last time.

'How was your holiday?' he asked as they knocked on the door of the Kirby house.

'I was on suspension,' she said, ignoring his attempt at humour. 'I'd hardly call it a holiday. By the way, what did Ian say about the diary?'

Lachlan looked sheepish. 'I only told him about it yesterday, but he was very grateful.' He paused. 'It was bizarre though. He hasn't stopped calling me since, asking when I'm going to drop it around. I've known him for years and he's never been like that.' A dog from a nearby yard let out a piercing howl and Lachlan winced. 'I didn't say you gave it to me … I thought it was best if he believed I was the only one who'd seen it.'

Chrystal opened the door, dark rings under her eyes and the baby on her hip.

'Come in,' she said. 'Paul's in the shower.'

They followed her down the hallway into the kitchen where she began turning sausages in a pan on the stovetop. Billy-Violet was in her school uniform watching TV.

'Smells good.' Lachlan smiled.

'Thanks.'

'You look tired,' said Dana. 'Can I help with anything?'

Chrystal readjusted Rubi on her hip and opened the fridge. 'I'm okay.' She nodded for them to take a seat in the lounge room.

Dana sat down, bothered about the way cooking and tending to the baby seemed second nature to Chrystal and about the scent she'd detected on her. The combination of spice and musk. So familiar and yet—

Paul came into the kitchen, his wet hair spiked in a fringe and a towel around his waist.

'Sorry, folks,' he said. 'I can't stay long. I've got to drop Billy off at school on my way to work.'

'This shouldn't take long,' said Dana. 'We've been instructed to close your case. Not something I fully agree with, but …' She shrugged with the futility of the situation.

'So you should.' Paul puffed himself up, pulling his shoulders back. 'I could never understand why you lot kept visiting. There are kids out there whose parents are bashing them every weekend and you guys are visiting me. When I was telling you all along, we're fine!' He rested his hand lightly on Chrystal's shoulder. She switched off the stove and gazed up at him. Dana's stomach dropped. She knew that look.

'I need to use the toilet,' she said, excusing herself and rushing up the hallway. As she stepped into the small white bathroom and shut the door her mind was racing. A mirrored medicine cabinet hung over a small sink. She slid open the misted doors of the cabinet and rifled through the shelves. After a minute, she started on the drawers under the sink. In the middle drawer she found what she was looking for – a white glass bottle with the Old Spice logo and blue ship. She sprayed the mist into the air and took a deep breath. She finally realised not only what Chrystal smelt like, but *who* she smelt like.

The pulsing of blood in her ears reached an oceanic roar. How could she not have seen this? How could she not have predicted Paul's interest in Chrystal?

She recalled Ian Steinmann's words the night of Sandra's wake when the fog had swept through Crows Nest. *There's something about him women like. You get a girl like that, with all that burgeoning sexuality and you've got a problem.* Dana now knew who Ian had been referring to.

She made her way back into the lounge room and stood behind the sofa stalling for time. On the mantelpiece was a stack of *Guns and Ammo* magazines.

'Enjoy a bit of shooting do you, Paul?' she said, remembering what Alisha had told her about Paul teaching her how to shoot.

He turned around to see what she was referring to. 'Course I do, it's the country. Everyone shoots around here.'

Lachlan was looking at her quizzically. He lowered his voice. 'What are you doing?'

Paul took his hand away from Chrystal.

'Okay,' Lachlan said, standing up and passing Dana her handbag. 'We've said what we came to say. Now we'll leave you in peace. Come on.'

Dana remained fixated on Paul, as if they were the only

people in the room. Her mind was racing, but she forced herself to remember Paul's airtight alibi from his first police interview. That there was no way he was involved in what happened to Sandra and Debbie that night.

'We'll be in touch if we need anything.' Lachlan took Dana by the elbow, leading her down the hallway. 'What's gotten into you?' he said as they made their way back out to the car.

She searched his face. 'They're sleeping together. I know it. Nothing has ever been clearer in my life.'

Lachlan's brow creased. 'It's pretty disgusting, but she's sixteen. So, unless she makes a complaint, there's nothing we can do.'

'But it's worse than that. She's only just turned sixteen, which means that when they *started* sleeping together it wasn't legal.'

Lachlan rubbed his forehead. 'And here I was thinking we were going to be able to shut this case and forget all about it …'

'I'm going to drive over to the police station and tell them what's been happening. They need to charge Paul with carnal knowledge.'

'You can't. You've just been suspended. Is it worth risking your whole career for?'

Her eyes narrowed. They were discussing a major child protection concern and he was acting as though he didn't care. 'Ian's your friend. You need to tell him about Paul and Chrystal. Now.'

'Seriously? You want me to drive to the police station and tell Ian, *what*? Paul's been having sex with Chrystal and it might have started when she was fifteen? Oh, and by the way, I don't have one shred of evidence.' He laid a hand on Dana's shoulder. 'Just checking, you don't, do you?'

She looked away, her hands on her hips, then turned back to face him. 'I get that you don't want to get mixed up in this. That it's going to be bad if I'm proven wrong, but I just thought – the two of you are friends ...' She trailed off, too exhausted to go on.

'Dana, I'm worried about you. You're spreading yourself thin, staying up all night obsessing about this case. You've gotten involved in things that are none of your bloody business.'

'Well, it is my business. The child is in our care. Sleeping with a man acting in loco parentis. Surely that's everyone's business?'

'At what cost? As I said – she's over the age of consent, she's unlikely to make a complaint. You've almost lost your job and now you'd like me to lose mine, too. Is that it?'

She looked back at the flowering shrub near the door half dead from lack of water. 'Maybe you're right. Maybe I should just go back to work and start churning through the cases, like everyone keeps telling me to.'

Doubt and indecision passed over Lachlan's face. 'I've arranged to meet Ian at the pub for dinner to give him the diary. I'll mention this to him then. But just this once. And only because I've got a duty of care to Chrystal.'

'Great.' She breathed a sigh of relief as she got back in the car.

Dana pulled on her running tights when she got home that evening and jogged to the end of the street, refusing to let fear rule her life. She ran north, past the bunya pines along the boundary of the park and veered right towards the memorial cannon, an empire relic of cast iron that children loved to play on. Her breathing was good. She passed the obelisk, running diagonally along the path past the last of the roses – *Tamango*, *Floribunda*,

Oranges and Lemons. The breeze in the trees murmured softly, of things being put right.

As she reached the arch leading into the children's playground and completed a lap of the park, the sky was lit with brilliant pinks and oranges. She rallied again, up Godsall Street, past the worker's cottages, the grand Queenslanders sprawling across three blocks, and sped through the gate to her own house.

After midnight, the wind changed. Camphor laurels bent in the breeze and cold air seeped under the door. Dana woke suddenly as the windows rattled in their panes. Loud, brash propeller blades sliced the sky. *The care-flight helicopter.* She'd seen one land at the hospital a week earlier. The sound reverberated with her heartbeat, shaking her lonely home to its core.

The call came a few hours later in the early hours of the morning.

'It's Lachlan,' Helen said breathlessly. 'He's hurt. They've transferred him to the Royal Brisbane. His condition's critical.'

22

They headed for the Royal Brisbane Hospital as the sun rose over the mountains, Keely at the wheel and Dana in the passenger seat. Dana stared at the abyss down the side of the mountain feeling sick to her stomach. The bravado she'd experienced after telling Lachlan about Paul's behaviour had long since departed. *Why had she been so keen to catch him out?* When had her mind become so warped, so obsessed with being vindicated? And now for the sake of her obsession, she'd forced Lachlan onto a treacherous road late at night. She pictured him on his deathbed, machines and drips keeping him alive. His accident had been her fault. No justification about trying to nail a sleazebag could undo that fact.

'Do you know why Lachlan was driving back so late?' Keely asked.

'No idea.' Dana lied. Bile rose in her throat as she blinked rapidly to keep from crying.

'It's such a bad road. Remember when the fog was so thick that night we had to stay in Crows Nest?'

'How could I forget,' she replied. They entered the Gatton Bypass, a stretch of road as desolate as her heart.

Keely switched to cruise control and glanced across at Dana. 'I need to apologise. I was the one who made the complaint to Helen about you hitting Connor.' She tightened her grip on the steering wheel. 'Even though it was you sleeping with him that bothered me most.'

'How did you know we slept together?' Dana thought she'd been discreet.

'His text message came up on your phone when you ran back to the motel for your jacket.'

'Oh.' Dana cringed, remembering. She felt the heat rising in her cheeks as she wondered who else knew she'd slept with Connor. *Jacinta? Helen? The whole office?* She slumped her head against the window and pictured them laughing about it at work drinks. If only she could bury herself deep under her doona and never see them again. Something else occurred to her. 'And the Princess Diana nickname?'

'That was me, too. I'm sorry,' said Keely. 'It's just that I'd liked him for so long … I finally thought I was getting somewhere.'

'It's fine,' said Dana.

Keely exhaled, her fringe billowing in the air. 'I wish I'd known how much better I'd feel after telling you. I've been feeling guilty for ages.'

'I always try to apologise for the things I'm not proud of straight away … It's never stopped them from happening again though.'

'I can't image you ever making mistakes,' said Keely. 'Ever.'

'I do all the time.' Dana paused. 'Sometimes I feel as though I've wandered so far off track I'll never get back.'

Keely laughed. 'He really likes you, you know.'

'Who?'

'Lachlan.'

Dana was silent.

'He always talks about how smart you are. How you cut right through the crap to see the truth. He told me he enjoys working with you to see how your mind works.'

'I think that was his undoing.'

'What do you mean?'

'I'm just not sure I'm the beacon of truth he imagines me to be.' Dana shifted in her seat. 'Anyway, he's the one who's the amazing worker. When I'm with him he gets people to open up in a way I'd never imagined possible. I'm embarrassed to admit, but when I started in this job I'd barely worked with any men and was under the misapprehension that they could never be decent social workers. He completely cured me of that delusion.'

'He is pretty awesome,' said Keely. 'When I started, there was this rumour that he'd managed to get a disclosure from this farmer who'd been sexually abusing his daughter. Once Lachlan got him talking, the guy had so much to say that he was still rabbiting on while Lachlan was winding up the window and driving away.'

'That doesn't surprise me.' Dana smiled, remembering the times she'd revealed far more to him than she'd wanted to.

A flock of crows rose up from a mound of rolled hay bales in the crops beside the university campus. Dana's thoughts turned to Van Gogh's wheatfield paintings. The symbolism of birds in a menacing sky. The dead-end path to the end of life.

When they arrived at the hospital they navigated the multistorey car park, then made their way to the information desk. A woman wearing a lanyard around her neck gave them directions to Lachlan's ward and they set off in silence. After winding through endless white corridors, they came to the intensive care ward.

The nurse briefed them on Lachlan's condition. They were to enter the ward separately and only stay a few minutes. 'You need to prepare yourselves. He's suffered a major trauma. He's still very weak.'

They squirted soap into their palms and washed their hands at the basin.

'You go first,' Keely said to Dana. 'I'm pretty sure you were his favourite.'

The air conditioner inside the room was on high. Even so, Dana's face burnt with shame. When she finally brought herself to look at him, she was stunned. His face was waxen as he lay there and his jaw jutted into space like a mummy's. A cruel joke, bearing little similarity to the man she knew.

She sat in the chair beside him. 'Hey Lachlan, it's Dana.'

It hadn't occurred to her that due to him being intubated, there was no chance of him speaking. She stared glumly at the bouquets of flowers on the table, and recalled his popularity. She vowed that if he lived, she was going to make changes. She'd follow his example and let people in. Soften the polished stone of her heart.

She stroked his hair, surprised at its softness. She took his hand. He gripped her fingers. 'I'm so sorry,' she whispered. 'Can you ever forgive me?'

His breathing became laboured, as though he was trying to communicate with her. Though the sight of his bandages was terrifying, her intuition told her that he was still *in there* fighting for his life.

'Everyone loves you. They're praying for you to come back to us. We need you here.'

The raw emotion she'd been holding in all morning ripped its way through her chest. 'Please, Lachlan.' Her voice cracked. 'You told me once that there's a lot of good things in the world.' She loosened her hand and redoubled her grip. 'I need to believe that.'

She mumbled a prayer. If she could bargain her way out of this, she would.

The air conditioner hummed and she heard muffled tones. Someone coughed. Tears rolled down her face, though there was no hope of them washing away her guilt.

Dana went to the bathroom while Keely went in to see Lachlan. She dabbed her eyes and took a tissue from her handbag to wipe her nose. It was obvious that she'd been crying. Her face was blotchy when she glanced at herself in the mirror. There was no point trying to hide it.

On the way back from the bathroom, Susan was walking down the hall towards her. It was so strange to see her neighbour out of context that Dana almost didn't recognise her.

'What are you doing here?' said Susan, a look of surprise on her face.

'One of our work colleagues crashed his car. We travelled up this morning to see how he's doing.'

'Is he going to be okay?'

'We don't know. He was holding my hand pretty tightly before, so that gives me some hope.'

'That's terrible,' Susan said distractedly. Her hands trembled as she tried to keep the coffee in her polystyrene cup from spilling.

'Why are you here?' Dana asked, her heart rate jumping.

Susan pressed a hand to her forehead. 'Tina, Angus's mum. She's back on the heroin. I got a call from the hospital this morning saying she'd overdosed ...' She caught Dana's horrified look. 'Oh, it's alright. She was lucky apparently. She'll need to spend the next few hours on an IV getting some fluids into her and then she'll be spending a few days in the mental health ward to get on top of her depression.' She shrugged helplessly. 'You think I'd be used to it by now.'

'Had anything changed for her lately?' Dana asked.

'Everything came to a head after she stole some money from the bikie gang in Crows Nest and they started sending her threats.'

'I hope it's not Tony Mulhain?'

Susan blinked back tears. 'They were childhood sweethearts and he's had a thing for her as long as I can remember. If she did steal from him and he was trying to help her out, he would have taken it personally.' She took a deep breath. 'I've tried to talk her into coming home, but she's not interested. She's going back to her boyfriend, Wade.'

Dana shook her head in commiseration. 'And who's looking after Angus?' she asked, imagining how upset he'd be.

'I hired a babysitter and told him I was visiting a friend. I'm terrified that if he gets wind that his mum's here, he'll do a runner again.'

They stepped aside as a woman pushed past them with a food trolley.

'I think he might have grown up a bit in the last few weeks,' said Dana. 'He told me that he understands what he put everyone through last time, so hopefully he's learnt his lesson.'

'You don't know what he's like with his mum. The trauma that he went through left him with a warped attachment to her.'

They stood in silence.

'Anyway, I'd better run,' said Susan 'I only paid for two hours' parking, so if I get a ticket that'll just be another thing I have to deal with.'

'Okay, I'll see you at home. Let me know if there's anything I can do.'

Susan nodded and hurried away down the corridor.

When she got back home later that afternoon, Dana stripped off her clothes, took a valium to calm the chaos in her head and headed for the shower. She turned the tap to its hottest setting, letting the steam fill the room, and stood with her head bowed. The cascade of water was a relief for her stiff shoulders and neck. She washed her hair for the first time in a week and towel-dried it in front of the mirror. From the corner of her eye, she caught a movement in the lounge room.

'Angus!' she screamed, facing him, still naked. 'What are you doing?' She covered her breasts with her hands and turned away, rushing for the bedroom. She flung open the cupboard and pulled on her dressing-gown. The shock of seeing him quickly giving way to anger. *Could this awful day get any worse?*

She tightened the belt of her gown and returned to the lounge room where Angus was huddled in the corner. 'You need to tell me if you're coming over. Not just show up whenever.'

His words came in a rush. 'There was an emergency. The babysitter had to leave.' He gulped.

'Where's your nan?'

'In Brisbane, with her friend.' He was on the verge of tears, his bottom lip trembling. 'I told her it would be alright if I came over here.'

'It is alright,' she said, softening. 'There's no need to look like that.'

She managed to calm him down by letting him play Pac-Man on the computer. Later in the evening, she cooked his favourite – chicken fettuccine – and took two plates into the lounge room. They watched *Neighbours* and ate their dinner as the thunder rumbled and lightning lit up the trees in the park. During the ad break, she ran their plates under the kitchen tap as rain bucketed down outside.

She was looking out at the hedgerow along the laneway fence when, for a split second, as the lightning flashed, she saw the silhouette of a man at the window. She stumbled backward, her heart racing. When she looked again, there was no-one to be seen. The pasta she'd eaten curdled in her gut. She hurried to her bedroom and rifled through her handbag for the card the policeman had given her last time. As she drew the curtains, she dialled his number.

'Dana,' he said, after she introduced herself. 'I remember – the property damage to that beautiful Queenslander. What can I do for you?'

'Well, the thing is …' She tried to pull her scattered thoughts together. 'About five minutes ago, I saw a man outside.'

'Okay,' he said slowly. 'Did you know this man? Can you describe him to me?'

'I couldn't say for certain. It all happened so quickly.' She was unable to keep her voice from trembling. 'I caught a glimpse of someone staring through the kitchen window and then they were gone. But it was definitely a man.' She thought about Tony Mulhain, but she'd said so many crazy things lately, she couldn't bring herself to say the words out loud.

'Okay. Alright. And did he come onto your property? Did he threaten you in any way?'

'He did come onto the property, but he didn't threaten me,' she said, starting to feel ridiculous.

'Was he on the laneway side or the street side of your house?'

'The laneway side.'

The line was muffled as he spoke to someone. 'Yeah, we've had lots of problems with houses in your area as people can access properties off the laneway. Just a sec … sorry about that. And do you have a lock on the back gate?'

'Yes, but it's a low fence. It wouldn't take much to scale it.' She hesitated. 'I'm looking after a young boy at the moment, and I know his mother has gotten on the wrong side of some drug dealers in Crows Nest.'

There was an exhalation of breath on the other end of the line. 'On a normal night, I'd offer to send someone out and take a look around, but we're seriously understaffed. There's been a fatal crash on the range tonight and every spare officer's out there.'

She was momentarily unable to speak.

'I'll tell you what, if you're still worried over the next few days, let me know and I'll see what we can do.'

'Thanks,' she said, her heart swooping with despair. When she hung up, she felt worse than ever. Not only did she think she was crazy, but the local policeman clearly agreed with her.

She returned to Angus and sat next to him on the couch, her hands shaking. At the end of the eight o'clock news he looked up at her.

'Can't I stay here tonight? Just this once?' He yawned. 'I never get to have sleepovers.'

She paused. It was only for one night. And if there was the slightest chance someone was lurking outside, she didn't want to risk it. 'That should be fine. I'll have to give your nan a quick call to check that it's alright.'

After she'd spoken to Susan, Dana made up the spare bed. Angus made himself comfortable and she switched off the light.

'Will you be okay in here?'

'Yes.' His eyes were big in the dim light.

She patted his head. 'I'll see you in the morning.'

'Good-o,' he said, pulling the blanket over himself.

She dragged the kitchen door shut, locked the door on to the verandah and double-checked the windows. In bed, she turned restlessly beneath the covers, trying to ease the bursitis in her hip, right side then left, desperate for comfort. She thought about the man she'd seen in the laneway. Was it a stalker, or just a random person walking past? Had she become so paranoid, that every man was now after her? Her heart sped up suddenly as though it had switched gears. She flung the covers from her bed and padded to the fridge for a glass of milk. She read her book for half an hour then lay back down and closed her eyes. She was so tired and everything was going wrong. Lachlan in hospital, her mind unravelling.

She'd just started to drift off when she heard it. A blood-curdling scream, from the direction of the park. She lay still, wondering whether she'd dreamt it. She heard the distant squeal of the midnight train, the relentless hum of its engine and the wind whipping the trees outside. Before long she felt herself being pulled down like she was under water, a brick tethered to her waist. The sleep that overtook her was thick and dreamless.

Dana woke sweating under the heavy doona. The drone of machinery in the laneway outside vibrated through the house. She stumbled out of bed and called the hospital to find out about Lachlan. There was nothing they could tell her. His condition was stable and they were hoping to know more once tests were carried out later that morning.

She got dressed and headed down the hall to wake up Angus. The bed where Angus had slept was empty, the blanket he'd been sleeping under was on the floor and the door to the verandah ajar. She did a hurried survey of the house then rushed over to Susan's. Maybe he'd gone next door for breakfast.

The sun was out. Susan opened the front door and Dana was dazzled by the gold of her earrings.

'Angus hasn't come back home this morning, has he?' asked Dana. 'I can't find him.'

Susan was flustered. She ran down the hallway then returned a few moments later, her face pale.

Dana remembered the scream in the park. The outline of a man through the window. He'd watched her cosy dinner with Angus. She hoped it wasn't Tony. Now that Angus's mother owed him money, he knew that his best artillery for getting it back was to steal her son.

'Oh god,' she gasped.

23

After convincing Susan to go to the police station, Dana darted back home through the front yard. A low-hanging branch by the gate clipped her face and she shouted in pain. She put her hand to her forehead and her fingers came away red. She wiped them on her pants and applied pressure to the wound.

Who could she enlist to help her find Angus? Connor came to mind, but the thought of speaking to him made her feel sick. Surely there was someone else? Anyone would be better than the man she'd slept with in her first weeks at work. She cast around for an alternative, but there wasn't one.

Connor answered on the first ring.

'Hey, Dana,' he said in a long, languid tone. 'Long time, no see.'

'I know.' She paced up and down the rug, getting tangled in the cord of the landline as she reached for a tissue to stem the bleeding. 'Sorry about the way we ended things.'

'It's cool. I knew you'd call. I just thought to myself, treat 'em mean and keep 'em keen. And one day she'll be back. And I was right, you know—'

'Can you just focus for a minute, put aside your massive ego? I need to talk to you about something.'

'I already know about Lachlan. Sarge told me last night.'

Tears stung her eyes and she blinked them away. 'No, it's not that, it's something else. My neighbour Angus Fitcher is missing.'

'Him?' He guffawed. 'He'll be fine. I've had to drop him back at his nan's, like, a hundred times.'

'This is different.' She untangled the phone cord from her wrist. 'He was at my house last night and he didn't make it home. I spoke to him just recently about running away and he said he wasn't going to do it again.'

'You know what kids are like. Say one thing, do another.'

For the life of her, she couldn't remember why she'd been attracted to him. 'Look, I know that Angus's mum stole money from one of the bikies, possibly Tony Mulhain, and I'm worried they might have kidnapped Angus as some sort of bargaining tool, so they can get their money back.'

There was silence on the end of the line.

'They were childhood sweethearts. Apparently, it's personal for him,' she said, detesting the pleading tone that had crept into her voice. 'Connor, I need your help.'

'C'mon, Dana. It's my day off.'

'Great.' A sliver of opportunity had opened up. 'I'll meet you at Crows Nest pub in an hour.'

She hung up before he had the chance to argue.

~

Dana hurried through the bar of the hotel, past the publican who cast her a suspicious glance and on past the lunchtime pokie players wearing flannelettes and smoking. Connor was in the beer garden out the back where the weeds were even more overgrown than last time.

He pushed a frosted schooner of Fourex in her direction as she sat down. 'I recall you being rather fond of these the last time we were here.' He was in the uniform of the off-duty policeman – a polo shirt with sunglasses perched on his head. 'So, what's been happening lately?' he said, a note of flirtation in his voice.

She turned the cold glass of beer in her hands. 'Connor, I've said this before, but you and I … it was a one-time thing.'

He sat back wearily, his air of bravado seeping away. 'I know. You've got a husband. You're not ready.'

'I'm never going to be ready.' She paused, worrying she'd been too blunt. She needed his help. Her foot jiggled beneath the table.

'It's cool. I was going to say the same thing, but I was a bit worried about breaking it to you. I've started seeing someone else.'

'Who?' she said, trying to hide her frustration with how off-track they were.

'Keely.'

Dana choked on her beer then pushed her drink aside. 'This meeting's not about having a catch-up. Angus is missing and I need your help.'

He took a large swig of beer and eyed her over his schooner. He set it down with a thump. 'I am taking this seriously. I went over to Tony's place on my way here and had a look around. Strangely enough, your little friend was nowhere to be seen.'

Her eyes narrowed. 'So, Tony wasn't there?'

'No, but that doesn't mean that he's kidnapped Angus.' He drummed his fingers on the hard wood of the table. 'Someone needs to say this to you and it's gonna have to be me. You've just been suspended and if you keep on acting crazy, you're going to get sacked. I know you lost your own kid and that was a shit thing to happen, but this kid is fine. I had a chat to Ian and a few of the other officers and no-one is worried. They're all expecting him to show up at the hospital hoping to see his mum.' He leant forward, screwing up his face with disgust. 'Is that blood on your face?'

She grabbed a napkin and dabbed her forehead. 'This is not some paranoid delusion, Connor.' She hesitated. 'It was only for a split second, but I think I saw a man in my yard last night. And from where he was standing and the way the room was lit, he would have seen the evidence board.' She shook her head trying to remove the image from her mind.

'You have an evidence board?' Connor chuckled. 'Oh, man.'

'It was just something Angus and I were doing for fun.' She cringed, realising how improper it was for her to be allowing a child to participate in such an activity. There was no way to explain the fun they'd had, theorising about different motives, trying to solve the puzzle of who was the killer. To Angus it was just a game, of that she was certain.

Connor raised his eyebrows. 'My point exactly. You've taken this thing way too far.'

'Regardless of what you think, something's wrong, I know it.'

'There's nothing to suggest that the two of them being missing is connected. Tony's probably just gone into town for the morning with his missus.'

A man at the jukebox stood with his back to her. When he turned around and stubbed out his cigarette, a look of recognition passed over his face. He hiked up his fisherman's pants and came over. 'I remember you! Never forget a pretty face.'

She nodded slowly as it dawned on her. The tow-truck driver who'd come to her aid when she'd been stranded on the highway all those months ago. 'Jimmy, isn't it?'

'Dana!' He leant in for a hug.

She was so taken aback that she had no choice but to surrender. By the time he'd released her, she was certain that seeing him again was a windfall of good luck. Jimmy knew everyone in the drug community and could be a huge help. 'Pull up a seat.' He arranged his lanky body in the chair next to them. 'This is Constable Connor Morgan,' she said.

Jimmy ran a nervous hand through his shoulder-length hair, his collarbones prominent beneath his blue singlet. He looked like he was on the bones of his arse, as she'd heard the locals say.

'Connor. Right on, man. I've seen you around.' Jimmy's eyes darted around the table until he spotted an ashtray and lit a smoke.

Connor looked at Dana, confused. 'How do you two know each other?'

'Jimmy helped me out of a difficult situation,' she said, before Jimmy had the chance to answer. 'With my car.'

Jimmy gave them a toothy grin. 'Yeah, man. She hit a kangaroo and totalled her Benz. It was pretty messed up.'

He'd changed since Dana had seen him last. He was less threatening in the daylight. Less inclined to stare at her breasts.

'Were they able to fix it?' Jimmy asked.

She shrugged with resignation. 'It was a write-off.'

'Such a shame … that was one sweet ride,' said Jimmy.

'Can I buy you a drink? You were so helpful to me and I've never managed to repay you.' Dana got her purse and rose from her seat. 'What'll you have?'

'A coke, please. And a packet of chips. Thanks, Dana.'

'How've you been anyway?' she said, once she returned from the bar and placed the drink and food in front of Jimmy.

'Good, yeah. I've cleaned myself up since the last time we met. Been going to AA, NA, anger management, whatever I can get my hands on. Been trying to get my shit together. I want to get custody of my kids, or at least fifty–fifty. It's not right my ex gets all my child support and I barely get to see them.'

'Good for you,' she said, and meant it. The way people could rise up and make their lives meaningful was the reason she did this work.

'Jimmy, I know you grew up here and you know this area well – a young boy is missing and you might be able to help us find him. Tony Mulhain is also nowhere to be found and I'm worried there might be a connection.' Her eyes locked on his, hoping he'd understand.

He nodded. 'I know what it's like to lose a kid.' Emotion flashed in his amber eyes. 'And maybe if I help out, you could write something nice to the judge, for my court case?'

'I'm sure it can be arranged.' Dana looked to Connor for support before returning her focus to Jimmy. 'So, what do you know about Tony?'

He tilted his head. 'I know that he was into some bad shit when he was younger.'

'Such as?' Connor leant across the table.

'Break and enters, stolen cars, smoking drugs … he told me he was in jail down south once.'

'Do you know where he might be at the moment?' asked Dana. 'Connor's been to his home, but there was no-one there. It's getting desperate. Angus has been missing for over twelve hours.'

'I don't know where he is, but my cousin, Matty, might – those two are thick as thieves and Tony's with him all the time. If anyone knows where he is, it's Matty.'

'The Matty that has schizophrenia? That was in the institution?' asked Dana.

'You betcha. But he's a lot better now he's on his medication.' He ground his cigarette into the ashtray. 'I'll show you the way.'

They piled into Connor's jeep, Jimmy in the seat behind them. A Neil Young song was playing and his lyrics about the cost of lost love swept over her. She leant back as blackened gum trees whipped past and wondered why everyone she cared about was being taken from her. Oscar, Lachlan, Angus. She took a breath. The adrenaline of the past few days had been unrelenting, a slow drip of poison to her heart. She closed her eyes and pictured Angus's boyish expression, the smattering of freckles on his nose.

'The one thing I need to tell you about Matty is – he don't take kindly to cops,' said Jimmy.

Connor flicked a glance at him through the rear-view mirror. 'I won't tell him if you don't.'

That seemed to satisfy Jimmy and he sat back in his seat.

'So, how do you know Tony?' Dana asked Jimmy.

He paused. 'When we were younger, we did community service together, getting rid of weeds, overgrown grass and shit. I remember he told me this story once – he was on the run from the cops and he had to dive into a river. They were looking for him and there were searchlights everywhere, so he submerged himself in the water and used one of the river reeds to breathe through. He stayed like that for an hour until they were finally gone.' He paused thoughtfully. 'I've never figured out if it was true or not.'

'What do you reckon?' Connor asked.

Dana shot him a look. 'And how much can you tell us about the local drug scene?' she asked Jimmy.

He grinned at her. 'Well, Crows Nest is the feeder town for drugs for the entire Darling Downs region and you'll be happy to know that the drug scene was a bit of a specialty of mine.' He paused dramatically. 'The way it works is that the first tier are the farmers and the madmen who work for Tony Mulhain, who grow and pack the drugs. Then the second level are the sellers, regular people like bikies and tradies who can distribute the stuff and not draw too much heat. And the third tier are the coppers who look after them and take their cut. The untouchables.'

She stared despondently at a flock of black cockatoos ahead. If they couldn't trust the local police force, who could they trust?

'Connor, you're going to want to …' she said as they hurtled towards the birds, '… *stop*!' She screamed as the birds beat the glass like a kettle drum.

'They know the deal.' He flicked on the windscreen wipers. 'If you're a small creature wanting to take on a two-ton car – you better be ready.'

Jimmy stuck his head between them. 'No wonder they're on the endangered list.'

~

When they pulled up out the front of Matty's property, the sickness in the pit of Dana's stomach remained. But now, instead of worrying about the endless roadkill, she couldn't get her mind off Angus and the possibility that he had become involved in something way over his head.

A large sign on the front gate had blood-red letters saying: *Legal Notice. No trespassing on this property, under any circumstances.*

'He likes his privacy,' Jimmy said from the back.

Dana got out of the car and unhooked the chain on the gate. Connor drove through and she resumed her place in the passenger seat, her chest tight with anxiety.

In the front yard, a rusty swing set sat next to a weatherboard house. A black van and the wreckage of a lightweight plane flanked the side of the property.

'Before Matty went crazy he used to be a pilot,' said Jimmy. 'So, he sits in the plane sometimes, for the memories of how things used to be.'

Connor parked beneath a ghost gum. A loud bang rang out from a shed to the left making them jump. A thought rocketed through Dana's head.

I want to find you, Angus. But please don't be here.

Connor strode through the grass with long policeman strides. She briefly wondered whether she should stay behind, but Jimmy had begun to follow so she jogged to keep up with them.

The door to the shed was open and there was more banging against the wall – the same loud noise they'd heard earlier. Connor gave the door a sharp kick and it flew from its hinges, dust billowing as it came to rest in the dirt. They padded through the door in single file. She took shallow gulps of air. *The worst has already happened*, she repeated to herself. *Nothing can hurt you.*

In the corner of the shed, a man with a black beard and owlish eyes was sitting in a chair. Beside him was an overturned motorbike. His shirt was unbuttoned and a can of VB sat on his stomach.

'Matty.' Jimmy stepped forward.

Matty squinted his eyes, as if trying to see Jimmy clearly. 'Jimmy, man. I haven't seen you for ages.'

'What's been happening?'

'Not much. Having a few drinks.' His words were slurred. He gazed around and ran his hand through the black hair on his chest. 'It's a good fan this one.' He nodded meditatively towards the fan swinging slowly in front of him. He stopped suddenly. 'Who are you?' he said to Dana and Connor, as if seeing them for the first time. 'It says on the sign no trespassing! I'm just trying to lead a peaceful life here.'

He took a swig of his beer and then arched his arm back like a baseball pitcher ready to take aim.

'Look, mate,' Connor said, sliding a can of capsicum spray from his pants. 'Do you want to start behaving or do you want to cop some of this?'

Matty dropped his beer and the can echoed on the cement. Connor walked over to the motorbike and leant down to pick up a clip-seal bag filled with green on the floor nearby. He held it up to the light.

'C'mon,' said Matty, snapping to attention. 'It's just for personal use.'

'Yeah, c'mon man,' said Jimmy.

'Okay. Well, what I decide to do about it depends on whether you can help me. We want to know if you've seen this boy, or Tony Mulhain and any of his mates recently?'

Dana removed the photo of Angus from her handbag and showed it to him.

'I saw Tony and that Nenita chick when they dropped by to use some of my gear.' He gestured towards a workbench and vice set up at the back of the shed. 'They were pretty secretive, but I reckon they were using one of my hacksaws to cut down a rifle.'

'To make a sawn-off shotgun?' Dana gave Connor a pointed look.

'Something like that.'

'And what about the boy?' Connor asked.

Matty squinted at it and scratched his head. 'I might have seen him in the back of Tony's car. He was speeding, so I only caught a glimpse.'

'When was this?' Connor asked.

'Can't remember. This morning maybe?'

A chill went through Dana's body. Her shoulders became rigid with terror. She imagined Tony holding Angus at gunpoint. How ill-equipped he'd be at dealing with a man of Tony's menace. She stepped forward. 'Can you be more specific?'

He switched the fan off. 'My dog died yesterday and I've been out here ever since … Timmy his name was.' His face crumpled with emotion. 'He was my best friend.'

Once they left Matty's, they drove out to Tony's property and parked the vehicle parallel to the house so it couldn't be parked in. Dana stared at the A-frame house shrouded by pine trees and a deep sense of dread settled over her. She turned to Connor. 'I swear this is one of the creepiest houses I've ever visited.'

Tony appeared on the verandah.

'That man has got to have cameras,' said Connor. 'The way he predicts our arrival before we've even knocked. It can't be coincidence.'

Jimmy stayed in the car as Dana and Connor strode up the driveway.

'For fuck's sake,' Tony said as they came closer. 'What is it now?'

'A boy's gone missing,' said Connor. 'We're speaking to locals to see if they have any information.'

Tony scowled. 'And I suppose you want to trample all through the house again.'

'Something like that,' said Connor.

'Come on in then,' he said, sounding resigned. 'This is worse than bed checks in prison.'

They walked into the lounge room. Tony stood in front of a colour TV on a glass cabinet.

Connor pointed. 'Got yourself a new toy have you, Tony?'

'I've been saving up my dole money. There's no law against that.'

'Not as long as you've got a receipt.'

Dana cringed. Collecting evidence was a necessary part of police work, but she could never get past the feeling they were being disrespectful.

'I never hold on to those, but I got it from Brashs – in Toowoomba.'

Connor frowned. 'Well, I'll be looking into that later. Anyway, I'll get to the point. An eleven-year-old boy is missing. He's five foot and has white-blond hair and freckles. Name's Angus. Have you seen him?'

'Nah, mate. Never heard of him.'

'But what about his mother, Tina?' Dana interjected. 'Surely you know her? I'm told she owes you money.'

'Sure does. Thieving bitch owes a thousand bucks to me and my buddies. For yard work and stuff. But as for the kid, I haven't seen him since he was small.'

'Well, if you do, I'd like you to contact the station,' Connor said. 'It's very important.'

Tony cocked his head to one side, considering. 'Will there be a reward?'

'Don't worry, buddy. We'll make it worth your while.'

Dana looked out across the yard at a copse of pine trees where the grass had never managed to take.

Nenita emerged from the trees in overalls and gloves, her black eyes wide as she looked up and saw Connor.

Dana's heart raced. She continued to stare as Nenita remained frozen to the spot.

A look of panic skirted across Tony's face. 'There she is. She must have come home early.' He yanked the screen door with such force it nearly ripped away from its track. 'Nenita, come inside.' There was a note of desperation in his voice. 'These people want to speak to you.'

Nenita looked behind her briefly, then walked towards the house. Dana took a deep breath, trying to quell the adrenaline spiking through her body.

'Connor, you need to follow me,' Dana said. Her mind was paralysed with images of Angus, of kidnap and murder. Fear clutched at her throat.

He gazed at her strangely, without comprehension.

'Now,' she insisted.

The walk down the hallway and out through Tony Mulhain's

backyard was the longest she'd ever endured. When she finally arrived at the treeline she had to duck her head, pushing branches out of the way so she could navigate into the clearing. Beneath the pines the air was cool, her eyes taking a few moments to adjust in the dim light. She noticed the electrical wires first, running through the dirt and down through a trapdoor cut into the ground. It was the culmination of all her nightmares. She grappled with the clasp before flinging it open.

Down in the hole she could just make out a shipping container. Sweat trickled down her back and her chest constricted with panic. She took a tentative step onto the ladder and stared into the dimly lit space beneath. Everything was dark and grainy, like a scene from a horror movie. There were two tables, one with titration equipment she recognised from high school chemistry, the other with glass beakers and a bottle of poison marked with a skull and crossbones. A row of cannabis plants ran along one side, the leaves green under an overheard lamp. She caught the sudden movement of something below her and rushed back up into the light.

Connor was on the lawn wrestling with Tony. He flipped Tony onto his back and landed a blow to his face, turning him over and hand-cuffing him.

'Connor,' Dana screamed. 'There's someone down there.'

In an instant he was by her side, pushing her out of the way as he crashed through the trees and leapt through the manhole. She looked away, frozen with horror.

'I can see something,' he yelled up at her.

'What? What is it?'

'A hat. A small one. I think it's a kid's.'

The world slowed down. The greens and blues of the backyard

became molten. There was a scuffle. Shouting accompanied by the breaking of glass.

'Hands up against the wall,' Connor was yelling. 'Do it!'

There was silence after that. The longest moment Dana had ever endured.

'It's okay,' Connor shouted up at her. 'He's not here.'

She let out a long breath and stared up at the white sky with gratitude.

Two men in tracksuit pants emerged from the hole with Connor behind them, pointing his gun. Their fleshy faces were so like Tony's they could have been brothers.

'What was it?' she asked.

'The usual,' he said. 'Drugs and a few handguns.'

•

24

Dana watched as the police descended on the property. She waited for Connor as the men he'd detained were handcuffed and arrested.

When Connor started the engine and put the car into gear, he said, 'So, how did you know to go out there?'

'There was something about the way Nenita was standing,' said Dana. 'I knew she'd been caught doing something she wasn't supposed to. I couldn't have told you what it was though.'

'Anyway, the guys are impressed,' Connor said, pulling onto the highway. 'They've been trying to catch Tony out for five years. Do you know what his nickname is?'

She shook her head.

'Teflon Tony. 'Cause shit doesn't stick to him. Whenever something goes down, he's always a person of interest, but aside from his stint in jail ten years ago, we've never managed to nab him. Now that we've pinned him for trafficking, I'll be in line for a promotion.' He gave her a sideways glance. 'Seriously though, when there's a drug lab in a town the size of Crows Nest it affects the whole community.'

Jimmy stuck his head between them, making her jump. She'd forgotten he was there.

'Sorry Matty gave you a bum steer. Do you reckon you could drop me off here?'

Connor veered over to the gravelly side of the road as they drew closer to a vacant block dotted with caravans and cabins.

'That's my girlfriend's place,' said Jimmy, his face softening as he undid his seatbelt. 'Catch you around, Dana. Good luck finding that boy.' He got out of the car. 'I'll drop by the station in a few days to pick up my letter.' He winked at her, before slamming the door and loping away through the tall grass towards the tourist park.

As Connor eased back out onto the highway Dana realised that she would have to thank him even if the search for Angus had been a wild goose chase. 'I appreciate you helping me out. You didn't have to.'

He checked the rear-view mirror as a smirk curled at the corner of his mouth. 'You could always show your appreciation by having a drink with me?'

She knew he was joking and gave him a withering look.

'Yeah, yeah,' he said lightly, tapping his fingers on the steering wheel. 'Drop you at your car?'

She stared into the distance and chewed her nails. 'We need to keep searching for Angus. Can we check the house where the boyfriend of his mum lives, just to be sure?'

'No can do – my sister's in town. She just got back from London.'

'Surely you have time for a quick visit?' Her palms were

clammy at the thought of returning to Godsall Street without Angus.

'Sorry. She wants me at Harry's on the dot of six.'

'But I thought you had time for a drink?'

'A drink sure. But dragging me out on another job—'

'Jesus, Connor. I have to find Angus. Don't you understand?'

When she looked over at him, she suddenly felt guilty. His eyes were bloodshot and his shoulders drooped with exhaustion. It was his day off and all he'd done was help her.

'Fine,' she said. 'Drop me at the station.'

Dana brushed past Ian Steinmann's receptionist and burst into his office where she found him dunking a biscuit into a cup of tea.

'What the hell do you think you're playing at,' he said, leaping to his feet and causing the filing cabinets on either side of his desk to rattle.

She folded her arms across her chest. 'Angus Fitcher is missing. Has been missing for a substantial period of time now. And you're not doing a thing about it.'

'That's not true. I've spoken to the Toowoomba CIB and I've also sent one of my men to interview the mother to see if she knows anything. Because every time that kid runs away – and there's been plenty of times, believe me – he always runs back to her. Not to mention, I'm starting up a full-scale search from the pub if we haven't seen him come morning.' He walked to the door and stood beside it.

'Which I assume will be conducted with the high level of professionalism I've come to expect from your staff?' she said, unable to conceal the sarcasm in her voice.

'Of course.' He glared at her. 'Now I'm going to have to ask you to leave. We've had a gang of teenagers on the rampage all afternoon and I've got three of them in the lock-up out the back ready to be charged.'

She stayed put. 'I'm glad you've got people looking into it, but they're searching in the wrong place.' She ploughed on. 'Angus was at my house having dinner last night and I think I saw a man spying on us through the window. Now, there may be no connection between me seeing the man and Angus going missing, but given the timing of the two events, it needs to be investigated.' She paused, waiting for a response. When there was none, she said, 'Angus's mum also ripped off Tony Mulhain and I'm worried some of his buddies may have taken him so they can get their money back.' She took a deep breathe. 'And I'm starting to think that Sandra's and Debbie's deaths were linked to drugs.'

'That case is closed. The forensic evidence pointed to only two people being involved – Sandra and Debbie.'

Her anger flared, white hot in front of her eyes. 'That's because you made a mess of it. It was declared a murder–suicide straight away, the car and the women's bodies were removed that night and the crime scene wasn't secured against the elements. And now any hope of finding fingerprints, tyre tracks or any other forensic evidence is lost. All because you didn't want to pay up for overtime.'

His eyes narrowed. 'How do you know all this?'

'So, it's true then?'

'No, it's not true.'

Dana paced the room, pausing at a filing cabinet in the corner. On top of the cabinet was a gold trophy of a running man clutching a football under his arm. The words *Mixed C Grade*

Touch, 1970, Ian 'Rocco' Steinmann were engraved under it. Her head spun as though she was having an out-of-body experience. Suddenly it all started to make sense – his expensive watch and the new car were gifts from Tony Mulhain for turning a blind eye. Dana had a flashback to Debbie's diary. *The bikies doing drug deals while Rocco sat at the bar.* Rocco. Debbie's secret boyfriend.

'Don't you think it's strange that Lachlan's accident happened straight after he gave you the diary?'

His eyes narrowed. 'What are you saying?'

'That moments after Lachlan hands over Debbie's diary incriminating you in illegal activities, he mysteriously runs off the road. Where is it now?'

'What?'

'The diary.'

'I don't know. He never gave it to me.'

'Of course he didn't.' Dana was gobsmacked. He'd told so many lies since she'd walked in the door that she could hardly expect him to tell the truth now. 'Jesus, Ian. He was supposed to be your friend.'

He came towards her trembling with rage. His face had turned an unhealthy shade of red. 'How dare you cast aspersions on me. How *dare* you!' His voice was quiet, but threatening. 'I'm the head of this station. This case is closed. The community needs to move on.'

He returned to his desk and dragged out a packet of aspirin. He took two and crunched them down without water. Suddenly, his expression changed, as though a lightbulb had flicked on. 'Helen warned me about you. She said that you'd become obsessed with this case and she had to suspend you for it. She felt that the child protection work had become a bit too much.' He opened the door and said, with a show of kindness. 'Whatever personal issues you've got going on, you need to resolve them in your own time.'

'This is ridiculous. The fact that you'd rather believe I'm mentally ill than start looking for Angus is deplorable.'

He took a deep breath. 'You need to think about the scale of the search we'll have to do. The Darling Downs is endless and with all these isolated properties – there's so many places he could be. So, to try and find him without any leads, it's a big ask.'

A uniformed police officer appeared in the corridor. 'We've found the kid,' he said.

Dana's neck snapped around.

'The crows beat us to it. But, from the looks of it, I'd say it's that little fella we've been searching for.'

The walls were closing in on her, the air stifling. She lay on her bathroom floor, tears streaming down her face. What had she done to deserve this? First Oscar, then Lachlan and now Angus? And what the hell was Angus doing out at Emu Creek, thirty kilometres from Crows Nest?

She knew the answer. If he could find his way to Debbie Vickers's flat the last time he'd gone missing, he could easily make it to Emu Creek. She clawed her way up the bathroom vanity and splashed water onto her face. She paced the wooden floors, every room holding within it fresh memories of Angus. The computer where he'd sat checking her emails, the Persian rug where he'd lain watching TV. Even the refrigerator betrayed her with the small carton of chocolate milk illuminated on the centre shelf.

She called Hugh. His phone went straight to message bank. She hung up, flinging the phone onto her bed where it made an indent on the doona. In her darkest hour he was nowhere to be found.

What she needed, more than anything, was to speak to someone. Someone who wasn't part of the community she'd been trying to investigate. Someone who was neutral and, most importantly, who didn't think she was crazy. Her gaze settled on a small gold clock on the bookshelf that a friend had given her in high school. Suddenly, she found herself clicking through her contacts for Isabell's number.

'Dana, don't be ridiculous – you know what us journos are like. What's the problem?' Isabell said, after Dana apologised for calling so late.

Dana's heart thudded against her ribs. For a split second she considered hanging up, then finally took a deep breath and told Isabell about what had happened with Angus.

'God, that sounds horrendous,' said Isabell. 'I don't know how you've managed to stick it out so long. Don't get me wrong, your neighbour sounds like a cute kid, but if I was in that creepy place with some freak hanging around my kitchen, I would've been on a flight back to Sydney weeks ago.' The line went silent. 'Is there anything I can do? I can be up there with a camera crew in twenty-four hours. Just say the word.'

'It's fine for the time being,' said Dana, pulling her legs up under her. 'But I'll let you know if that changes.'

'Look, Dana. I know we weren't close in high school and sometimes I was a real bitch, but I want to let you know that things are different now. I'm here for you.'

After Dana hung up, she considered reaching for her handbag and cramming some valium tablets into her mouth, but decided not to. There was no way she was going to miss a call from the police if they had news of Angus.

Instead, she reflected on how nice it was to have Isabell on side, even though her fears, which had once been confined to Oscar's death, had now spread like a bushfire through all aspects of her life. And the words she'd wanted to say to Isabell – *I'm completely and utterly terrified* – were lodged in the back of her throat.

25

Dana was lying in bed, wide awake, when her mobile started ringing. She almost knocked her glass of water over in her rush to answer it.

'Connor,' she said breathlessly.

'It's good news.' He paused. 'At least, good news for you. The boy who was found wasn't Angus. It was a local teenager who'd been out riding and was bucked off his horse. His parents realised something was wrong when the mare wandered back to the farm, fully saddled, without their son.' There was silence. 'Anyway, I just thought you'd want to know.'

'Thank you,' she said, her voice wavering as she looked to the ceiling with gratitude. She closed her eyes. 'Thank you.'

'We're organising a search party for Angus, so if you meet us in Crows Nest tomorrow morning you can join in.'

~

Dana was stunned by the high-level operation when she stepped into the pub. As Ian had promised, the venue was transformed into a telecommunications hub. Dozens of volunteers in high-vis vests were gathered around him in the courtyard as he shouted instructions and pointed to a white board. On it was a map of the area and a large picture of Angus in his school uniform.

Connor was speaking into a walkie-talkie as dozens of SES volunteers in orange uniforms filed into the bar area behind him. 'You take Bald Hills Creek,' he was saying. 'And get Jonesy to check out the area leading down to the falls.'

Ian's assistant, Gail, hurried over with a tray of drinks. Dana's heart swelled with emotion as she watched the people in the room, united in their search for Angus. For the first time in as long as she could remember, she was part of something. Her Sydney office had been so large that, beyond exchanging pleasantries with her co-workers, she realised she hadn't known them at all. Here, in this community, was proof that if she was ever in need, these people would be the first to help.

Susan came towards Dana. 'I don't know what I'll do if they can't find him,' she said. 'I can't sleep.' The expression on her face was beyond panic. Her eyes widened as she looked at Dana gravely. 'If he … if something's happened. I'm not going to be able to—'

'It'll be alright,' said Dana, with more optimism than she felt. 'All these people are looking for him now. One of them is bound to find something.' Susan burst into tears and Dana put her arms around her.

When Susan pulled away, Gail was still standing beside them. 'Why don't you go have a rest in one of the rooms upstairs,' she said to Susan. She thrust her tray of drinks at Dana and took

Susan by the elbow, leading her over to the staircase. 'Number two's free. The bed was freshly made up this morning.'

Dana dumped the tray on a nearby table and Connor walked past in a police cap and bright yellow vest. She stopped him. 'Has anyone had any leads on Angus yet? Anything at all?'

He considered for a moment. 'Majorie, that neighbour of Paul's, rang the hotline saying she might have seen him at the bakery, but she can't be sure if it was actually him.'

Dana was desperate. She suddenly realised there was only one person who could help generate the publicity that was needed to find Angus. She left a message on Isabell's phone, giving her an update of the situation and telling her she needed to bring the *Sixty Minutes* crew to Queensland.

She hung up as another pair of SES workers, one with silver hair, entered the pub. Dana tried to remember where she'd seen him before. She watched his broad shoulders and muscular calves as he walked into the kitchen and retrieved milk from the fridge.

Richard Beutel? Was this the same man she'd seen at Alisha's cabin? She felt as though she was grasping at so many pieces of the puzzle at once and none of them made sense.

'Richard?' she said tentatively, following him into the kitchen.

The man turned around, his silver mane glinting under the bright fluorescent light. The creases around his eyes made him look older than she'd first thought.

'I'm Dana Gibson. I work for the Department of Families. I need to speak to you about Alisha Lawrence. About why she's living in your cabin.'

He put the milk on the bench, gazing around to see if there was anyone within ear shot. 'We should have this conversation outside.'

'Here's fine,' she said, blocking his path.

He gazed at her steadily. 'I'm happy to explain it to you, but I have a wife and kids to think of – Crows Nest is a small town. People are narrow-minded.'

'Fine, then.' She stepped aside to let him pass.

He made a mug of instant coffee and she trailed after him as he paused to shake hands with the SES coordinator and went outside. They sat at a table in front of the pub as a westerly blew around them. He angled his legs towards hers. Now that she was closer to him, she saw that his eyes were tired. He removed a handkerchief from his pocket and wiped it across his brow.

'Listen, Alisha came to see me in her final year of high school when I was acting as the guidance officer. She was having problems at home with her sister, Sandra, and her family. She'd started drinking too much, shoplifting. Truanting more often than not. Anyway, it turns out that before Alisha moved in with Sandra, Paul had sexually abused her. It was a one-off apparently – when they lived in New South Wales – but he started to show interest in her again when she moved into his house.'

Dana wanted to ask why Alisha had gone to live with Paul and her sister. Why didn't she go and live somewhere else? Then she remembered what Alisha had said. *It's not as though I had some fairytale family to return to in New South Wales. My grandfather died and my mum was pretty much useless.*

'I don't understand.' She searched his kind, creased face. 'Why didn't New South Wales inform the Department?' As soon as the question was out of her mouth, she remembered the blank pages in Alisha's file.

'They probably did. But if what Helen's told me about how busy you all are is true, I suspect it might have been shelved.

Alisha refused to make a complaint, so I assume it wasn't a high priority.'

'Did you tell Ian Steinmann about this?'

'I had a word, but I never knew if he took it on board. He and Paul went to the same church, moved in the same social circles. On some level they were friends.'

Her mind was racing, her thoughts coming so thick and fast her intellect could barely keep up. 'Do you think Sandra found out and confronted him?'

His face darkened. 'Look, he's a womaniser for sure, but killing two women? I don't know.'

She stared at a leaf scudding along the path and began to doubt herself. She'd heard so many stories in the last couple of months she no longer knew who to trust. 'Do you have any proof of what happened to Alisha?'

Richard toyed with the coffee cup in his hands. 'Before Alisha moved into the cabin, I asked her to request her DOCS files.' He paused. 'So I could find out her story, without making her tell me what happened and re-traumatising her all over again.'

He fumbled through his pockets for his keys before going to a gold Citroen parked across the road. When he returned with a swathe of documents he handed them to Dana and directed her to a police transcript marked with a fluorescent yellow tab. She started to read.

Alisha Lawrence had been interviewed by Senior Sergeant Brett Tindle and Department of Communities Officer Janette Lynchfield on 29 March 1994.

On New Year's Eve, Alisha's half-sister Sandra and husband, Paul Kirby, came to stay at the home where Alisha lived with her grandfather in Blacktown, New South Wales. In the outdoor pergola that night, the adults engaged in celebratory drinking games while the children remained inside watching TV. At one point during the night, Paul came inside and encouraged Alisha to join the drinking, saying she was almost sixteen. She joined the adults however, after vomiting and feeling sick, retired to bed at approximately 0100 hours.

At approximately 0400 hours, Alisha awoke to discover Paul having sex with her. She remained silent, paralysed with fear. She did not tell anyone about the incident that day or in the following weeks. Paul and his family returned to Queensland the next afternoon.

Dana stopped reading, a familiar queasiness churning in her stomach. 'Oh god.' Her eyes met his. 'I had no idea.'

'Now you know.'

Dana's heart went out to the girl. 'You'll have to excuse me,' she said, jumping up. 'I have an urgent matter to attend to. I have to go.'

As Dana was jogging to her car she remembered the photo of the three sisters. The eldest one with her arms around the younger ones. A lioness protecting her cubs.

She turned and sprinted back. 'Richard,' she said. 'Did you ever find out anything about Chrystal?'

'I asked on a number of occasions if she was okay, but she never said anything. You can save one child …' He looked defeated, as though all the energy had drained from him. 'But you can't save them all.'

She pursed her lips. 'I need to find them.'

'They were at the cabin this morning.'

~

Dana gunned her car along the highway all the way to the tourist park, then down the gravel driveway. When she arrived at the last one in the row, she yanked on the handbrake, hurried from the car and knocked on the front door. Alisha opened it, a cigarette in her hand.

'What do you want?' she said without smiling.

'Is Chrystal here?' asked Dana.

Alisha sighed. 'As usual, everyone wants to talk to her and I'm just' – she took a drag of her cigarette then waved away the smoke – 'chopped liver.'

'I'm sorry,' said Dana. 'I'd like to speak to both of you. It's extremely urgent. Is she here?'

'Chrystal,' Alisha called out over her shoulder. 'The social's here.'

Chrystal came out of the bedroom in a ratty jumper, her eyes red from crying. She slumped down in the recliner.

Dana hesitated. 'Chrystal, I'm sorry to have to ask you this, but I'm worried about you. Because it's come to my attention that you and Paul might have been …' Dana searched for the right word. 'A couple.'

Alisha turned around from the counter where she'd been buttering toast. 'She won't say a bad word about him. She was in *love.*' She mimed quotation marks. 'Until she realised what he was like.'

'You knew about this?' Dana asked. The physical confrontation they'd had outside the pub suddenly made sense.

'I tried to warn her.' She shot Chrystal a withering smile. 'But Little Miss Angel Face over there wouldn't have a bar of it. Things will be different for her,' she said in a singsong voice. 'She was special.'

'Shut up,' Chrystal said. 'I couldn't help it. I *was* in love.' She turned towards Dana, a look of wonderment on her face. 'I'd never felt that before.'

'And the next thing she knew she was a full-time house cleaner and babysitter,' Alisha said, before taking a bite of her toast. 'He is such a user … just like with Sandy's life insurance. He made her sign the forms, then acted all heartbroken when he dressed up to go to Toowoomba to claim it.'

Dana's stomach roiled when she realised it must have been the same day Paul had asked her out to lunch.

'It wasn't exactly like that—'

'Oh, don't defend him Chrystal,' Alisha cut in, her voice rising. 'He knew exactly what he was doing.'

Dana said gently, 'Perhaps you could give us a minute?'

'Fine.' Alisha yanked a basket from under the bed. 'I've got washing I need to get anyway.'

The door slammed and Dana and Chrystal were suddenly alone.

Dana leant in towards Chrystal, elbows resting on her knees. 'When did the two of you get together?'

Chrystal stared hard at the floor, unable to meet Dana's eyes. 'Not long after Sandra died.' She was visibly shaking. 'I know how it looks. I don't think I'll ever forgive myself.'

Dana had no doubt that the grooming had started earlier, but there was no time to find out all the details. 'And were you with Paul on the night Sandra and Debbie were murdered?'

Chrystal's eyes remained downcast. 'No.'

'Jesus Christ, Chrystal. Then why did you lie about it?'

'Because he asked me to.'

Dana took a deep breath. 'What did he tell you?'

'That he was going to speak to the builder about the termites in the new house and he didn't want anyone to know.'

'And you believed him?' she asked, then reminded herself that Paul had another alibi, the neighbour who'd seen him through the window.

'At first,' she said tentatively. 'I knew that they'd been stressing out massively about the house ... then as time went on, I didn't know what to believe.' She looked forlornly out the window. 'He used to be so kind. I was so sad when I first arrived, missing my friends, missing my grandfather. Paul used to comfort me.' She let out a long breath. 'I barely noticed the point where he stopped comforting me and we started having sex.' She stared at her hands. 'It's my fault. I led him on, I just feel so guilty.'

Dana was glad Alisha was no longer in the room. 'I'm sorry, Chrystal, but that's bullshit. He was a seasoned abuser. He knew exactly what he was doing.' She leant over and clasped Chrystal's hand. 'When was the last time you saw him?'

'Two days ago. He was being a real dickhead. He said if I didn't want to help out with Rubi and Billy-Violet, then I wasn't part of the family and I wouldn't get to see them anymore.' She burst into tears, heavy sobs racking her petite frame. 'I miss them so much.'

Dana reached into her handbag for tissues and passed them to Chrystal. 'And where are Rubi and Billy-Violet now?'

'I was so tired, I took them to Carol's.'

'The foster carer?'

Chrystal nodded.

'Well, thank god for that.'

'I feel like shit,' Chrystal said, blowing her nose and dabbing her eyes. 'I need my tablets, but they're still at home. Can you help me get them?'

Dana was about to say it would have to wait until it occurred to her that the Kirby house was one of the few places where they hadn't searched for Angus. 'Do you have a key?' she asked.

'Yes.'

'Before we go,' Dana said, reaching into her handbag for a photo of Angus. 'Do you know this boy?'

Chrystal looked at the picture blankly. 'No.'

Dana's heart sank, but she gathered her coat and hurried to the car, Chrystal trailing after her.

The sky was grey. An abrupt gust of wind whipped around the hills and the temperature had dropped, a clear sign that a storm was on its way.

They were driving out of the car park when Alisha stepped in front of the car. Dana slammed on the brakes. Dirt and gravel sprayed up from the undercarriage. She wound down the window.

'Can I get a lift?' Alisha asked.

'We're going to Paul's.' Dana tapped the steering wheel in agitation.

'That'll do.' Alisha slid into the back seat and they sped away.

26

Alisha stayed in the car and Dana rushed for the front door, leaving Chrystal hurrying to keep up. They knocked and when no-one answered they let themselves in. Dana's boots echoed down the hallway as Chrystal headed to her room to retrieve her medication.

Dana stood in the lounge room and took in the clinical neatness of the kitchen and living room. It suddenly dawned on her that something was wrong. *He's cleaned up.* On instinct, she made her way into Rubi's bedroom where the change table and elephant mobile remained untouched. On a hamper in the corner, a piece of clothing lay crumpled on a pile of sheets. A blue shirt. It was too small to be Paul's and too big to be one of the children's. When she looked at it more closely, her heart contracted with fear.

Dana took a coloured pen from a container on the bookshelf and used it to hold up the shirt so her fingerprints didn't contaminate the evidence. She leant closer to examine the logo on the small blue shirt. *Ansett.*

Chrystal was suddenly at her side.

'What do you think this is?' Dana pointed to a black splatter near the neckline, knowing, but desperately hoping she was wrong.

Chrystal leant in closer, a frown on her face. 'It looks a lot like ... blood.'

'But the neighbour. She said she saw Paul that night. He still had an alibi for the night Sandra and Debbie were murdered.'

'Marjorie?' Chrystal looked unconvinced. 'She's a bit of a crackpot ... I just figured she was excited to be part of the murder everyone was talking about.'

'He has him,' she said to Chrystal, barely registering the girl's look of shock. 'He's got Angus.' She grabbed the girl by her shoulders, more roughly than she'd intended. 'Is there anywhere Paul used to take you when you were together? A secret place you used to go?'

'Well, the creek, sometimes. He'd get us fish and chips. But there's nothing there, just bush.' Then her eyes narrowed. 'A few times he took me to the pistol club, to practise shooting – it's on the way out of town.'

Dana flouted the speed limit all the way to the pistol club, dust flying high into the air behind them. Alisha had insisted on coming. In the end there wasn't time to argue. Dana reached for her phone as she drove, her fingers flying through her contacts to find Connor.

'I was just at Paul's,' she said, once she had him on the line. 'I found one of Angus's t-shirts in the Kirby house. Meet me at the pistol club.'

She reached a wooden sign with *Crows Nest Pistol Club Inc.* painted in white. Behind it, a smaller sign: *Danger Live Ammunition.*

Dear god what had led her to this? Her son had died and now she was staking out a murderer. Maybe Hugh was right. She barely knew Sandra and Debbie, but once again she was running towards danger, on an impulse to self-destruct. She should have focused on her own life. Stared into her own cesspool of need.

They screeched to a stop at the gate and Chrystal rushed to open it. Up ahead, bunya pines flanked the road where a large aluminium structure sat in front of a grassy knoll. She sped up the dirt track approaching the rifle range. The sky was darkening overhead. What Dana saw next turned her blood icy cold. Paul's Ford Falcon parked outside the shed. She had a terrible image of Angus's body in the boot.

She pulled over and turned to face the girls. 'Stay in the car. I'm serious. If I need your help, I'll come and get you.'

Alisha wound down the window as Dana was walking away. 'Be careful.' Her face was etched with fear. 'He's a real psycho when he's pissed off.'

Dana's heart was thumping, but she pushed her emotions down, approached Paul's car and stared through the windows. Once she'd ascertained there was no-one inside she darted around to the boot. She attempted to open it, then knelt pressing her ear to the lock. She tried to calm her own breathing, listening for any movement or sound.

'Angus,' she whispered, her voice trembling. 'Are you in there?'

In the next instant, a police car was speeding up the driveway. Connor pulled up and leapt from the vehicle, armed and in full uniform. She was flooded with relief.

'I've called for back-up,' he said, his face tight with tension. 'They couldn't say how long it would take.'

'Paul's car is here,' Dana said, nodding towards the vehicle. 'But I'm not sure where he is.'

Connor looked at her as though it was obvious. 'He probably wanted to make sure the place was deserted before he dragged your little friend up there.'

'Anyway,' she said, fearful she was losing her mind. 'We'll have to be careful – Alisha said he's a skilled shooter.'

'No joke.' A look of annoyance flashed in his eyes, then he directed his attention to the road. 'So, here's what I'm going to do. Up there is a large shooting shelter that opens on to a lawn. And there's a small hill fifty metres in front that's used for a back stop. I've been here before, for training.' He checked to see that she was paying attention. 'And behind this and to the left is a storage shed. My plan is to run alongside the shelter using the eucalyptus trees for cover, then if there's no-one around, I'll duck over to the shed.' He put a firm hand on her shoulder. 'And what you're going to do is stay in the car.'

'No way.' She shook her head vigorously. 'If Angus is up there, I'm coming too.'

'We're about to confront a dangerous man, possibly armed. And even though you think you're super smart, you're not trained in police work. If you're hurt, it's my head on the chopping block.'

'I'll keep behind you. I'll do whatever you say.'

His expression was closed. 'No, mate. You're going to stay in the car.'

She stalked back to the car, banging her backside down hard against the bonnet. The breeze whipped her hair around her face as Connor hurried up the track. He slowed as he reached the pistol club. She turned and pointed a finger at the girls. *Don't move*, she mouthed. When she turned back, Connor was out of sight. She put her thumbnail to her mouth, chewing as the minutes passed until she reached the quick.

A shot rang out. A whip-like crack that sent a mass of birds into the sky.

A scream.

Angus.

He's hurting him.

She sprinted towards the sound, only slowing as she approached the shooting shelter from behind. As she rounded the corner where the front of the building opened on to the range, she braced herself. Was this Paul's plan? Watch her zigzag across the grass before pulling the trigger? She hesitated, then went across it. Fast.

At the far edge of the shed she found Connor on the ground, blood spreading out beneath him. Dana realised Alisha was behind her, pulling up short when she saw him as though she'd been shocked with a cattle prod. Dana tore off her jacket and knelt down beside him, pressing it firmly against his chest. With her other arm she dragged Alisha next to her.

'Put pressure on the wound.'

Another scream.

Dana jumped up and threw Alisha her phone. 'Call triple zero.'

'Don't leave me,' Alisha cried.

Dana glanced back at her. 'I'm checking the shed.'

A few metres ahead she saw the corrugated-iron storage shed with a lean-to verandah. The slats on the verandah creaked as she walked across them. She opened the metal door, then eased it shut behind her. It was dark. Pinpricks of light shone through where the roof had worn away. She dropped to her hands and knees figuring it was better to stay low. She could smell the blood rising up from the dust. Dizziness set in. She buried her nails into her palms, trying to bring herself back. More blood.

A moan from the back of the shed.

'Angus? Is that you?'

'He's got a gun.' She heard his small voice. 'He said he'd kill me.'

She tried to move in the direction of his voice, her pulse racing. She needed to tell him it was going to be alright. *Would it ever be alright?*

'I've called for help.' Her voice stuck in her throat. 'It'll be here soon, I promise.' She gasped for air, breathing in dust. 'Angus, where's Paul?'

'I don't know. Get these things off my arms. GET THEM OFF!'

'Shh, Angus. Please.' Her throat was thick with emotion and her eyes were struggling in the darkness. 'I need to think.' The only option she had now was to get him outside or sit tight and wait for police back-up. Paul was out there, watching and waiting to see what she'd do – her moment of reckoning. She forced herself forward, crawling in the direction of Angus's voice.

A shutter opened; a sliver of light. Alisha at the window, signalling wildly. Eyes bigger than Dana had ever seen them.

Then she was gone.

Dana swung around as the door opened with a clang. Paul, backlit by the grey sky. Monstrous in the glare.

In that moment Dana's doubt was extinguished. She *knew*. His devilish expression, his red eyes. If the murder of Sandra Kirby and Debbie Vickers had benefitted anyone, it was him. In the midst of a gigantic police stuff-up and theories of a community rife with drugs and the occult, he'd tried to replace his wife with a younger, more attractive model and claim Sandra's life insurance in the process. His financial woes wiped clean and an alibi with benefits.

He'd killed those women.

And unless something happened soon, she was next.

27

Paul stepped into the shed, a rifle in his hand. 'Dana,' he said. 'You're finally where I want you. On your hands and knees.' He laughed and cocked his gun like an outlaw. 'Now, get outside.'

She glanced around, trying to locate Angus, then scurried outside onto the lawn. She kept going until Paul told her to stop – ten metres in front of him. She could see Connor where he lay near the shooting shelter. There was nowhere to hide. Eucalypts to the right, acres of grass between. Every sinew in her body screaming with terror.

'What have you done to Angus?' she said, thankful he had the sense to stay quiet.

'What are you talking about? Your little friend's fine. You took my kids, now I've got yours. An eye for an eye, hey?' Paul gave an exaggerated shrug, then aimed his gun at her. 'I'll do you first and him next.' He paused, considering. 'No. I'll do him first and you can watch. You'd like that, wouldn't you?'

She forced a painful breath into her lungs.

Connor, hidden from Paul's sight by the shelter, let out a low moan.

'Oh, shut up, would ya,' Paul yelled. 'These coppers, they're so cocky. Then you pit them against someone with a weapon and they run away like little boys behind their mothers' skirts.' His voice dripped with sarcasm. 'Women are attracted to power. It's disgusting. You're willing to fuck him, but you look at me like I'm some sort of dog turd. Well, how do you like me now, Miss Dana?' He wiggled his hips and danced, the smile never leaving his face.

Her knees throbbed from crawling on the ground and her hands were shaking. She considered reasoning with him, but had a desperate feeling that nothing she said would help.

Paul fired at the earth beside her and she cowered as dirt rained down. Her ears shrieked with the shots.

'That one got away from me.' He chuckled. 'But maybe it's a sign. Perhaps we should go for a drive?'

The question hung in the air as she flattened herself against the grass. She began to shiver, as though an electric current was passing through her. *Don't let him take you.* The taste of blood was on her lips. If he took her, she knew her chances of survival dropped to zero. If she was going to die, it would be here, in these hills, beneath a grey and unforgiving sky.

She prayed. *Let Angus live.*

'Come to think of it. I'm not sure I can be bothered. All these women telling me what to do. Smiling and happy one minute. Pissed off the next. Come on. Up! Get up!'

She dragged herself up.

'Hands behind your head.'

Alisha came into view behind Paul at the edge of the shooting shelter in her singlet top and work pants. Dana gave a tiny shake of her head, but Alisha came closer, surveying the scene. Her eyes were focused. Ready for battle. A gust of wind swept the hair from her face. Dana stood perfectly still, shutting down any instinct to move.

Alisha took another few steps towards Connor.

'This isn't going away, Paul,' said Dana. 'Too many people know about what you've done. Lachlan, my manager Helen, Ian Steinmann. Not to mention, I sent a file of evidence to my husband after I saw you in my yard the other night,' she lied.

'Yes, nice house you've got there,' Paul said. Dana watched as Alisha leant down. 'Not as nice as Susan's, but pretty good all the same.'

Dana's breath caught in her throat as she pictured Paul spying on Susan, creeping around her house as she tended to her roses.

'People are starting to realise what happened,' Dana pressed on. 'They've put two and two together, after seeing that lemon of a house you built and the financial ruin that came with it. After discovering that you'd had sex with Sandra's sisters, they've figured you've got more than enough motive.'

'I'll miss that,' Paul said wistfully. 'Those young girls … there is something gratifying about fucking virgins, giving them their first orgasms.'

Dana willed Alisha to keep her cool as she moved slowly beyond Paul's sight.

'They were so grateful,' he said.

'You made a mistake though,' said Dana. The rifle was pointed at her chest. There was a tightness in her throat. 'Sandra and Debbie knew. They found out and confronted you. That's why you had to kill them.'

'It's a nice theory. Unfortunately, it lacks this one little thing called evidence.' He wagged his trigger finger. 'And soon the only person saying any different is going to be dead.'

She faced him. Stared down the barrel, taking desperate gulps of air. She closed her eyes.

The shots came from the right and she opened her eyes in surprise. Paul clutched his neck. Made a gargling sound. Blood rushed from his mouth.

Alisha was standing in front of Connor, holding his gun. She started screaming, a sound straight from hell. She unloaded the entire round from the pistol as Dana covered her ears.

Paul jerked and shuddered as the bullets took him. He collapsed to the ground.

Without thinking, Dana dropped to her knees beside him and pressed her hands on his neck, trying to cover his wounds. Blood leaked between her fingers; the light was fading from his eyes.

'Did you kill them?' she yelled. 'Did you kill Sandra and Debbie?'

He looked at her, a serpent sliding beyond her reach.

She shook him by his shoulders. 'Did you do it?'

'Dana.' Connor's voice was weak.

Paul looked up, suddenly noting Alisha's presence. 'Course I did.' He grabbed Dana's wrist, his eyes still on Alisha. 'Course I killed those stupid bitches.' He released her wrist, his hand falling into the dust.

'Angus,' Connor gasped. 'He needs you.'

She realised Paul was dead. Like the kangaroo she'd hit all those weeks ago. There was beauty in surrender. And in closure.

Dana snapped to her senses and sprinted over to the shed. In the dim light she could just make out a mattress in the far corner, a slim figure stretched out on it. Her breath caught in her throat. 'Angus?'

He was tied up. Paul's blue bandana twisted tightly around his wrists, rope around his feet. Her stomach churned as her fingers grappled with the knots. Seconds passed like hours before she finally managed to set him free.

Angus's lips were cracked and his skin was cold. His arm was streaked with blood. She drew him to her, breathing in the scent of his hair. She had a flashback to Oscar. His chubby cheeks and soft skin. Her cheeks were suddenly wet with tears and she had no idea where they'd come from.

A crack of lightning split the sky and the heavens opened up. Helicopter blades and the shrieking of sirens sounded in the distance. Angus pulled back from her embrace. Rain pounded on the tin roof above.

'I'm so glad you're okay,' she said. She touched her hand lightly to his cheek.

He gripped her arm, his eyes revealing the horror of what he'd been through. 'We got him,' he said. 'Didn't we?'

'We did.' She stroked his hair. 'We absolutely did.'

Dana held Angus's hand as he was loaded onto a stretcher. When she next looked up, Ian Steinmann was striding towards her in a hooded raincoat, an expression of shock on his face as he surveyed the scene. She heard voices and turned around to see Isabell hunched under an umbrella, picking her way through the weeds in her high heels, a cameraman in tow.

'What happened?' Ian asked, taking in Paul's dead body on the ground and a swarm of paramedics who were attending to Connor's wounds. A catatonic-looking Alisha was being led away to a police car.

'Murder–suicide?' Dana muttered.

'Don't be a smart-arse,' said Ian. He did a double-take when he caught sight of the news crew. 'Who gave you permission to be here?' Ian shouted across at Isabell. 'This is a crime scene.'

'You haven't done a very good job of sealing it,' said Isabell. 'We walked right in. No questions asked. Besides, I'm checking on my friend.' She stared at Dana's bloodied blouse. 'Jesus, Dana. Are you okay? What happened?'

Dana glanced at Isabell then back to Ian. She no longer cared what he thought. She'd been trying to get the Kirby case re-opened for weeks. But as she went to tell Isabell, the words wouldn't come. Her brain was dull with shock, the bitter tang of nausea in her throat.

Isabell raised her eyebrows. 'Well, if this isn't the scoop of the year, I don't know what is.' She rushed over to where Connor was being loaded onto a stretcher and pushed her microphone in his face. 'Is there anything you'd like to say about what's gone on here today?'

'Get out!' Ian waved his hands at the cameraman. 'Move.'

Dana stepped aside as the paramedics took Angus's blood pressure and shone a torch into his eyes. The wind blew her hair and she shivered, thinking over the events of the day. What a waste. The violence and suffering Debbie and Sandra had endured, their potential would never be fulfilled.

As she climbed into the ambulance, Dana could hear Isabell's voice behind her.

'In breaking news, there's been a stunning development in the murder case of Sandra Kirby and Debbie Vickers … The families of these victims might finally find closure knowing what has transpired here today in the small town of Crows Nest …'

'All good to go?' said the paramedic, before slamming the doors of the ambulance.

28

After it was established that Angus was unhurt, Dana left him with Susan and made her way down the hospital corridor to see Connor. Though he'd suffered a significant wound to his shoulder, it was clear that the main injury had been to his pride.

'Yippee-ki-yay!' he said, gingerly taking a sip of water. Dana sat down in the chair beside him and smiled for what felt like the first time in forever.

They both turned when they heard a knock on the door.

'Come in,' said Connor, struggling to sit up.

Keely stepped into the room carrying an enormous bunch of freesias. She paused when she saw Dana, then came over and arranged the flowers in a jar on the bedside table.

'How are you feeling?' Keely said to Connor, her face bright with emotion as she brushed a lock of hair from his eyes. He gave her a lopsided grin and she leant down to kiss him.

Dana said her goodbyes and slipped from the room, sneaking one final glance at them before closing the door. On her way out she spotted a staff bathroom. She scanned the corridor and darted inside, locking the door behind her. She stood at the basin, staring at the mirror. Her hair was dusty and matted from crawling through the storage shed and she had a dark smear across the pocket of her blouse and another on her shoulder. She washed her hands under the tap, cleaning her blood-caked fingernails until the water ran clear. Then she splashed her face until the tense muscles in her neck began to relax.

Volunteers in blue t-shirts and doctors with stethoscopes around their necks rushed past as she made her way up the linoleum corridor to the reception area. Soft light filtered through the large glass panels of the foyer as she turned the corner to the reception area. She recognised the familiar gait of a figure entering through the main doors. She paused, shocked. Her instinct was right: Hugh was coming towards her.

'What are you doing here?' she asked him.

He stared at her stained blouse and matted hair. 'Your boss, Helen, got in contact and said you needed help after that boy went missing.' He peered at her more closely. 'Jesus, Dana. You look like you've been through the wringer.'

'That's accurate.'

He smiled. 'After I got off the plane I drove to Toowoomba and came straight to the hospital.'

'That was good of you.'

'I wanted to see you. I couldn't wait any longer.' He glanced around. 'Is there anywhere we can go to talk?'

'I'd love to, but I promised the sergeant I'd go to the station to give my statement. I can chat for five minutes though.' She gestured to a row of seats by the window. 'So, what else has been happening?'

He wrung his hands and sat beside her. 'Antonia moved out a week ago. She's back with Philippa.'

Dana raised an eyebrow. 'That must have been a surprise.'

'Not really.' His expression was suddenly serious. 'I promise you, I never slept with her.'

'I believe you,' she said calmly. 'After Oscar, there was a period of time when I just went a bit crazy. I hope you can forgive me for just up and leaving. I know how hard that must have been.'

A sudden hopefulness passed across his face. 'I want to start over. We can go back to Sydney, pick up our old life in Castlecrag and be a family again.' He touched her upper arm gently. 'If it all works out, and if you wanted, maybe we could have another baby? There's still time.' His eyes were wet. 'We don't have to be defined by what happened to us.'

Her heart beat faster. She hadn't expected him to say that. Surely he deserved someone who loved him more than she could? Who could look at him without remembering the agony of what they'd been through? And what about Angus? Could she really abandon him, to try for a child of her own?

'I'm forty-two. Even if we did decide to have another child, it would be a long shot.'

'It doesn't matter if we do or don't – it's up to you. What I'm trying to say is – I want you to come home.'

She stared past him towards the car park, wondering whether the prospect of returning to their home filled her with dread or longing.

EPILOGUE

Dana was standing by the kitchen window feeling good about herself after speaking to her mother. In the park across the road, a child scootered along the footpath and a border collie raced towards its owner with boundless joy. After the shock of winter, the park was lush and green. The garden in Susan's yard was filled with dazzling perennials. Delicate tulips signalled the carnival of flowers was around the corner.

The shrill sound of her mobile interrupted her thoughts. 'Hi, Lachlan,' she said, holding the phone to her ear. 'How are you feeling?'

'Good, actually. I was thinking that I was almost ready to return to work, but my doctor's just signed off on another six weeks of leave.'

She could hear his mirth down the line. 'Enjoying the beach too much?' she said. She could picture him smiling.

'Something like that.'

It had been a miracle he'd survived the crash, but a specialist who happened to be visiting the hospital had been able to assist and Lachlan was on the road to recovery.

'Has Hugh visited?' he asked tentatively.

'He dropped by yesterday. He's staying at Vacy Hall.'

'And?' Lachlan said expectantly.

'And what?'

'For god's sake, woman. Are you taking him back?'

She gazed at the bunch of roses that Hugh had given her, now in a vase on the kitchen table. 'I honestly don't know … we're working through things,' she said finally. After all the tears and recriminations an exhausted peace had settled between them. A new equilibrium. She didn't know how long it would last or where they'd end up.

'Well, that's good.'

When they'd finished talking she walked over to the bookshelf and picked up a photo of Oscar. Her boy, the beautiful bird she'd only been allowed to hold for a short time. Though she was sad, she knew she was fortunate to have known him. And all her lovely memories would remain part of her. They would not amount to nothing.

Angus lay on the rug, his white-blond hair shimmering in the light. She had a vision of what her son might have looked like, had he lived.

Sensing her gaze, Angus looked up. 'I guess you'll be going away soon, won't you?' His bottom lip began to quiver and he turned his face into the cushion.

She knelt down to his level, struck with a sudden clarity. *He needed her.* She could see the difference she'd made, right before her eyes. And while she couldn't help Oscar anymore, Angus had a chance at a good future. She took his shoulders and turned him squarely to face her. 'I hope you like watching *Sherlock Holmes* and going for milkshakes. Because I'm staying where I am. From now on you'll be seeing a lot more of me. Okay?'

His smile when it came was small but beautiful. 'Okay,' he said softly.

Outside, the soothing sound of bird song rang out. She'd grown to like Toowoomba, more than she'd believed possible. And the house that she'd once thought of as pokey and eccentric had become as familiar as her home in Castlecrag.

Angus propped himself up on his elbow and asked, 'Is it lunchtime yet?' A small dimple formed on his cheek.

She gazed at the cuckoo clock on the wall and nodded. 'I was thinking, chicken fettuccine?'

'Good-o.' He smiled up at her and went back to watching TV.

ACKNOWLEDGEMENTS

When I look back on how much encouragement and assistance I've been given along the path to writing this book I'm incredibly grateful and humbled. Writing a book is a marathon and I could never have done it without the support and guidance of so many people along the way.

Thank you to my incredible agent Benjamin Paz at Curtis Brown for your enthusiasm and hard work. I'll always be grateful to you for plucking my manuscript from obscurity and turning my dream into a reality.

A heartfelt thanks to my publisher, Aviva Tuffield, for taking a chance on an unknown author and believing in my work. I'm also deeply indebted to the staff at UQP and to my editor, Jacqueline Blanchard – thank you so much for your intelligence, attention to detail and for helping make *Crows Nest* the best book it could be.

I wrote most of this book while sitting at my kitchen table after my children had gone to sleep, but some of my favourite chapters were written during the writing residency I attended in 2018. To this end, I want to thank the Katharine Susannah Pritchard Foundation, who awarded me a fellowship which gave me the time and space to write at a point in my life when I had very little of either.

Thanks to my insanely wonderful writers' group, the Dead Darlings Society: Deanna Antoniolli, Mary Chan, Dan Fallon, Karen Hollands, Kaja Holzheimer, Nicky Peelgrane, Isabel Prior, Fiona Reilly, Fiona Robertson, Paul Thomas and Warren Ward. Meeting you was one of the most fortunate things to ever happen to me. Thanks for all the laughs, Christmas parties and your invaluable insights.

I couldn't have written this book without the encouragement of friends and family. Special thanks to my parents, Barry and Frances Mottram, for your unconditional love and support. To Chris Brophy, Dr Carol Major and Justine Lutkin, for your insightful editorial feedback. And to close friends Shideh Faramand and Shadi Faramand Gomez, Lynne Smith, Liz Chenoweth, Jennifer Loakes and Karina Lewis.

I'm grateful for my children, Emily and Jack, who are the reason for everything, who are endlessly funny and inspiring and make me want to be a better person.

I'd like to save the biggest and most profound thanks to my husband, Alex. This book would never have been written if it weren't for all the endless help and encouragement you've given me along the way. I'll always be grateful for your unwavering support and love.

And, lastly, to all the child protection workers who do the work day in and day out with little recognition. You make a world of difference.

MONEY-BACK GUARANTEE

If you bought *Crows Nest* and didn't find it a great read, UQP will give you your money back.

Here's how to claim your refund:

1. Keep your proof of purchase.
2. Detach and complete the form below.
3. Cut off the book's front cover.
4. Send the above to: University of Queensland Press
Sales Department
PO Box 6042
St Lucia, QLD 4067
Australia

✂---

Name ....

Address...

....

Email address ....

Telephone number ....

Account name ....

Institution name ....

BSB.................. Bank account number ....

Please allow up to one month for your refund. This offer is valid to 30 June 2023, and is open only to Australian and New Zealand residents. To be eligible for the money-back offer you must provide proof of purchase, the book cover and the completed form above.